ALEXIS BASS

An Imprint of HarperCollinsPublishers

HarperTeen is an imprint of HarperCollins Publishers.

Love and Other Theories
Copyright © 2015 by Alexis Bass

Library of Congress Cataloging-in-Publication Data
Bass, Alexis.
    Love and other theories / Alexis Bass. — First edition.
        pages   cm
    Summary: Seventeen-year-old Aubrey and her three best friends have perfected
the art of dating in high school, but their theories on love will be put to the test when
gorgeous senior Nathan moves to town.
    ISBN 978-0-06-227532-5 (hardcover)
    [1. Dating (Social customs)—Fiction.   2. Love—Fiction.   3. Friendship—
Fiction.   4. High schools—Fiction.   5. Schools—Fiction.]   I. Title.
PZ7.B29255Lo   2015   2013043140
[Fic]—dc23   CIP
                                                                        AC

Typography by Carla Weise
14 15 16 17 18   CG/RRDH   10 9 8 7 6 5 4 3 2 1
❖
First Edition

FOR MY PARENTS, BOB AND JENNIE,
FOR ALWAYS ENCOURAGING ME

*"A wise girl kisses but doesn't love,
listens but doesn't believe,
and leaves before she is left."*
—MARILYN MONROE

CHAPTER ONE

There's one major reason I'm ready to be done with high school, and it's all culminating now, the first day back from winter break, in Senior Drama. Because where else, right?

"Aubrey Housing!" Mrs. Seymour yells, her mouth full of potato chips. From her seat in the center of the auditorium, she points to the stage—as if I really didn't know where I was supposed to be going—and the grease on her hands glimmers in the spotlight.

I take my time walking down the aisle, not only because standing alone on the stage is the last place I want to be, but because *I can*. I can take my time if I want to because I'm someone people will wait for at this school.

I walk up the small staircase on the right, leading up to the stage, and make my way into the spotlight. Yes, for this first-day-of-the-semester exercise, Mrs. Seymour has set up the actual spotlight. It was her TA, Melvin's, idea. Clearly annoyed that Senior Drama wouldn't provide him with much real theater experience, as everyone in the class is about to graduate and more interested in the lack of homework than the betterment of their acting skills, he's trying to squeeze in as much as possible. Melvin is going to be the rock in my shoe this semester, I can already tell.

"Tell us your name and three things about yourself," Mrs. Seymour says loudly, the same thing she's said to the last eleven students to have a turn. "And remember to speak from your diaphragm."

I nod at her, but I don't smile. "I'm Aubrey Housing." The only things people need to know about me, they're already completely aware of. I'm Shelby Chesterfield's best friend. Trip Chapman's final conquest before he graduated last year. The only student from Lincoln High in seven years to be accepted to Barron University.

I reveal the same asinine information everyone's been divulging. "My favorite color is purple, I work at the French Roll, and—" I stop only because it gets noisy. There's a rush of whispering and squeaking—the sounds of butts moving against chairs. It's weird being up here, how aware you are of everything the audience does.

It doesn't take long for me to notice what the big deal is. It's a boy. A boy none of us has ever seen before. No one can be cool. They all stare—their typical reaction when someone new, good-looking, and unapologetically male makes an appearance.

"And my favorite vacation spot is Lake Geneva," I say—projecting from my diaphragm—to bring everyone's attention back to me and away from the new boy walking obliviously down the aisle toward the stage. He's even holding his schedule out in front of him like he's studying it. Like there might be another auditorium and he's in the wrong place. But then he looks up at me.

I'm not the first person to notice the new boy, but I'm arguably the first person he notices. Like, *really* notices. And it might just be because of the spotlight.

"And what did you do this winter break?" Mrs. Seymour calls to me.

"I went skiing and—" I keep the new boy in my peripheral vision. He takes a seat up close. Not like most of the other students, who are perched carefully in the back. The glow from the spotlight makes him exceptionally visible to me. Too visible, maybe. "And I visited Barron's campus."

The new boy smiles. That's when I know I'm in trouble. His smile is amazing. It fits perfectly on his face. Which, from what I can tell, is also amazing.

"Robert Jules!" Mrs. Seymour shouts, again with her mouth full. Next, she smiles. Robert Jules has a solid reputation of being a class clown. She's probably thinking, *Finally, some entertainment.*

Robert walks to the stage slowly—because he can—and there's this awful lull of time when the room is quiet as I head back to my seat.

It's weird. The new boy has chosen the seat exactly three seats away from the one my stuff is resting on. I'm the only one sitting that close to the stage—just five rows away—and had I known better, I wouldn't have sat there. But I didn't know, until Robert Jules laughed at me and asked if I needed glasses, that Senior Drama wasn't like all the other classes—real classes—and it was actually not going to help my grade to sit toward the front.

"I'm Robert Jules," he says. "I love beautiful women, parties, and beautiful women." Thanks to the spotlight we can all see Robert wink. I shake my head because he just did *that*. But he's Robert Jules, so he can do whatever he wants. "And over winter break I partied with beautiful women. Right Aubrey, baby?"

Whatever he wants.

I cover my eyes with my left hand and continue shaking my head. It's expected of me to do this. I saw Robert Jules twice over winter break, which is twice more than I've ever seen him over any of the twelve winter breaks that have passed since I met him in kindergarten. We took Jell-O shots—that was a first. And he tried to get me to make out with my friend Melissa. That was obviously a bust.

The first thing I do when I uncover my eyes is glance at the new boy. I don't mean to, but I'm glad I did. Just as I'd suspected, the new boy is staring at me.

Robert is tall, dark, and muscular, and the consensus at Lincoln High is that he's attractive. Everyone knows he's a jokester. That he calls everyone "baby." They also know there never has been and never will be anything romantic or sexual between Robert and me. But the new boy doesn't know any of this. He might think I'm Robert's only *baby* when really Robert's been hooking up with my friend Danica for the last few months. This might have really hurt any chance I have with the new boy.

Or it's just guaranteed that I've got his undivided attention.

Robert saunters down the aisle right as the new boy is walking up it. The new boy turns into the row where Mrs. Seymour is sitting and leans toward her. She waves her hand toward the stage, and, not taking his time at all, the new boy positions himself directly in the center of the spotlight. Everyone gets unnervingly quiet.

He struggles to look at us, which is overly dramatic because I didn't really think the spotlight was so bad. "I'm Nathan Diggs," he says loudly, but he's definitely not projecting properly from his diaphragm. "I just transferred from San Diego, I'm eighteen, and my favorite food is chicken parmigiana."

Nathan Diggs.

Nathan Diggs is attractive in a way I'm not familiar with, and it's not just because he's practically the only boy at Lincoln High I haven't known since I was five. Sure, he's different. He's not wearing the usual Guys-o'-Lincoln High outfit of jeans, sneakers, T-shirt, hoodie. He's not even opting for the I'm-Country-and-Rugged faded flannel and lamb's wool that some of the seniors sported last year. The Chapman Look, Shelby calls it—named for the style of Zane and Trip Chapman. The new boy is in a leather jacket. I thought leather on a guy might look tacky. I was so wrong. I thought a leather jacket over a sweatshirt would look boxy and uncomfortable, but apparently I was wrong about that, too.

"I spent my winter break moving," he concludes. I wait for the depression to come out, to hear the self-loathing in his voice at having had to move the second semester of his senior year. What kind of parents would do that? But he seems perfectly pleasant. That's another thing about him. Even though his eyes are really dark—darker than his deep brown hair—he still manages to look congenial.

He shrugs—he's probably gathered that he shouldn't wait for applause—and descends off the stage. I watch out of the corner of my eye as Nathan Diggs returns to his chair. Three seats away from me.

In all honesty, I'm uncomfortable. I stay perfectly still, though, because it's against everything I believe in to show how physically altered I feel just because of a boy.

"Hey," he whispers to me, leaning over the seat next to him.

Normally, I'd pretend I don't hear him right away, make him work a little harder for my attention. But my gut reaction is to look at him, so that's exactly what's happened. He's staring at me expectantly, so I lean in toward him.

"Has she handed out the syllabus yet?" he whispers.

"Oh. No. There's no syllabus." He looks confused, which I find refreshing because usually everyone pretends they already know everything. "We're graded on participation only," I explain. I want to point out to him that this isn't a real class. There's no assigned reading, no reason to sit in the front, and the teacher eats potato chips while she's teaching.

One of his eyebrows hitches up, like he's still a little surprised. "We'll really get a chance to show off our theater skills, then."

It takes me a minute to realize that he's joking. I laugh and am appalled at how breathy it is.

"Tough first day, eh?" he says.

Another joke. This time I'm ready for it and laugh appropriately.

"So who transfers the second semester of their senior year?" I ask him. It's a legit question.

"I do." Legit answer. He shifts forward like he's seriously debating getting up and moving to a seat closer to me. I tilt away from him, encouraging this.

Before Nathan can try to speak to me again and I can pretend not to hear him, forcing him to move closer, Mrs. Seymour begins addressing the class, telling us something about improvisation. Melvin is handing us sheets of paper. Nathan reaches across the seats to pass me the handout and I hesitate, waiting for him to use this as an excuse to move closer still. But he shakes it at me like he's afraid I don't understand that he's passing it to me. I snatch it out of his hand.

Mrs. Seymour tells us to spend the final fifteen minutes of class studying the sheet so we'll be prepared for tomorrow. She brushes the potato chips off her skirt and exits stage right with Melvin.

There are three bullet points on the sheet. Because describing a game in which everyone stands in a circle taking turns acting out various scenes requires only three bullet points to describe, and definitely not fifteen minutes to study.

"This is so lame," I say, just loud enough for Nathan to hear me. It is lame. Acting. Pretending to be someone else in a make-believe scenario. As if high school isn't fake enough. Especially Lincoln.

"We could . . ." Nathan pauses thoughtfully. He shakes his head, smiling.

"What?" I ask, and I'm genuinely curious, though I try to play it off like I'm more annoyed that he hasn't finished his sentence. "Tell me."

"I was going to say we could leave." He's still smiling; still shaking his head. He's joking.

Because leaving is absurd.

Rephrase: Usually, for me, ditching class is crazy. I didn't get into Barron by cutting class.

I steal another glance at him, at this face I've never seen until today. It occurs to me that Nathan doesn't know who I am at this school, or that I've never skipped class before, ever.

"It's going to be lunchtime soon anyway," I say, as if he wasn't diligently studying the schedule just minutes ago. The casualness in my voice scares me, but I soldier on. Nathan's head is slightly cocked, his smile shrinking. "Do you want to just leave?"

He gives me this look then. *The* look. The one that says, *I'm all yours.* It's weird when a boy seems vulnerable like this. It was especially weird when I got this look last year from Trip Chapman, who wasn't really ever vulnerable. I was always at Trip's mercy; everyone was. So when he gave me this look—eyes wider than usual, waiting for their cue; lips pressed together, too unsure to smile—I knew I had all the power. It felt good.

"You think we'll get away with that?" he asks. "You don't think we'll get in—caught? You don't think we'll get caught?" He repeats himself, but it's too late. He was about to say, *You don't think we'll get in trouble?*

I like that he knows he's not supposed to show he's afraid of trouble.

I look back at the stage one last time. There's no sign of Mrs. Seymour or Melvin. I take a deep breath and repeat in my head the mantra Shelby told me last week on Monday night before handing me a homemade margarita. It was exactly twenty seconds before our favorite show, *Mercy Rose*, was about to start, so she spoke quickly. "Now that you've been accepted into Barron, you need to join the rest of us and get a real life. It's your senior year, Brey, time for you to party it up." I normally never joined in on Monday nights when my friends decided to drink during our weekly viewings of *Mercy Rose*, but I'd polished off two margaritas by the time the show was over.

Shelby was right. She always is.

I can't look at Nathan when I say, "I think if you don't follow me, you'll be sorry." I shove past him, not even waiting for him to move his legs, and walk briskly up the aisle toward the exit. I know people are staring. They must be. But I just keep walking. As I burst through the back doors of the auditorium, I don't even turn around to see if Nathan's following me. I already know he is.

CHAPTER TWO

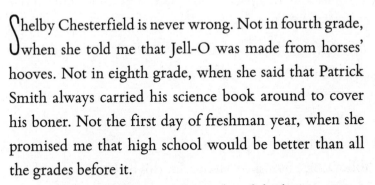

Shelby Chesterfield is never wrong. Not in fourth grade, when she told me that Jell-O was made from horses' hooves. Not in eighth grade, when she said that Patrick Smith always carried his science book around to cover his boner. Not the first day of freshman year, when she promised me that high school would be better than all the grades before it.

And she wasn't wrong the night of the homecoming dance junior year. The night we officially learned that everything we'd theorized about boys and high school and love was, in fact, true.

"What time is it?" I'd asked. Again. We were standing

in the middle of the football field. It was dark, but I knew Shelby was rolling her eyes. I heard an annoyed sigh and assumed it was Danica.

"Chill out," Danica said, her voice muffled. There was a clicking noise, and a flame appeared in front of us, flashing light on Danica's dark brown eyes and dark, wild curls. Too close for Melissa's comfort. She backed away, shrieking a little.

"Jesus," Danica said, lighting the cigarette sandwiched between her lips. Her voice was raspier than normal from the cold and from having spent the past three hours singing along with the music at homecoming, but she also kept it raspy deliberately. "For seduction purposes," Shelby claimed, but I think that voice just came with Danica and was part of her fierceness. She didn't move here until fifth grade, but even then, her voice was on the gruffer side. I think that's why Shelby started talking to her, just to hear her talk back.

"Be careful." Melissa returned to our huddle but gathered her long blond hair in a side ponytail. Away from Danica.

Danica punished Melissa for this by blowing smoke in her face. But the smoke was warm, so it wasn't exactly a punishment. The embers from her cigarette fell in flakes, the light fading before it hit the ground. We all watched it flicker in front of us. We didn't have anything else to watch.

"I don't think they're coming," I finally declared. Someone had to say it. I was sure we were all thinking it.

"I thought you were supposed to be the smartest one out of all of us," Shelby said. Danica's cigarette floated a few feet and landed in Shelby's mouth. She took a long, slow drag. The same amount of time it took for her insult to sink in.

"And speaking as the smart one, I think it's time to bail before we all get pneumonia," I said.

"Maybe we should wait in the car?" Melissa offered. Her teeth chattered on the word *the*. She was probably the coldest since she was the skinniest, even though she was almost as tall as Shelby and me, hitting five seven when we were five eight. Shelby claimed to really be five nine. It was because Melissa was such a picky eater—a picky person, really. We knew she'd been born like this, because Shelby and I had known her since kindergarten.

"If we wait in the car, Chiffon won't see us," Shelby said. "Were you paying attention to the plan at all?"

"Yes. I was. I just think . . ." But Melissa knew better than to finish.

The plan. For Shelby it was a plan. It might have been a plan for Danica and Melissa, too. For me it was a test. Weeks before, when the four of us had decided to turn down anyone who asked us to homecoming and instead go to the dance with just one another, snag a bottle of champagne (or three) from Shelby's mom's stash, and invite our senior crushes—most of whom already had dates anyway—to meet us at midnight for an exclusive homecoming after party, we didn't consider the weather. October in the Midwest. Cold with a chance of freezing.

"Maybe we should open the champagne," Danica suggested. A sedative to shut me up and calm Melissa's nerves.

"They'll be here any second," Shelby said. She frowned at us. "Do you really think they won't come?"

"Not if they're at Celine's." An indoor after party. I had to make sure Shelby had considered all the options. "Not if they're getting laid." Because that's what boys did after homecoming. Or at least that's what they tried to do.

"Gross," Melissa moaned.

"They're not getting laid," Shelby said. I could hear a smile in her voice. "Or if they are, they're probably done by now. It's not like they need very long."

We all laughed, even though at the time only Danica and Shelby weren't virgins. We hadn't laughed in twenty minutes—a record for the four of us. *You sound like witches cackling*, Celine McGillicutty told us once. We took it as a compliment.

"Come on," Shelby said, taking a deep breath. "You know they don't want to spend the entire night with those girls." Those girls. Who wouldn't dream of attending homecoming without a date. Those girls who wanted too much, an *I love you* after sweating in the backseat of the car, to be taken to breakfast, to be kissed tenderly and promised, *You're the only one*. Those girls we were not.

Before I could doubt Shelby again, bright lights shone on us through the chain link fence. Headlights from a vintage blue-and-white pickup.

We stood in a line, staring. I imagined we looked like withering ice queens. Long formal dresses covered by puffy coats, our breath vaporizing around us, our faces white, our noses red. The cold had made our styled hair go flat. The jewels that were once on top of Melissa's head had drooped with the fallen strands dangling around her face. The bottom of my green dress was muddy.

"Let's go," Shelby whispered. She almost sounded surprised. She approached the guys, shaking the bottle of champagne and smiling.

"Shelby!" called a voice I couldn't place but still knew belonged to one of the invited.

Melissa and Danica sauntered toward the figures staggering in the headlights. They were just a few feet away, walking through the open fence connecting the football field to the parking lot, but I was frozen in place.

J. D. Donovan, Forest Lester, Liam Poole, and Trip Chapman. Everyone was accounted for. I watched as Shelby sprayed them with champagne and the boys ran after her. They picked her up and turned the champagne bottle on her, soaking her and leaving wet spots that looked like pools of tar on her silver dress.

Trip stared at me and I stared back. I wanted to run to him. I wanted to hug him and kiss him and be as free with him as Shelby was with Forest Lester. But I couldn't. It had been two hours since he'd winked at me across the dance floor. Three days since he'd leaned against my locker and complained to me about the knee he'd sprained during football practice and made me feel the places where he thought the muscle was torn. One day since he'd whispered in my ear after German class, *You look beautiful in green.*

It had been a week since I'd kissed Trip in the hallway at Dion Matthews's party. It was the first party of junior year and I'd left him midkiss, Shelby dragging me away so I'd make it home in time for my curfew, all the while reminding me of what didn't feel true at the time but what we now know to be an irrefutable fact: if you want more, you've got to give less.

"Brey, get over here!" Shelby yelled, tangled up in Forest, who was using one hand to hold the champagne bottle and the other to hold Shelby.

I was grinning like an idiot as I jogged toward them. Trip was smirking at me, so I slowed my pace.

Past Trip, another figure appeared, a girl in a pink dress and a red coat, with dishwater blond hair pulled back in a French twist. At first I thought I was the only one who'd noticed her, but then Shelby asked with faux innocence, "Hey, Chiffon, what are you doing here?"

Chiffon took one more step, putting herself right in the brightness of the headlights. She was probably more visible to us than we were to her.

Chiffon's face paled and she stumbled back a little, tripping on her dress. She opened her mouth like she wanted to say something, but we knew Chiffon was horrible at firing out comebacks on the spot. Especially when the boy she liked was around. Especially when that same boy had his arms around Shelby.

"Did anyone invite her?" Shelby asked, her eyebrows raised, an expression of exaggerated naïveté on her face. Shelby is most insulting when she's playing dumb. "I know Melissa certainly didn't." Melissa shook her head, her jeweled hair swinging around her. She enjoyed this. "And I didn't, of course. Forest, did you?" Shelby shifted to face him, giving him an evil grin, but she stared at him only for a moment before she turned to see Chiffon's reaction.

Chiffon didn't give her this satisfaction. She ran away, bolting into the dark night.

Shelby laughed. "Oh, don't leave angry!"

"You're such a bitch," Forest said to Shelby, but he was smiling, pulling her closer.

"Harmless fun." Shelby said. It was the same thing she'd told us when we'd slipped the fake note from Forest into Chiffon's locker, inviting her to meet him here after homecoming. "Besides, she deserves it."

Everyone knows we hate Chiffon Dillon. They just don't know why.

"There you are," Trip said, pulling on the bottom of my jacket. Pulling me closer. "Are you cold?" he asked, even though I was in a coat and he was only in his tux jacket, wet from the champagne.

I shook my head. Trip slowly pulled my hands away from their position clasped in front of me. He put his hands on my face, and even though they were freezing, I didn't flinch. "I've been waiting to see you." He leaned in closer, like he might kiss me.

Melissa's voice rang in the distance, high and easy to hear amid the light country music coming from the truck, and over the laughing and flirting. "We need more champagne!" Melissa was the hardest to get. That's why she drank the most. She was standoffish and easily offended by anyone who wasn't us, and she hated being looked at. Shelby said it was because Melissa watched one too many episodes of *Dateline* with her mother and thought that if someone—a guy especially—was looking at her for too long, he was devising something evil. This was a problem, considering Melissa was always attracting the usual suspects with her looks. Long, layered, California-blond hair, a paid-for nose, and big brown doe eyes. If a guy was going to get with her, he had to be someone Melissa didn't mind having stare at her—someone who was exactly her type, the way Ronnie Adams had been sophomore year, or persistently charming, the way Liam Poole was being that night. Normally, though, they'd have to catch her right after her third drink, post-cigarette, before she took three sips of her fourth and started puking or passed out—a moment that had to be perfectly timed and therefore hardly ever occurred.

"We left the other bottles on the field," Danica said.

"I'll get them," I said, breaking away from Trip. He sighed. It was the same noise I'd heard him make when Shelby had pulled me away from him in the hallway at Dion's party. This time the noise didn't disappoint me. It *excited* me. And the sound of footsteps, of Trip coming after me, was even more thrilling.

Keep moving and he'll keep following. Stand still and he could be the one to move away.

My name was what stopped me. Made me turn around. "Aubrey." He said my name so carefully, like it was breakable. He was a few paces behind me and getting closer still. When he caught up to me and stepped in front of me, he was looking at me like I was a million miles away. He stared at me like I was the only person he'd ever wanted.

I picked up both bottles of champagne and brushed past him as I walked back to the group. It wasn't as hard to walk away as you might think. I knew for certain by then that what I liked more than kissing Trip was being pursued by him.

He caught my arm, took the bottles from me, and carried them by their tops with one hand. His free hand he put around me as we walked back to our laughing friends.

"I've been looking forward to this all night," he whispered into my hair.

I'd been looking forward to this my whole life. But Trip had never been attainable—none of those boys had, with their lean muscles, perfect hair, and pensive smiles.

Now that we finally understood the only thing we needed to know about high school boys and love and how you couldn't have both, we could have anyone we wanted. *If you want more, you have to give less.* This logic seemed backward compared to the you-get-what-you-give crap we'd always heard, but it worked. Maybe it was a backward time in our lives and that's why. High school brought people together; graduation tore them apart. Love wasn't forever; it was for a moment. And the only thing that made anyone special was the ability to spread out the moments of bliss. To savor them instead of gorging on them.

All our theories were right—tonight had proved that. Maybe I was the last one to really understand because I didn't get to go to all the parties the three of them went to. I'd hear the stories the next morning, when they'd stumble into the French Roll hankering for coffee and a cinnamon twist, with tales that provided me with a collage of all the fun I was missing and gave me a glimpse into the teetering, fleeting, reckless, selfish people these boys turned into when they were mesmerized by a girl— correction: *girls*.

I was there that summer afternoon sitting on a blanket on Shelby's front lawn, just weeks before the start of our junior year, when we came up with the theories. Melissa wrote them down on the back of a magazine and Shelby laughed, telling her that writing them down was such an Aubrey thing to do. She asked me why I didn't think to write them down. She didn't expect an answer; she was joking. But the real answer was that writing them down would make them official. And I wasn't sure these theories were more than that. *Theories*. The night of the homecoming dance proved they were everything.

True and specific to high school boys:

1. Don't expect anyone to fall in love with you, because even if they do, it doesn't matter. They're just going to leave you. You have to leave them first, or treat them so casually that there's nothing for them to leave at all.

2. Sex is only for fun, and only for the moment. You can demand a good time, but you can't demand anything afterward. If you don't expect anything, you won't be disappointed.

3. High school guys are not capable of commitment,

so don't assume there's something you can do to make them commit to you. You can't. But it's actually better and more fun this way because then you don't have to give anything in return. Being a female free agent in high school is pretty much the best thing you can be. Embrace it.

4. Boys will do whatever they want, no matter what you say to them and no matter what they tell you. You should never believe them.

5. Don't ask for an apology from a boy, because you absolutely will not get a sincere one.

6. It's only a matter of weeks (two weeks is the average dating cycle at Lincoln High) before he'll get distracted by someone else. So it really doesn't matter who the guy in question hooks up with, be it one of your friends or any other girl at Lincoln— it's just a blip of your time and his. Nothing to waste more time fighting over. It's definitely not worth it to fight with girls over boys—especially not your best friends—because boys really do come and go, and they definitely go.

Trip's arms were around me, his eyes fixed on me. I let myself smile. He was beyond good-looking, and a notorious serial dater, but none of that mattered now. It didn't matter that I didn't go to as many parties as he did. I didn't have to worry about whether he'd ditch me for the girls who did. I was in no position to be left. I was already gone. I didn't have to be nervous. I didn't have to be scared. It was a relief.

Shelby was right.

Even losing Chiffon as a best friend in the process of discovering the theories was worth it.

SHELBY WOULD APPROVE of what happened next with Nathan, of me leaving class early on the first day back from winter break. Of me climbing into Nathan's car, because he insisted he drive. Of me telling him to hurry but acting like I didn't really mean it.

Nathan and I are driving down the road and I picture what Shelby will do when I tell her—her mouth falling open wide in a shocked smile, her hands poking me, trying to get the story out of me as fast as possible, shrieking the way she does sometimes that makes Celine McGillicutty call her an attention whore but makes the rest of us laugh. I can't wait to tell her. I almost want Nathan to turn around and go back so I can tell her right now, how much I'm being like her and Melissa and Danica. We always say that the four of us belong together, and it's so, so true.

"Where to?" Nathan says. He keeps both hands on the steering wheel and his eyes on the road. But he smiles, this boy who doesn't know I was never like this before, and it makes my insides pulse. There will be no going back to school now.

CHAPTER
THREE

I walk into my house around midnight. On school nights I'm supposed to be in bed by now. My mom looks up at me from the kitchen stool she's sitting on, a place that allows her a perfect view past the living room and the staircase, of the front door. She's got a cooking magazine out, like maybe she's been just been casually reading with a cup of tea. But I know better.

She squints at me and bites her lip. Waiting. Under normal circumstances she would yell, tell me that coming home this late on a school night is completely unacceptable and that I've probably woken up the entire household, i.e., my dad and two younger brothers. But this is my last semester of high school. I've already received my early decision acceptance letter from Barron. Circumstances have changed.

I still have a full schedule, but instead of taking all AP classes, I've got a few breezy, minimal-study courses on my schedule as well. Exhibit A: Senior Drama. I'm still student council committee chairperson, but by now most of the committees are assembled and self-sufficient. Swim season is over, I didn't sign up for debate team this semester, and my volunteer work for Key Club ended with the holiday toy drive. Even my work schedule has slimmed. The French Roll, a bakery owned by one of my mother's college sorority sisters, is where I've worked every weekend since I was old enough. Five a.m. to two p.m. is my shift. I only ever took time off for family vacations, swim meets, or volunteer work. After I got my Barron acceptance letter, I asked my mom if I could ease up on my schedule. She hesitated. I could tell she didn't like the idea, but my dad piped up right away. He thought I could use the rest. I'd earned it, after all. Ms. Michel, the owner of the French Roll, was fine with me changing my schedule to every *other* weekend. She even gave me the entire month of January off, claiming it was a slow month anyway. I can't remember the last time I had this much free time.

25

All my friends work too—short shifts, adding up to about twelve hours a week, that produce at least enough money to pay for stuff our parents wouldn't approve of. Booze. Cigarettes. Birth control. Brazilian bikini waxes. Shelby waitresses once a week at one of her mother's boyfriend's restaurants, and Danica and Melissa work at Target. Mine is the only job that infringes on my social life. I think my mother hooked me up with this job on purpose, to keep me from staying out late with my friends. To keep me from having the kind of fun you're supposed to be having in high school. If it wasn't for Barron, I'm not sure it would have been worth it.

Throughout all these easements made on my once-rigid schedule, a school night curfew was never discussed. On the weekends my curfew only changed from eleven to midnight, but I planned to get around it the way Melissa escapes her curfew, the way I, too, had avoided mine before on those few special-occasion nights I'd been out with Danica, Melissa, and Shelby: I stayed the night at Shelby's, and because she had no curfew, I'd have no curfew.

I can see the wheels turning in my mom's head. She doesn't know if my coming home late on a school night should be something she's "cool" with.

I sent her a text, of course, so she would know I wasn't bleeding to death in an alley, the place she always seems to think I am if she doesn't hear from me. She knew I'd be later than expected. Though I can tell by her tight forehead that she didn't expect I would ever come in this late during the week.

"Try not to stay out so late on a school night," she says, giving me a forced smile. But tonight was one of the best nights of my life. "Well, I hope you had fun with your friends," she says. She lies.

"I did," I say.

It's pure assumption on her part that I've been with Shelby, Melissa, and Danica, because with my break from extracurriculars and Trip away at college, who else would I be with? If she knew I'd spent the past several hours skipping school to hang out in the backseat of a BMW with a boy I hardly knew, she wouldn't be smiling at all.

I trudge up to my room and get ready for bed. I pull my long dark brown hair into a ponytail and check for signs that Nathan's lips haven't left love prints along my neck. All clear. For some reason this disappoints me. My hair still smells a little bit like his cologne, which is the same Calvin Klein Eternity stuff all the boys wear, but for some reason it smells better on him.

I crawl into bed and turn my iPod on low volume. I am still buzzing. Booze and cigarettes be damned. This Nathan high is my new favorite.

My phone beeps and I read a text message from a number I don't recognize, but am now destined to remember forever.

YOU'RE INCREDIBLE AUBREY, NATHAN.

It's the third text I've received today. The first was from Shelby, around noon: **DUDE, WHERE ARE YOU?** I could see it, the three of them looking for me in the cafeteria. Melissa getting worried; Danica telling her to knock it off, I was probably fine. Shelby telling them to shut up, she was going to text me. The next two texts were from Ella Benson and Marnie Rickard, informing me of what I'd missed in AP Physics and American Lit. Ella's message ended with **I HOPE YOU FEEL BETTER.** It makes me smile to think Shelby might've planted this in Ella's head, covering for me before I've had the chance to cover for myself— looking out for me when I didn't know I needed looking out for, like in fifth grade when she told me to carry tampons around even though I hadn't gotten my period yet.

Three seconds later I get another text from Shelby that says, **WHERE HAVE YOU BEEN? SPILL!**

I text back, **IN THE MORNING.**

Because what I want right now, more than to talk about it and rehash it out loud, is to let the tingles take over just as they did the second I left the auditorium. And as soon as I tell Shelby, or anyone, what I've done, I'll be opening up the gauntlet. *Aubrey, you're doing it, you're living, finally!*

It does feel like that. *Living.* Nathan followed me out of the auditorium after I told him that if he didn't leave with me, he'd be sorry, and when he caught up with me he said, "Are you always this threatening?"

I had to suck on my bottom lip to keep from smiling like a moron. No one had ever called me *threatening* before. And I'd never threatened anyone before, especially not with something as daunting and bitter as *regret.*

"My car is this way," he said, and I was so glad he was talking so I wouldn't have to. I was sure my voice would shake and give me away. "Where to?"

The theories were in the back of my mind, calming me. *So what* if this was the only time I got to threaten him? *So what* if after today Nathan Diggs moves on to a cheerleader or a sophomore? Today, he was mine. I got him for nearly ten hours.

I fall asleep reliving every second.

CHAPTER FOUR

'm late this morning. I slept in.

But for once, I'm actually glad. I'm a little nervous, a little shaky, and a lot afraid of being seen this way.

Shelby, Danica, and Melissa have been assaulting my phone with text messages all morning, demanding an explanation as to why I defected after fourth period yesterday and was never seen or heard from again. Shelby threatens not to forge me a note excusing me if I don't tell her what the hell I've been doing that I couldn't be bothered to call and fill her in. It's just a threat, though.

They text me the rumors floating around about my

drama class skip-out. Almost all of them are true.

I see Nathan's silver BMW parked in a third-row spot as I walk through the parking lot to school. It makes me smile, imagining Nathan arriving early enough to get the spot. I used to always arrive early enough to get one of the close spots. My friends all park way, way in the back of the lot, where, as Shelby so delicately put it, *Those of us who are normal and have lives, and don't go to bed before ten, park.*

I press my lips together so that anyone who sees me right now won't catch me smiling and assume that the new boy is the reason.

So I left with the new guy?

So we hooked up?

So what?

I lost my virginity to Trip Chapman. *This* is not a big deal.

The second I sit down in first period, Mr. Johnson hands me a note bidding me to go to the counselor's office. Ella Benson rolls her eyes at me like she feels my pain. Marnie Rickard starts chewing on her mechanical pencil. Ella and Marnie have been in most of my honors classes since freshman year. Marnie is student council vice president. Ella is the rumored valedictorian. Danica is in a lot of our classes too, and she winks at me from where she's seated in front of me, because even though I haven't yet had time to fill her in on what happened with Nathan, she's heard the rumors. She probably helped spread them.

Really, the counselor probably just wants to chat about college stuff—classes, my major, work-study programs—the usual crap they always want to discuss. But when I get there, Nathan's there too, sitting with his hands in his lap on one of the three plastic chairs lining the wall outside Mrs. Harris's office.

I act casual. "Hey."

He does not. "Hey, you." He grins, large and with his teeth showing.

And then, damn it, I'm blushing, and probably smiling, though it's hard to tell because my face is on fire.

"Hi, kids, how you doing?" Mrs. Harris greets us. It's the first time I've ever been glad to see her.

Nathan and I exchange a look, and I can't help but let out a laugh. How am I doing? I'm sitting next to Nathan; I'm flying. Nathan's looking at me like he's flying too, so it's all right.

Mrs. Harris tilts her head and her glance shifts between the two of us. "Well. Isn't that sweet. Come on in."

"Both of us? Together?" I ask.

"Yes." Mrs. Harris seems annoyed, but the I'm-your-guidance-counselor-you-can-tell-me-anything smile doesn't leave her face. "Come on, get in here and we'll have ourselves a little chat."

Nathan is no longer the reason my heart is racing—the reason I feel like I need a trash can to vomit in. We've totally been caught. Skip school once and it will ruin your senior year. *Screw* my new mantra.

We sit in the chairs positioned opposite Mrs. Harris's desk. I can't stop fidgeting with my sweatshirt drawstrings. Nathan seems nervous too. He's folded and unfolded his hands at least three times since taking his seat.

"So, I gather you two have met," Mrs. Harris says, like she's expecting a response but never gives us a chance to speak. "Which is fantastic, I think. It's good to know others when you move away from home, and before you got here, Nathan, Aubrey was the only one from Lincoln attending Barron University in the fall."

I'm shocked. I catch that my mouth is hanging open and slowly shut it. It seems weirdly coincidental that Nathan Diggs—who's just moved from an entirely different state—will be attending the same college as me next year. And not just any college. Barron.

Mrs. Harris is rambling on about Barron University's orientation programs, but I'm not listening. The truth is slowly sinking in, and it stings just as badly as when I thought that the fake note Shelby wrote to excuse me from missing school yesterday didn't work.

The truth: I've just skipped school with a guy I hardly knew. I took off his shirt, he peeled away mine, and I let him undo the top button on my jeans. And I was overly impressed by his BMW. But the worst thing is, I haven't been able to stop thinking about him since.

CHAPTER FIVE

Nathan and I leave the counselor's office and walk side by side slowly in the direction of our respective classes.

"So you're going to Barron next year too," I say quietly. It sounds less like a question and more like an accusation.

"Yeah. Sorry I didn't tell you." Nathan's eyes shift to the floor, to the ceiling, and finally to me. "Are you mad?"

His face is apologetic. He's lied to me and been caught. It was a lie of omission, but a lie nonetheless. Yesterday, when I told him, like I tell everyone—and like he'd heard me announce to the entire class during Drama—that I'd be attending Barron next year, he didn't say anything.

I remember the way his hands so carefully caressed my bare back and the way the windows fogged, and think, *Yes, actually, I am mad. Why would he bother hiding something like that from me?* But even before the question can fully root itself in my mind, I'm already aware of the answer.

I don't really matter to him.

"Whatever." I give him a smile, but it's not exactly friendly. It says, *I'm onto you, Nathan Diggs.* I don't stick around to gauge his reaction. I quicken my pace down the hall.

"Because it's not set in stone yet," he tells me, catching up to me. He steps in front of me so I'll stop walking. "I *hope* to attend Barron next fall."

"But haven't you already been accepted? That means you don't need to hope anymore. You've got a guarantee."

His hands look so white against the dark of his hair as he runs his fingers through it.

"The reason I'm enrolled in Lincoln High is because I need the credits. I complete this year and I'm in. Until then I'm taking Spanish and a bunch of bullshit classes like Senior Drama and AP Physics."

I don't allow myself to smile at this even though my lips are begging me to. I like the way Nathan jokes about AP Physics being bullshit. "Okay." I try to shake away the confusion as to why I didn't find this out yesterday. Why I didn't ask, why it didn't come up, why he didn't feel the need to tell me.

The few facts I know about Nathan: His parents are both chemists and both got jobs at our local plant. His favorite milkshake flavor is strawberry. He really likes HBO shows. He drives a new BMW that his parents bought him for having a perfect report card last year. He would rather have the superpower of flying instead of the ability to be invisible. His kisses start out light and build slowly into passionate.

Nathan takes a step closer to me. "I'm sorry I didn't tell you, but—"

I put my hand up to stop him and shake my head. The theories dictate what to do. *I'm sorry* is synonymous with *good riddance*, and I don't want to say good-bye. I've just met him.

"You don't have to explain. It's okay."

Nathan's big brown eyes light up. Relief washes over his face, followed by something else. Gratitude. It's a look my friends and I always receive from boys when they realize they've met a girl who has evolved—a girl who's not going to throw a bunch of drama in their face. A girl who's not going to waste their time.

"I don't usually skip class, but yesterday . . . you—you told me to go with you and I thought, what the hell?" He can't stop touching his chin. He smiles, waiting for my response, blushing slightly.

I smile back at him and forget he ever made me mad. When I start walking down the hall again, he follows me.

CHAPTER SIX

Shelby finds me in the hallway after second period. She grabs me by the shoulders like she thinks I'm going to run away.

"There you are," she says, pushing me toward the lockers. I don't have to look around to know that everyone is watching her do this. Even if they're still talking to their friends, even if they're still walking to their next class or getting a book out of their locker, they're still also watching her.

"Where have you been? Who is this Nathan? I hear he's gorgeous. Like, insanely gorgeous." She goes from swooning to swearing all in one breath. "And goddamn it, you're my best friend. My fucking best friend. I even forged you an excuse! I'm supposed to know about this already!"

"He was cute. We skipped class." I shrug.

"Oh no, you don't." She crosses her arms. "Spill. Immediately. Go."

But I don't have time to spill. Nathan's exactly three feet away, walking down the hall and looking a little lost. I smile and blush the second I see him. Shelby's eyeing me, gathering all this as evidence, when she spots him too.

"Well, hello," Shelby says playfully. I can't help but laugh.

Nathan hears my laugh and looks over like he's just found the point on the horizon that's going to lead him home. "Hey," he says. To me. It's like he doesn't even see Shelby. But then his eyes shift toward her. I have the urge to cover them.

Shelby is beautiful. More than just silky blond hair, big blue eyes, pouty lips, perky boobs, longer-than-life legs—though she has all that, too. "Beautiful" is probably an understatement. Last year scorching senior Ryan Sparrow, with a reputation for waxing poetic, announced at a party that Shelby was so beautiful, it broke his heart to look at her. Whatever that meant. Trip's older brother, Zane Chapman, who is not at all poetic but equally as scorching, elaborated and said Shelby was so beautiful that it was hard to make sense of how someone could look so perfect.

I've known Shelby since I was six. I've never been able to make sense of her beauty either.

"I'm Nathan Diggs." Nathan sticks out his hand for Shelby. So formal. So adorable.

Shelby takes it loosely, just grabbing his fingers. Her blue eyes study him. "So I've heard."

I feel an ache in my stomach as Nathan smiles at Shelby. He's seeing Shelby and her beauty for the first time. I wonder if *he's* able to make sense of it. I wonder if he'll want to try.

"And you are?" Nathan seems so genuinely curious, I feel like I'm going to die.

"Shelby," she says, not at all hiding that she's eyeing him up and down. "Nice leather."

"Thanks?" Nathan says like he's suspicious of her comment.

"So do you ride a bike, or what?" Shelby asks.

I'm royally confused. A bike?

"I wish." He touches his jacket and I make the connection. Leather biker jacket, thus a motorcycle. Nice of Shelby to assume that Nathan's jacket had a functional purpose other than making him look freaking sexy.

"What's stopping you from running out and buying the first CB that catches your attention?" Shelby asks.

"You know bikes?" Nathan looks suspicious again.

"My sister's ex used to have a 1973 Honda CB350." I remember Sienna's fling with the boy with the bike. The one who let Shelby drive it in circles in the mall parking lot late at night when he was too tired to tell her no.

"And he let you drive it?"

"Of course—I mean, I demanded to, and it was worth it." Shelby puts her hands over her heart—over her left boob, really. "Why didn't you get one?"

Nathan shrugs. "Bribery from the parents. They bought me a car, would never have forgiven me if I'd traded it in for a bike."

Shelby nods, looking strategically bored. "Any regrets?"

His eyes stay locked on hers for a moment and I feel my heart beat five times before he finally looks away. He shakes his head. "No . . . I don't have any regrets." His next lingering glance is reserved for me.

I purse my lips to keep from smiling. It's no use.

"Well, I think that's crazy," Shelby says, ignoring that Nathan and I are having a moment. "You're really missing out."

"His car is nice, trust me," I say, this time letting my smile all the way through so it's obvious that I have fond, fond memories involving Nathan and that car.

Shelby ignores this, too. "The dealership on Amherst Boulevard carries tons of bikes. We should test-drive them sometime." She puts her hands in the front pockets of her jeans, which is a classic flirtatious move because it does two things: (a) it draws attention to her stomach and what's below it, and (b) it presses her arms to her side in a way that pushes her boobs up. It's a good technique, actually. I should really use it more.

"Maybe." He turns to me and I try not to act like I've been waiting for this. "I'll see you later?"

I barely have the chance to say "Sure, I guess" before he walks away, the bell echoing around us. When I look back at Shelby, she's got the faintest pout resting on her lips.

"Nice ass," Shelby comments as we stroll down the hallway. Nathan's a few paces in front of us, but I don't think he hears.

"I know."

You're probably thinking I should be furious at Shelby. She obviously wants Nathan. But who wouldn't? If I've learned anything, it's that in high school everyone is fair game. If you want to lose friends over it, get ready to be friendless.

"So what happened between you guys?" she asks. She wiggles her eyebrows up and down.

"Not that," I tell her. *Not sex*, because that's where her mind goes, always.

"But something?" She does the thing with her eyebrows again.

"Yes. Something. Some things."

Shelby lingers in front of the doorway of her next class. She's waiting for me to freak out about fooling around with someone so quickly after meeting them. I panicked before prom last year, locking her in the bathroom with me at the salon where we were getting our hair done to squeeze her hands and hyperventilate hours before the dance even started, when it occurred to me that having sex with Trip was a probability. Just last week I called her, flustered, because Tommy "the Riz" Rizzo tried to take off my underwear when we were messing around in his living room while the angel on top of his Christmas tree stared down at us.

When I don't freak out right now, I get her nod of approval. "You little minx!" she calls, cackling as she disappears inside the classroom.

THE WAY ELLA Benson and Marnie Rickard stare at me as I walk into third period, I think they've finally heard the rumors about Nathan and me.

"Why did you get called into the office this morning?" Marnie asks, her voice high and girly, as always.

I sigh. I should have known. *This* is why they're looking at me like that. This is what they think is the most exciting, unexpected thing going on in my life right now. My ongoing flirtation with Trip earned these wide-eyed stares, too. When they heard about our first kiss at Dion Matthews's party last year, their mouths were slack for an entire week. I expected that Nathan might garner the same reaction, but no. They're worried only about my visit to see Mrs. Harris.

"Just college stuff," I tell them.

They smile at me and their faces relax. Ella was on the swim team with me. Marnie and I were on debate team together. I have a lot in common with them, and I'm glad they're my friends. But they'll never understand me the way Shelby, Danica, and Melissa do. And to top it off, Ella has a boyfriend. It's going to blow up in her face any day now. It'll be just like what happened with her former boyfriend, Ivan Gunderson, who dumped her after he got into Stanford. She couldn't wear eye makeup for two weeks last spring, because her chances of smearing it were 100 percent. I tried to comfort her but couldn't give her any real advice. Ella is always the first one to finish her test in AP Calculus, and she always sets the curve, but she would be stumped by the theories. I had to correct her constantly last year when she would refer to Trip as my boyfriend. And she's holding the title of girlfriend again this year, so clearly she learned nothing from the Ivan Gunderson fiasco.

"That girl has one of the worst cases of TGS," Danica says sometimes about Ella. She knows Ella better than Shelby or Melissa do, because she was in AP English with us sophomore and junior year.

The Girlfriend Stigma (TGS): a scientific term

describing the disgrace girls face from guys when the girls appear to want to hold the title of *girlfriend*.

TGS. There isn't anything more pathetic.

This is why I sit with Shelby, Melissa, and Danica at lunch whenever I don't have to study or go to a student council meeting. They are my home base, my best friends in a way that Ella or Marnie will never be. Because how was I going to talk to Ella or Marnie about how Trip Chapman could unhook my bra with one hand? Or how it was impossible to kiss Tommy Rizzo for less than an hour? It didn't matter that Shelby, Melissa, and Danica spent so much time together without me, or that I didn't go to all the parties they went to, or that I didn't always have classes with them. Shelby came into the French Roll every Saturday morning to fill me in on what I'd missed the night before. So I knew what everyone was whispering about in the halls, gossiping about at lunch. Almost as if I'd been there too. Shelby kept me in the loop. She kept me relevant. And she did it because we're best friends.

CHAPTER
SEVEN

The falling-out with Chiffon happened when we were sophomores. It was before we knew how to talk to boys without smiling and blushing.

Before we understood that we had all the control. This was back when Chiffon was one of our best friends.

Melissa was in love with Ronnie Adams. Obsessed in a way that had her switching her class schedule to spend more time with him, and she wound up enrolled in Science Fiction Writing and Woodshop. Her obsession started the second day of high school and stayed strong and steady. But Ronnie was two years older than us. Our sophomore year was her last year with him.

He found us at Maria Vasquez's party—the only party I attended that year—strategically standing in a circle between the kitchen and the living room. The place where everyone could see us.

Melissa beamed as he spoke and laughed at his jokes as though he was the funniest person she'd ever known. We all laughed, but not too hard. We smiled at Ronnie but weren't too friendly. Because he was Melissa's and we were just in the background. We were following rules—the wrong rules. Rules no one had ever told us but we somehow all knew. We were to be polite, but not inviting. Friendly, but not intriguing.

The problem was Ronnie. He wasn't following any of these rules. He was being flirty, overtly friendly, and he couldn't stop staring at or smiling at or leaning toward Chiffon.

Chiffon did what any one of us would have done: She pretended she didn't notice. She ignored his gestures. She avoided eye contact. She didn't laugh too hard at his jokes.

This behavior, of course, is ultimately what made him decide to pursue her. But this was before we knew how it drives boys crazy when they think you don't care.

After Maria's party, Ronnie started hanging around us a lot more. It was obvious that Chiffon was the reason. He tried really hard to make her laugh. He noticed stupid details, like what her favorite Starbucks drink was, and sometimes he even brought it for her in the morning.

Melissa was silent about the issue at first, and after she started to speak up, we tried our best to keep her safe in the arms of denial.

Melissa, don't be ridiculous.

Of course he likes you.

It's soooo obvious.

He's playing hard-to-get.

He's afraid of how he feels.

This was all behind Chiffon's back, of course. Even we weren't stupid enough to lie when the truth was standing right in front of us. Because the truth was, if Ronnie wanted Melissa, he wouldn't have repressed his desire for her.

We were the ones suffering from repression.

It all came to a head the night Ronnie Adams graduated and we could no longer pretend he hadn't chosen Chiffon over Melissa.

He begged for Chiffon's number after the ceremony. Right in front of us, too. He grabbed her hand. Told her he'd miss her. Insisted they hang out over summer break before he left for college. Chiffon was smiling, but you could tell she was trying not to. Caught between a rock and an older boy, she ultimately gave him her phone number.

He made her laugh. He made her feel special. She wanted him, too. This is how it works. This is how simple these things are.

All I remember about that night, besides being shocked that Chiffon would make an awkward situation even worse, was the sound of Melissa's sobs drowning out the gravel crunching under our feet as we walked through the nearly empty parking lot.

Chiffon was silent because there was nothing for her to say. Her face was limp, drained. Not the way you're supposed to look after a boy you like begs for your phone number and you give it to him.

Finally she said, "It's not like I'm going to do anything with him, Melissa." There was a hint of annoyance in her voice, enough to set Melissa off.

"You're a bitch," Melissa said, choking on a sob. Melissa never said things like this about people, so when she did, she really meant them. Shelby pulled her close and put her arm around Melissa. That's when I knew something was about to change. I grabbed Melissa's hand.

Shelby, Melissa, Danica, and I had been through a lot: Melissa's surgery to fix her deviated septum, otherwise called "the nose job of the decade" by Shelby. The time Shelby's dad unexpectedly showed up to see her and we helped slide her under her bed and told Shelby's mom that she'd snuck out to see Zane Chapman—which was a much less worrisome lie when we were nine and Zane was twelve. The time in sixth grade when Mrs. Bergdorf gave me detention for texting during class and Melissa started crying so I wouldn't be the only one crying over it, and Danica called Mrs. Bergdorf "the most unreasonable teacher I'd ever had," so I wouldn't have to be in detention alone. We'd known Chiffon our whole lives too, but we hadn't really been friends with her until seventh grade, when she made Shelby laugh so hard that Diet Coke spewed out her nose in the middle of an assembly.

I felt mad. Hurt. This was Melissa, *my Melissa*, who didn't start cursing until she was fourteen, who hated spiders and fire, and who always drove below the speed limit. Back then, it was much easier to relate to the girl who'd been ditched than to the girl who'd stolen someone else's crush.

When we reached Danica's car, she hesitated before unlocking all the doors. That's when Chiffon started to look scared. She put her hand on the door handle, and Danica shook her head.

"Why don't you get a ride home with Ronnie?" Danica said, her voice darker than I'd ever heard it before. Some people say Danica always looks like she's scowling. She's perfected this look, but it's especially effective when she wants to use it.

Chiffon's eyes started to water. "Are you serious?" she said with a depressing laugh.

To be honest, I don't know what would have happened if she had fought harder to apologize. On some level she probably recognized she shouldn't have had to.

Chiffon rolled her eyes and walked away. But not

before I noticed the tear fall down her left cheek.

It should have made me feel bad, leaving one of my best friends in the parking lot at night, not knowing how she was going to get home, but at that moment I was just glad I couldn't see her anymore.

The rest of the summer, it was easy to avoid her. It was too easy, in fact. Ignoring phone calls. Deleting texts. Blocking her online. School was out, so there were hardly any accidental run-ins, and if there were, we took care of them.

Chiffon is a bitch. Don't let her in.

Chiffon slept with the entire baseball team at the community college and probably has an STD.

She's desperate.

Have you seen her in a bathing suit? She never shaves.

She'll fuck your boyfriend.

She'll fuck anyone.

It was hard to feel bad about saying these things. Everyone wants a reason to hate on someone, even if it's not a good reason, and everyone loves a good slut-villain. She didn't help her cause either when she dressed in clothes that were either too low or too short. And Chiffon actually did start going out with Ronnie Adams that summer, so sometimes it felt like everything we'd said about her might have been true. Not the "facts," of course, but what the lies insinuated about her character.

Chiffon Dillon was the sacrifice. We had to go

through the Chiffon-Ronnie ordeal in order to discover the theories. Had we known the theories, what happened with Chiffon wouldn't have been cause for friendship annihilation or social slaughtering. It's ironic, yes, but it's just what had to happen.

"It's a Catch-22," Danica said once. "Some things in life just *are*."

That's why we tried to apologize, the summer before junior year.

With the Ronnie Adams situation, Melissa had been losing too many points for Team Girl to even count, and the rest of us were no better, tossing points and throwing the game. We'd talked about how we would have handled the Chiffon and Ronnie situation in a much different way, now that we had the theories. We would have winked at Chiffon and told her to go for it. Melissa would have already moved on, lost interest in him the second it became clear he wasn't impressed with her. Chiffon should never have allowed Ronnie to call her his girlfriend for the entire month of July. And she should never have cried all the tears I know she must've shed for him when he dumped her. She should have spent those summer months kissing boys, no strings attached, and laughing with us in the sun.

It's so easy to look back, but sometimes it's no use.

Shelby was the one to attempt the apology, which was fitting because she'd been the worst to Chiffon. Chiffon didn't care to hear it. She didn't forgive us. She stuck by her new friends—the girls with too much eyeliner and not enough hemline. So it's not surprising that we've seen Chiffon crying in the halls over a boy on more than one occasion.

We hate Chiffon because she chose to fight back with eye rolls, giving us the finger, and calling us bitches instead of forgiving us when we tried to explain. But mostly we hate her because she's everything we do not want to be.

CHAPTER  EIGHT

After school I walk slowly to my car. Of course, I'm
looking for Nathan, as I've been doing ever since he
took off for the library after Drama to study Spanish
during lunch, but this time he finds me.

He pulls up alongside me in his car and rolls down
the window.

"Where do you think you're going?" He looks like a
movie star in his leather jacket and aviators. I picture sliding his jacket off his shoulders and unbuttoning his shirt,
and feel my knees start to buckle.

I shrug and smile at him.

"I'm parked way in the back of the lot." *Where the*

people with lives park.

He gives me a playful frown. "Get in. I'll take you." A part of me really loves that to Nathan Diggs, parking in the back is terrible and not a confirmation that I'm cool.

"Okay." I smile—I can't stop myself—and I climb into the front seat of his car. I point him in the direction of my red Honda and he pulls up behind it.

"Are you doing anything right now?" he asks. Before I can answer, he tells me, "I could follow you home so you can drop off your car, then we could go grab some food. I'm in the mood for Italian."

I really like that Nathan has a well-devised plan for us. Trip's plans usually included the word *whatever*. And the only food he was ever in the mood for was micro-wave pizza.

"Right. Italian food. Is that what the kids are calling it these days?" He has to know that I'm onto him. I'm not completely naive as to why he's tracked me down again. He wants more kissing, more foggy windows, more shirts being tossed on the floor.

He laughs. "You're going to be so embarrassed when you witness firsthand just how bad I'm craving chicken parmigiana." Nathan's eyes linger on me as I open the door.

He follows me the ten-minute drive to my house. He parks behind me in the driveway. I'm making my way to his car when my dad pulls up, toting my two younger brothers. It's unusual for my dad to be getting them from school, as he's usually at work until five thirty, but I notice my brother Gregory and my dad have matching PEACE, LOVE, AND PALEONTOLOGY shirts, and I remember something about a field trip to the science museum. I wave at them as I walk to the passenger side of Nathan's car. They note that I'm on my way out and simply wave back. My mother peeks her head out the front door, and I'm not sure if it's to greet my father and brothers or to get a look at the boy whose car I'm climbing into. Nathan waves at them—the polite thing to do—but then he gets out of the car.

"What are you doing?" I ask.

"Your parents don't want to meet . . . You don't need to check in, or something?" There he goes looking confused and adorable again—and finally uncomfortable, which is what I'd expect. Boys do not want to meet your parents unless there is absolutely no way around it.

"What they don't know . . ." I say. He knows the rest of the cliché.

He looks unsatisfied with this answer, and smirks like he finds *me* adorable. "Come on."

I groan but follow him up the path to my house.

"This is going to be fun," he says into my ear once I've finally caught up to him. "I'm curious about the people who bumped uglies to create you."

"You did not just say that." One hand swats at him, the other covers my face. "Vulgar!"

He tilts his head back and laughs lightly. "Your best friend is Shelby Chesterfield and you think *I'm* vulgar?"

I smile and roll my eyes and pretend that I'm not slightly perturbed that he's only been at Lincoln High for two days and he already knows Shelby's full name and that she's vulgar. Of course, that's what anyone would learn the moment they enter Lincoln. That Shelby is someone whose last name you should know. That she has no filter when she speaks. That I am her best friend.

"Just be good," I say, pushing the front door open. But I already know he will be.

CHAPTER NINE

From out Nathan's back window I can't see anything. It's so dark. All that's visible is his face right in front of mine, and all I can feel are his hands, moving under my shirt.

Thanks to urban sprawl and suburban spread, the best place to park your car, if your intention is to fool around in the backseat, is in a vacant housing development still under construction. All the roads have been paved, but the houses aren't built yet because the developers are still selling off the lots. I could have taken us to the actual lookout point, where we'd have to share the parking lot with other couples, or into the woods along the outskirts of town, but I'm not sure his car can handle the back roads.

Just like yesterday, Nathan finds it incredibly hilarious that this is the location we *park* at. And, just like yesterday, I kiss Nathan like I've been doing it for weeks instead of days.

We spent a good twenty minutes inside my house talking to my parents but rushed through dinner at the Italian joint Nathan picked out. Nathan wasn't craving chicken parmigiana as much as he was craving me.

I press my hands into Nathan's bare chest and grind my hips into him. He slips his hands under my bra straps, lets them dangle around my shoulders, but doesn't take off my bra.

With my parents, Nathan was courteous and charming. They were impressed, naturally. Especially that he'll most likely be attending Barron next year. Nathan wants to be a civil engineer, which is what my father is, and, surprisingly, the insta-bond they established just seconds after they shook hands pleases me. Nathan also succeeded in distracting my father from that whole I'm-the-guy-hooking-up-with-your-daughter thing that Trip could never pull off. Even my younger brothers loved him, because unlike Trip, Nathan didn't try to get them to go outside and play catch. Nathan asked them to explain the video game they were playing—which is all Gregory and Jason are capable of talking about anyway. Gregory is twelve and Jason is nine, so video games are still their number one priority. And better yet, Nathan actually seemed to understand what they were saying. He was even able to give them advice for advancing to the next level. My mother liked Nathan too; her loose smile and lax posture made it obvious she was relieved he was so easy for everyone to talk with. I know what she must have said to my father after we left: *I like him—he's so well mannered.* And my father said back to her, *Anyone who knows about structural design is A-okay in my book.*

Nathan's hands are in my hair. Nathan's hands are on my hips. All I can think about is how impressive he was with my family. I kiss him as hard as I can. I bite his lower lip.

"You're amazing," he tells me in between kisses.

"I know" is what comes out. Shelby has always told me to be cocky in bed, and apparently I've been listening.

He laughs into my mouth and it's the best feeling ever. His hands travel up my neck and he grabs my face, pulling back a little so he can he can look into my eyes. "I'm serious," he says. "I feel like I can talk to you for hours. And *this*. I could do this for hours too."

My heart starts to hiccup as his lips move down my neck.

"I'm so glad I met you."

He's not lying. I'm straddling him and practically topless.

I pull his head up so I can reach his lips and I kiss him hard, but I don't say anything. I know better. It's perfect that he's here, now, when I finally have the time and freedom to live out these wild and blissful moments before I have to be a serious Barron freshman. And it's the same for him, which makes everything about him feel wonderfully familiar. It makes all this even better.

Nathan cups his hands against my cheeks again. I watch his eyes tick back and forth over my face. "You're so fucking beautiful."

The last boy to tell me I was beautiful—and actually use the word—was Trip. I forgot how much I loved hearing it.

CHAPTER TEN

There are several reasons Nathan Diggs is adorable. He spends his lunch hour catching up on Spanish so he's fully prepared come fifth period. He wants to bet before Drama about what kind of potato chips Mrs. Seymour will be eating while she teaches. He flies back to San Diego for his best friend's birthday because, according to Nathan Diggs, when your best friend turns eighteen you don't miss it. While it's adorable, it also means he's gone for the weekend, leaving straight after school on Friday.

My head spins a little with questions, specifically: While you're seeing your best friend, will you be hooking up with other girls? As in, girls you could talk to for hours and make out with for hours and who you think are beautiful?

I practice the art of suppression. I restrain these questions, and after a while they exist only in the form of a mild stomachache.

Luckily, it's the beginning of the weekend and I do not have to work this month. My friends and I have big plans.

After school we all go to Shelby's. It's the best place to go because Shelby's mom, Sandra, is never home on the weekends, especially since she started dating Phil three years ago. Sandra spends her weekends out of town with Phil, venturing north to the casinos or south to the lake.

"There you are!" Melissa shrieks when I walk through the front door. "I was starting to forget what you look like."

Shelby and Melissa were the first to arrive since they drive together every day. They're in the kitchen mixing drinks, and I join them after ditching my heavy winter coat in Shelby's room.

"Sooooo . . . spiiiilllll!" Melissa says, dangling a freshly mixed glass of vodka and diet tonic in front of my face as though she's not going to give it to me until I do what she says. I snatch it out of her hands and a little drips on the counter.

"Is that Brey?" Sandra appears in the kitchen wearing a black dress and heels. Must be a casino kind of weekend. The diet tonic is sitting out on the counter, and Sandra must know what we've mixed with it. She doesn't say anything. She never does, but I always expect her to.

"In the flesh."

Shelby giggles.

"I hear there's a new man in your life."

I blush the way I always do when Sandra Chesterfield talks to me about boys. It's like I'm thirteen all over again.

Phil walks into the living room and greets Sandra with a peck on the cheek.

"Get a room," Shelby teases, looking only mildly disgusted.

"Hands where we can see them!" Melissa chants—something we used to say to embarrass Sandra whenever she had a guy over.

"You girls have fun," Sandra says, rolling her eyes. "And don't drink all of Phil's beer!" she calls to us as she's shutting the door.

We laugh because we would never. We like Phil. He's not creepy like some of the other guys Sandra dated. Sure, he doesn't have a whole lot of hair left, and Sandra is two inches taller than him when she wears heels, but, as Shelby puts it, "Sandra doesn't lose as many points with Phil." We certainly like Phil more than Shelby's dad, who only comes by to drop off money, which means he's never around.

"You've been holed up in the back of that BMW for, like, two days—what the hell?" Shelby holds out straws for each of us. Melissa is quick to grab the pink straw and I'm stuck with the yellow one. She smiles like she's won.

Shelby's phone rings. Saved again.

As soon as I hear Shelby yell, I know she's on the phone with her older sister, Sienna. "But we don't want to leave that early—since when do you go to the bar at nine? Fine! Whatever—at least I'm not twenty-three and still completely dependent on my *mother* to pay my rent."

Melissa and I laugh as Shelby slams her phone onto the counter.

"That was harsh," I say in between giggles. Really, it's not that harsh. It's true. Sienna is twenty-three and constantly borrowing money from Sandra. And always to pay rent even though she works three days a week filing for the records department at the plant and is also a waitress at a restaurant by the highway.

It's Sienna's on-again-off-again-so-many-times-it's-impossible-to-keep-track boyfriend, Allen Lysander, who's the problem. Shelby says he's a mooch, and that he only comes back to Sienna when he needs money. "It's like she's learned nothing from Sandra's past male-misdemeanors," Shelby says, and we all agree.

"She's back with Allen," Shelby informs us. "Minus twenty points."

We're keeping score. Because when one girl is stupid, it affects girls everywhere. Boys tell all their friends—anyone who will listen, really—when a girl does something foolish or degrading or crazy involving them. Pretty soon the idea that girls act ridiculous spreads like a rolling snowball.

And if boys think girls are stupid, that's how they'll treat them.

Our theories stop boys from thinking girls are crippled by their emotions, and needy, and dramatic, and dependent. We like to think that our evolved behavior is saving girlkind. Because let's face it, we need saving.

"So how many points does Brey lose for hooking up with Nathan on his first day at Lincoln High?" Melissa says, bumping me with her hips.

"We didn't have sex," I tell them, my hands up, surrendering.

"Yet!" Both Shelby and Melissa say at the same time. They say "cheers" to this even though their drinks are still too full. Clear liquid splashes everywhere.

"She'll gain ten points for being the first one to bed Nathan Diggs." Shelby winks at me.

This makes us laugh, and we're still laughing when Danica breezes through the front door. Her hair is wild and she's got a ridiculous smile on her face. "What's so funny?"

"Well, well, well, where have you been?" I ask, even though it's so obvious. Danica has a poker face, but her hair always gives her away. Down and wild and obviously *handled*. She's been with Robert.

"Whaaaat?" she says. Her smile fades slightly when she looks at Shelby.

"God, Danica, couldn't you have waited until after the party to hook up with him?" Shelby frowns. "Sienna ditched us and we need a ride." I've learned recently that it's always easier to get a ride from Robert if he's getting something in return, i.e., Danica.

"Maybe Nathan Diggs can give us a ride?" Danica says. "I saw him in the library today looking all studious and sexy."

"He's out of town," I tell her.

"So what did I miss?" Danica takes a huge sip of her drink, then purses her lips together to keep a straight face. "Did you spill the dirty details about Diggs yet?"

"If someone says the word *spill* one more time, I'm going to lose it." I press my fingers against my temple.

"Spill, spill, spill," Melissa says, knocking into me, and once again, some of my drink trickles out of my glass.

A smile creeps onto my lips. "What do you heathens want to know?" Usually we just cover the basics: what was done, how long it lasted, and of course, how big it was. I didn't tell them that Trip actually blushed the first time I saw him naked. Or that the first time he put his hand up my skirt, it felt so good that I thought if he was going to stop touching me I'd have no choice but to rip out all my hair.

"Tell us everything!" Shelby slams her hand on the counter, impatient.

For some reason I don't want to share. Nathan's still a mystery at Lincoln High. This isn't like when I started hooking up with Trip and everyone already knew what he was like between the sheets.

The first thing I think of to share is that Nathan was also accepted to Barron; that he was just as nervous about skipping school and getting called into the office as I was. How he insisted on meeting my parents and tried really hard to impress them. And that he succeeded. But this isn't what they're after. If I exposed this, they would assume I thought Nathan was different, when I'm smarter than that. I love that right now I'm the only one who really knows anything about Nathan, with or without his clothes on. I'm not ready to give that up. Not while it's still mine. It's not going to be mine for long.

"Let's just say it was awesome," I tell them, clamping down on my straw.

They all cheer and laugh and give me high fives. I always feel like a lame frat boy whenever we do this, but whatever. 'Tis better to be the lame frat boy than the sorority girl getting used.

CHAPTER
ELEVEN

By the time Patrick Smith and Leila Court arrive to pick us up for the party, it's nearly ten thirty, and even though we've eaten two large pepperoni pizzas, we're still pretty tipsy.

"Hey, *my* lovelies!" Leila says. That's the way she talks, as though everything is hers. "*My* lovelies." "*My* bestie." "*My* Steve Maddens." "*My* Patrick."

"*My*, oh *my*," Shelby says, and we all burst out laughing as we squish together in the backseat of Patrick's Jeep Cherokee. Shelby always makes fun of Leila, sometimes right in front of her, because she never gets it, and if she does, she doesn't seem to care. We actually like Leila, though. And it's not because she's more popular than us, because she definitely is. Not by much, but she's a cheerleader and her best friend is Celine McGillicutty. We like her because she's seriously fun and nearly evolved.

"I brought my cherry vodka," Leila says, swiveling around in the front seat to show it off.

"You're *my* favorite person tonight," I say to Leila. Shelby shakes from laughter next to me, and soon I'm laughing so hard I can barely keep my eyes open. Everything is whirling around me.

Leila claps at our excitement and leans over to kiss Patrick on the cheek. When I say Leila is nearly evolved, Patrick would be the hiccup in her growth. She was completely cool when Shelby lost her virginity to Patrick two summers ago during one of Leila and Patrick's many, many breaks. Very evolved of her. Leila's only downfall is TGS. After about a month of being on with Patrick, she always demands to be his girlfriend. When he ignores this demand and rebels against it by either flirting with a big-breasted junior or forgetting to return Leila's phone calls, it's always the same: Leila cries, sometimes in public. Sometimes she even throws stuff at him—yes, in public too. And predictably, he tells his friends, and girls like Shelby, Danica, Melissa, and me—the only females at Lincoln who understand that this is unacceptable—that Leila is a "crazy bitch." We gave up trying to defend her the day she threw a tennis ball at his face during PE and gave him a black eye. And to think, it all could have been avoided if she'd just kept the g-word out of her mouth. Say "girlfriend" and boys say "good-bye."

We get to the party and some guy I don't recognize greets us as we walk into the shabby apartment. Unidentified guy waves and says, "Who's getting lucky tonight?"

Patrick high-fives him. Leila is too busy hugging her vodka to know what's going on. Melissa frowns at the boy. Danica glares at him. Shelby rolls her eyes, but as soon as we're away from him, she turns to me and says, "Speaking of getting lucky."

She points across the party to Tommy Rizzo. His curly black hair is tucked under a white baseball cap and he's teaching some skinny blonde wearing dark red lipstick how to pump the keg.

There's a moment when our eyes meet. He's got his arm around the girl and he's leaning into her, and I've spent the last few days making out with someone else. There's an unanswered message from him on my phone from two days ago. But that doesn't matter now.

"That's over," Shelby says, but she still glances at me, waiting for confirmation.

Tommy Rizzo raises his glass in my direction, freeing his arm for the moment. He motions to the keg. An offering. But since we've brought our own vodka, I shake my head. He nods and turns away.

We've detached. Just like that.

"That's over," I tell her, looking away from him.

"Kiss that Wintermint breath good-bye." Danica giggles. We've all made out with the Riz at one time or another because he's an amazing kisser and always chews Wintermint gum. I was the last one to kiss him.

Full disclosure: I spoke to Tommy Rizzo via text every day over winter break, and the day after Christmas we went to second base. I was semi-using him to distract me because Trip hadn't called, even though he'd been in town at his dad's for Christmas. I'm fairly certain Tommy Rizzo was using me, too.

Sometimes I'm still amazed at how easy it is to move from hooking up over winter break to being distant acquaintances at a party. Like after Shelby had sex with Forest Lester, he stopped calling her, but he would still high-five her during football games and give her piggy-back rides to Spanish class and pick her up for parties. It was like, no harm, no foul. He still wanted to hang out with her, he just didn't want to be with her—and that wasn't her fault. He was a high school boy: he didn't want to be with anyone. At the end of the day there was no awkwardness, and Shelby could say she'd screwed Forest Lester.

I know that with all the frat-boy high-fiving and how the four of us pass Tommy Rizzo around like a good sweater, it must seem like we're really slutty. That's completely wrong. Danica has only had sex with four people, which is two more than Shelby, three more than me, and four more than Melissa.

Shelby puts her hands on my shoulders and smiles at me. "At least you didn't have to use Nathan as your Exit Strategy."

Shelby always knows how to cheer me up and remind me that what's irking me isn't something I should care about at all.

The Detach is simple. The Exit Strategy is hard. It means action, sometimes a conversation. It means you have to be cruel. Melissa cried last year when she had to employ an Exit Strategy. I don't blame her. She'd been making out with Todd Ahlstrom pretty consistently for about a month, but she was over it.

To Melissa's credit, she detached from him in the exact way she was supposed to. She stopped texting him and stopped returning his texts. She was aloof in the halls and didn't indulge in conversations lasting more than three minutes. Todd should have taken the out, backed off, and moved on to some other girl like most boys would have done. But he didn't. So there was no other choice.

The night Melissa employed her Exit Strategy, I was her accomplice. One of Trip's best friends, Liam Poole, had mentioned he thought Melissa was hot, so the four of us went to a basketball game together. Trip and Liam stood behind us on the bleachers with their arms dangling around our shoulders, kissing our necks whenever they felt like it and rubbing up against us as though no one could see.

But of course, everyone could. Including Todd. I'll never forget the way his face looked when he noticed Melissa and the six-foot-four senior god with his lips pressed against her cheek. He looked like his heart was breaking. Melissa closed her eyes and let Liam kiss away her guilt.

Yes, I never wanted to make anyone's face look the way Todd's did the night Melissa employed an Exit Strategy. But I never wanted be on the receiving end of an Exit Strategy, either.

After about an hour at the party, I'm sick of hearing Nathan's name. Everyone's asking me about him. And they won't just call him Nathan; they all say "Nathan Diggs," like he's famous, which I guess at Lincoln he is, but still.

My friends get tired of it too.

"This party is so typical," Shelby complains.

It's not typical to me, but I can see what she's saying. Dingy apartment. Filthy carpet. Flat screen sitting atop an entertainment unit from IKEA. Posters taped to the whitewashed walls. Rap music, cheap beer, smoky air, and lame locals.

We quarantine ourselves in a corner of the living room near an open window.

Shelby and I are nestled together on a large recliner,

and Melissa and Danica sit across from us on an ottoman. We've taken the cherry vodka, since Patrick is making out with Leila and she's completely forgotten about *her* alcohol. We pass it around, sipping it slowly because we're all already pretty hammered.

"Oh my God, no!" Shelby bursts out. Not so discreetly, she points to the far end of the room, where Chiffon Dillon has made an appearance. This is the first time I've been here to witness a Chiffon run-in since Tommy Rizzo's barbecue last summer, when Shelby was unsuccessful in calling a truce. I don't know if my friends will ignore her or chase her away or provoke her, since they're bored. I take another sip from the bottle, but it does nothing to calm me.

"What is she wearing?" Melissa says, leaning toward us. Danica snorts with laughter. "Her boots! Ew!" Melissa continues, wrinkling her nose but smiling like she's on the verge of laughter herself.

"Those are townie-hunting boots!" Danica says.

They all start to laugh, and I join them—I can't help it. I don't know if it's the vodka. It must be. I can't stop laughing about how Chiffon only dates the guys who haven't moved out of their parents' houses since high school—who wouldn't have looked twice at her when they were *in* high school. Shelby clutches my arm and looks right at me, like she wants to make sure I'm really here with them. It's been so long since I've stayed out late laughing like this with my best friends.

"Didn't you hear?" Shelby says, out of breath. "She's caught one!"

We try to contain our laughter because we don't want to miss Shelby's gossip. Shelby is always the first one to hear anything worth repeating.

"And surprise, surprise, he's keeping their 'relationship' a secret." Shelby rolls her eyes as she makes air quotes.

"Who?" Danica squeals.

"Guess!" Shelby yells back, and we all groan because we're too impatient for this right now.

"I'll give you a hint," Shelby says. "Chiffon should really be wearing a shirt that says 'Stepmom in Training.'"

"Zane Chapman?" Danica and I guess at the exact same time. Shelby confirms that we're right by repeating his name loud enough for everyone in the living room to hear over the music. Besides being the legendary older Chapman brother, Zane Chapman is also the father of a one-year-old named Billy—he knocked up his on-again-off-again girlfriend, Jamie, just four months after meeting her at the community college. He used to be the hottest senior at Lincoln, but that was three years ago, so since he still lives with his dad and is *still* gossip around Lincoln High, he has adapted to townie status.

"Oh hell, I need a cigarette!" Danica says this

whenever she hears something shocking. She means it only about 50 percent of the time. She digs a cigarette and a lighter out of her purse. Melissa makes a big deal about moving the bottle of vodka away, like it's going to ignite into large flames if it gets anywhere near the lighter.

"Better paranoid than sorry" has always been Melissa's motto, and she screams it at Danica after Danica not so subtly rolls her eyes at her.

"'Cowards die many times before their deaths,'" Danica says.

"Huh?" Melissa's mouth hangs open.

"From *Julius Caesar*," Danica says.

"*Obviously,*" Shelby says.

We laugh so hard and loud that there's no way everyone doesn't assume we've just lit up a joint instead of a cigarette.

Chiffon makes the mistake of walking past us. To get through the living room, she's forced to. My stomach takes a quick dive. The last time there was a Shelby/Chiffon face-off, Shelby told Chiffon her chlamydia was showing.

When Chiffon is close enough to hear, Shelby says, "So they're just letting in strays; are they immune to the smell of trash?" Her voice melts immediately back into laughter. The kind that makes it hard for her to breathe.

It's contagious, that kind of laughter, and we all bust

up. I don't feel uneasy when I'm laughing like this, and I take another sip to chase the last of my nerves away for good.

Chiffon glares at us before leaving the room. It's a look that, thanks to that night at Tommy's barbecue, we know means *Die, bitch*. We're laughing even harder now. I'm so glad she's gone.

I'm dizzy. From booze. From happiness. From the smoke lingering in the air from Danica's cigarette. But this is my favorite moment of the entire day. Melissa topples over, drunk and giggling, and we all pull her up, the four of us collapsing into a BFF pile on the chair. This even trumps watching Nathan attempt an Irish accent in Drama, and the way he stared at me the whole time. Like I was the only audience member who mattered.

The three of them have been having this kind of fun all through high school. This is what they've done countless nights. Every weekend. I can finally join them. Just in the nick of time, too.

You could have left for college a lightweight, Shelby used to joke.

You could have left for college without knowing what a good drink was and been one of those girls who order nothing but Midori.

You could have left for college a virgin.

It was all true.

You could have left for college with a boyfriend. And this would have been my worst offense by far.

I love my friends because my friends are real. We can be loud and destructive and crazy, but there's nothing fake about us. So even though we're just laughing and drinking—and in about an hour we're going to bum a ride off of Celine's forever-sober little sister and pass out in Shelby's room—it still makes me feel happier, and more successful, than I've felt all week. Maybe all year. Because getting into Barron is a huge accomplishment, but having good friends, real friends, the kind you keep forever, is an even bigger triumph.

"Good night, *my* lovelies," Shelby says well after two a.m., as we lie in the California king-size bed Sandra handed down to Shelby when Phil bought her a new one last year. We laugh at Leila's expense one last time before drifting off. Right before sleep takes over, I think, *This is what I'm really going to miss when I'm at Barron next year.*

CHAPTER TWELVE

"You look amazing," Nathan says Monday morning when he passes me in the hall on the way to fourth period.

I *do* look hot—it's not an accident. Nathan spent an entire weekend away doing God knows what with God knows who—so of course I'm going to remind him of what he's been missing. Of course.

He stops me and tugs on the bottom of my low-cut shirt that hugs me in all the right places. It's made of a lace material that no doubt reminds him of lingerie. "I like this."

"Oh, this old thing?"

Nathan tries to stare back at me, but his eyes drift down. I can't blame them.

In Drama we sneak away. Mrs. Seymour has left the class to its own devices again, and no one's in the mood to act. Melvin gave up trying to corral us for a reading of *Hamlet* after Robert Jules asked if we could use the fake blood. The idea of wasting drama supplies seemed to terrify Melvin as much as saying no to Robert Jules. Nathan and I slink backstage and find an old couch shoved into a corner with the rest of the furniture props.

"I had the best weekend," he tells me. He's got his arm slung over the back of the couch. I'm tingling because he's so close, and I don't want anything to spoil it. I do not want to hear about his weekend.

"Me too," I say, leaning into him ever so slightly.

Nathan leans into me, too, but then I notice he's only leaning my way to pull something out of his back pocket.

"This is my best friend, Bobby—it was his birthday," he says, holding his phone in front of me, scrolling through pictures of his weekend. "Why he wore that stupid crown I don't know. Must've seemed like a good idea after all that gin. . . ."

We flip through several pictures of a redheaded boy with thick-rimmed glasses and a cardboard crown on his head (from Burger King, I guess) smiling ridiculously with Nathan and a slew of other people who Nathan's more than happy to tell me about. He even lets me hold the phone and tells me to scroll through the pictures. It's like he has absolutely nothing to hide.

The photos of Bobby's party are very different from the photos of any of the parties I've gone to with Shelby, Danica, and Melissa. These are the kinds of parties Ella and Marnie—and boys like Ivan Gunderson—attend. Sure, everyone's having fun. And they're drinking. They hold up their cups proudly. They stick out their tongues. Their heads are pressed together as if they don't understand how much of the room the camera actually captures. San Diego is a much larger town, so I expected his parties to reflect that. These photos reveal what I suspected about Nathan. There's a bottle of gin sitting next to a game of Scrabble. It's the same eight kids in all the pictures. This confirms that he spent most of his time in high school studying; that when he did hang out—which probably wasn't often—he did it with only the other AP students. I'm an AP student, and no, I'm not insulting myself—I believe there are exceptions to every rule. The exception for me is that I have Shelby.

Nathan didn't have anyone to keep him from turning into what Shelby calls "the lame brains." Nathan didn't have anyone to take him out of that world. He does now.

He catches me smiling at him. It's a small smile, but still. I feel so busted.

He tilts his head toward me like he's got a secret.

"You have to visit sometime," he says. "You've never been, have you?"

I shake my head and try to look bored.

He gives me a sideways smile that makes me want to kiss him. "I told my friends about you. They think I'm making you up."

He turns the phone on me and I hear a click.

"There," he says. "Proof."

Luckily, it's a good picture. Nathan basically calling me one of a kind shouldn't surprise me—few girls at Lincoln High are evolved.

He teases me, hovering close and letting his hot breath tickle my lips before he goes in for the kill.

I pull away when I hear my phone buzz and retrieve it from my purse. It's something I would normally ignore, but if I've learned anything, it's that just the right amount of unavailability has the potential to prolong the typical hookup period.

I stand and walk a few feet away. As though my text message is personal and I have to be alone to read it. Really it's just an excuse to stand so he'll have a full view of me. I hear him clear his throat.

The feeling creeps over me—the same feeling I got last year when we first used the theories and they started to really work. Satisfaction and excitement, but also the comfort of knowing that I am in complete control.

Ironic because the text I receive is from Trip Chapman. The last boy to make me feel like this.

THE TEXT FROM Trip was followed up shortly by a phone call, which I ignored on my way to lunch. No voice mail because Trip has never had the patience to wait through the greeting.

"Trip called?" Shelby is appalled. We're all at our usual table in the cafeteria at lunchtime.

"The nerve." I roll my eyes and laugh, but Melissa still gives me a look that's dripping with sympathy.

"Well, he did pocket-call you in December," Melissa says. "Oh, and he sent you that 'Happy New Year' text."

"He sent that to all of us," Shelby says, her mouth full of turkey sandwich.

Before any of them have a chance to think it, I announce, "I'm not going to call him back. I don't even want to talk to him. I don't care."

"What did his text say?" Melissa asks.

I show them.

I'M BACK THIS WEEKEND, COME BY MY HOUSE ON SUNDAY. I WANT TO TALK.

Danica twirls her finger around the straw hanging out of her Diet Coke. "You're not even a little bit curious about what he wants?"

"We know what he wants." Shelby sighs and pouts a little. She's bored with this. "Where's Nathan? Why doesn't he ever eat lunch with us?"

"He's studying."

"Laaammmeee," Melissa sings.

I'm about to defend him, explain that he partied so hard last weekend that he didn't study for the Spanish test he has next period—even though that's not true—but they've already switched topics. Not that they would recognize that as a legitimate excuse anyway. Especially not now, with graduation creeping up on us.

CHAPTER THIRTEEN

'm lying on Nathan's bed, on top of my open physics book, while he kisses me. I stare up at the ceiling. Snow slowly covers the skylight.

"I've never met anyone like you," Nathan says against my cheek.

This makes me smile. I keep my mouth closed, so it comes off looking like more of a smirk. "I'm exactly like you."

He laughs. "You think so?"

Nathan's room matches his house. Big. Clean. Dare I say, *lavish*. His bed has actual posts. And a painting of the ocean in a thick brass frame hanging above his desk—a full-size desk that looks like it belongs in a CEO's office. But apart from that, his room is exactly like mine. Textbooks littered with Post-its marking the important pages. Highlighters, red pens, pencils. Stacks of note cards. A dictionary and thesaurus piled up next to *The Elements of Style*. A stress-relief ball sitting next to his laptop on the desk. "Yes. Exactly."

I notice a Barron college sweater hanging on his wall next to his bookshelf. Nathan notices me noticing.

"Both of my parents have PhDs from Barron," he tells me.

"Impressive."

He twirls his fingers in a circle on my shoulder, but it's not romantic, it's more like a nervous tic.

I turn so I can see him better, careful not to move out of his reach. His grip on me tightens slightly when I shift, as though he thinks I'm going to roll away.

"You don't seem very excited."

His lips form the tiniest smile. He stares up at the skylight even though the sky isn't visible anymore. "I think Barron is what I want."

He *thinks*. As in, Barron wasn't his first and only choice. His front-runner goal. The light at the end of the cram-session tunnel. The best alternative for going away to college and not attending one of the two state schools—cleverly referred to by everyone as "State" and "the University," because this is as creative as it gets around here. I realize in one horrible second that there seems to be this gaping hole in my college experience when I think about strolling Barron's campus without the possibility of bumping into Nathan. I'm disgusted with myself for this.

"Why did you decide to go to Barron?" he says, as if Barron was something I chose. As if I didn't work my ass off so they would choose me.

"Because, it's Barron." That should be enough of an explanation for him. It should be enough of an explanation for anyone.

He lowers his eyebrows and nods.

"If not Barron, then where?" I ask. I don't especially want to know the answer. I don't understand what the alternative could possibly be.

"I don't know, really. There are a lot of great schools out there," he says. His smile widens just slightly and he looks down. "Some of the state universities in California are part of this program that allows engineering students to intern on huge private projects supporting new technology. Plus, not going to Barron is the most efficient way to rebel against my parents."

He laughs, so I do too—because it is adorable that he's talking about *efficient rebellion*, especially when I get the sense that skipping school with me is the most he's ever colored outside the lines.

"Yes, but"—I prop myself up so we're face-to-face— "why would you ever turn down the opportunity to go to Barron?"

Nathan smiles like he's amused and pushes my hair behind my ear. "I wouldn't," he says, pulling me closer and kissing me until I forget all about Barron.

You have to live moment to moment, I remind myself. *The theories exist because moments like this are fleeting. And I only get to have this moment because of the theories.* I let myself soak into him.

There's a noise then, the sound of the door opening. Followed by a woman's voice.

"Why is this door closed? Nathan, you know the rules."

Nathan and I both stand. Carefully. I'm at the side of the bed and Nathan's at the end. Mrs. Diggs is petite, delicate. Short black hair curling at the ends, a peach cardigan draped over her tiny shoulders. She's looking at me like she's already offended.

"Who's this?"

"This is Aubrey, Mom."

"Pleased to meet you." She's not eager to shake my hand, and she's looking at it like she's wondering where it's been.

"We're studying." Nathan's hands are in his pockets, but he nods at the books scattered on the bed. There's a piece of paper that crumpled from where my head leaned into it when we were making out, and I want to die. Nathan's blushing. He's not at all smooth, though I have to appreciate his embarrassment because sometimes Trip wouldn't even bother getting off me when his dad walked in.

"I've heard a lot about you," she finally says. She even gives me a small smile. "You're going to Barron."

I glance at Nathan, who is also smiling. It's my cue to smile too.

"It's a great school," she says. "Nice to meet you."

I echo this to her, but I end up interrupting her a little.

"Dinner's at six," she says to Nathan, and the silence that follows—the place where she doesn't invite me to join them for dinner—fills the room, so I lie and say, "I have to be home early." It's awkward again, and *again* I'm the cause.

"It's a school night," she offers before leaving, making a point to keep the door wide open.

"So that was your mother."

"I didn't know she would be home so early," he says. I'm not sure if it's an apology. He pulls out the desk chair and takes a seat. A proper place to sit. I don't blame him—I don't want to go anywhere near the bed either, now that the door's open and his mother hates me.

It's when I'm standing there, shifting my weight from one foot to the other and watching Nathan slide his chair over to the edge of the bed, using the bed like it's a desk, that I realize none of this is right. I shouldn't have to worry about impressing Nathan's mother, or about what I should do to get her to like me, or have to walk on eggshells now that the door is open. Nathan and I are not in a relationship. We're not falling in love. We just happen to enjoy hanging out and messing around, and there's really no reason that *his mother's* opinion should be relevant at all.

If the theories exist to make the boys more comfortable, they also exist to make things more comfortable for us.

I flop down on the bed, lying on my stomach, the same way I was lying side by side with Nathan an hour ago, before he started kissing me. He looks a little surprised to see me sprawled out like this, but I ignore him. I turn my attention back to the theory of relativity and pretend not to notice that now he might be irritated with my lightheartedness and actually care that I failed to impress his mother.

"You're reading that book at an incredible rate," Nathan says, noticing that I'm flipping the pages haphazardly before I realize I'm doing it. Apparently I'm no good at fake reading.

"I'm skimming."

Nathan gives me a kind smile. "She'll be much better the next time. It just takes her a while to warm to people . . . to anything new." His voice is quiet, and I wonder if she's listening.

I shrug and I mean it. The name of the game is indifference, and Shelby, Danica, Melissa, and I are pros.

"You look comfortable," he says. He seems amused, and I can't tell if he's also hinting at me to change my position, lest his *mother* walk by.

"I am. Thanks."

I leave at five o'clock because I can't stand to stay any longer than that.

CHAPTER
FOURTEEN

The abnormality of my new life is easy to adjust to. I know it hasn't really been that long; I've known Nathan for only two weeks, but I'm actually having trouble remembering what life was like when I wasn't spending all of Drama class searching for opportunities to make out with him, and every hour after school either talking with my friends about making out with him or actually making out with him, in the backseat of his car or in his bedroom that precious hour before his mother comes home from work. I used to have student council meetings or debate team or study sessions with Ella and Marnie after school. All those things seem so strange and foreign now.

Nathan and I do spend a lot of time studying. Because being accepted into Barron means you still have to take a few AP classes your senior year.

With Nathan, it's enjoyable, though. Not that I didn't find some pleasure in it before, but I'm pretty positive that without Barron to motivate me, any academic obligation this semester would seem like just that. Obligation. There are some things that almost never go together—i.e., boys and studying—but when they do, it's surprisingly spectacular. Like bacon ice cream, for example. Shelby dared me to order a scoop one afternoon when we were bored, and we fought over who would take the first bite, then fought over who got to finish it off because it turned out to be outrageously delicious.

"You're falling asleep," Nathan says into my ear. We go parking during lunch. The word *parking*, like we're living in the fifties, makes us laugh every time. But that's really the most accurate description for what we're doing.

"This book." I sigh. I have to have it finished by Monday. It's Friday. Nathan's the only one who understands this urgency, who knows without my having to explain it that I want to finish the book today so I can write notes on Saturday and spend Sunday evening reviewing them.

"Here," he says, helping me sit up. "Come here." He puts his arm around me. My body battles with itself for a second: the heat of his skin versus the chills (the good kind) I get whenever he touches me.

He takes the worn school copy of *As I Lay Dying* and holds it out in front of us.

"Where'd you leave off?"

I point to the end of the second paragraph on the right page, curious whether he's going to do what I think he's going to do. And he does. He reads to me.

At first I want to laugh. I know that's what Shelby would do. But the truth is, I like it.

It feels personal. Everything Nathan does feels personal.

AFTER SCHOOL I'M meeting Nathan at his house. His parents will be gone until seven. He's sure this time.

"Bring him to Robert's when you're done with him," Shelby says to me. That's where all the fun is happening tonight.

I nod at her. "All right."

"*Somebody's* a little eager," Shelby says in Melissa's ear, but loud enough that I can hear.

"She can hardly wait—look at her." Melissa giggles.

I grin, despite myself.

I'm outlasting the two-week mark with Nathan. Trip was mine for a long, long time, thanks to the theories. But that's also because he wasn't entirely mine. And I was never entirely his. After I take Nathan to Robert's tonight more people will know what I know: that Nathan is perfect. And he'll start to learn about them, too.

"You know what?" I interrupt Shelby in the middle of a story about Leila and lost girl points. "I don't think Nathan and I are going to make it tonight, after all."

"That's bullshit!" she says, then gasps. "Wait! Are you finally going to do the deed?"

"Probably," I tell her. It's not the truth, although I suppose it could be. Nathan and I have always kept one layer of clothing—even it was just underwear—between us and *the deed*. We've never even attempted to cross that barrier.

The two of them proceed with the usual screaming and cheering, along with "Get it!" and "Remember to wrap the pickle!" and "No glove, no love!" Because, as Shelby always says, we're "condom advocates."

"Calm down!" I yell at them. My heart has already started to race. They laugh, so I laugh too. Just the thought of having sex with Nathan makes my palms sweaty.

"Have fun, be safe" are Shelby's parting words.

NATHAN GREETS ME at the front door with a kiss. "There you are."

"Here I am." Then Nathan is kissing me again. And pulling me up the stairs, into his bedroom.

I fall back onto his bed while he locks the door, and I stare up through the skylight. The snow has melted, and the sky is gray and cloudy. Nathan lies down next to me on his side; he puts his hand on my stomach as he kisses me. Night comes faster in the winter, but it feels better, more romantic, more intense, being with him like this while the world outside is dark and sleepy and cold.

When we've reached the point of one layer and he's kissing my neck, I whisper in his ear. "Do you have something?"

He rolls to his side, keeping one hand resting on my rib cage.

"What?" But I can tell by his face that he understood me.

He doesn't move, so I do. I sit up. My purse is across the room, and yes, I've got a condom in it. Shelby gave them to us last year when she told us we should always have one on us because you never know when you might need it. She was right. "I have something, I think—"

Nathan puts his hand on my shoulder, stopping me.

"Wait," he says. "Are you sure?" He sounds calm, which I expected, but he also doesn't sound like he really believes I want to have sex, or that I have a condom in my purse.

"I'm sure," I tell him. He takes his hand off my shoulder, but he uses it to rub under his chin. He doesn't look at all excited that I'm ready to give him the one thing *everyone* wants. "Do you not want to?" I sound irritated. I was trying for confident.

"It's not that." His lips turn up a little, and I'm glad.

"I know. I mean, I *know* you want to."

He looks at me, confused, so I let my eyes travel down. He's only wearing one layer, after all. He blushes, but he also smiles.

"You got me," he says, laughing lightly. "Us guys, we're all so transparent."

"You all are, actually."

He stops me again when I move to stand.

I stare at him. Waiting. He looks flushed—*flustered*, maybe—and he takes a deep breath. So I just ask him. "Have you never . . . before—"

"No, I have. Once. Have you?"

"Well, yeah." It shocks me a little that he thinks I haven't.

He nods and looks to the ground.

"With just one person," I add, even though it shouldn't matter to him. There's a pull to tell him I have a *one* in the equation of experience too. Just like he does.

He nods again. "Your ex-boyfriend?"

"No, not exactly." I fix my eyes on my purse across the room. We're not supposed to be discussing it like this, explaining ourselves. It's supposed to be one of the impulsive moments that we get to keep after time and high school have pulled us apart.

"Aubrey." I feel his hand brush against my cheek and I look at him. "I want to . . . but—not—"

"But not tonight."

He shakes his head. "I'm too afr—I'm apprehensive. My mom could come home early again. And I want it to be perfect." He's holding my hand, and I don't even remember when he grabbed it. His thumb traces circles on the inside of my wrist. It's one of his nervous tics, but it is romantic sometimes too.

It feels like my whole body is smiling. "Okay," I say. "Another time." After a moment I add, "When you're not afraid." I can't help myself.

Nathan covers his face with his free hand, but he's grinning so wide I can see his teeth. He playfully pushes me back, and then he's hovering over me, kissing my neck, my cheeks. "I said *apprehensive*," he says. "I was very careful."

I laugh. It's nice this once to feel like the reckless one.

CHAPTER FIFTEEN

"I'm bored!" Shelby proclaims on Saturday night. We're doing what people do when they're bored on Saturday nights. We're wandering the mall drinking cherry Slurpees mixed with vodka and waiting for something to miraculously entertain us. But this time Nathan is with us.

"We could go to Paul's," Patrick says. The first time he said this, we pretended we didn't hear him. This time we don't give him that same courtesy. Shelby groans and Melissa gasps like he's just suggested we spend the night committing murder. Danica sighs and puts her hands on her hips. Paul Detrick wasn't cool when he went to

Lincoln High two years ago, and he still isn't cool. But now he has his own apartment and buys a keg every weekend. His parties are always heavily attended when there's absolutely nothing else to do, which is why Shelby named him Last-Resort Paul.

"I'm never going to another one of Last-Resort Paul's parties again," Melissa says loudly. "I made a vow, remember?"

It's true. In November she got doused with beer by one of Paul's loser friends and vowed loudly and officially, with one finger in the air, that she would never set foot inside Paul Detrick's apartment again. None of us took her seriously, of course. She goes where we go, and none of us made that vow. Although we probably should have. The one and only time I've been to Paul's, my feet stuck to the linoleum floor.

"You could take us, right, man?" Patrick nudges Nathan.

Nathan picked us up from Shelby's and drove us here, where we met Robert and Patrick.

"You could drive my car," Patrick says, addressing the problem of how seven people would fit in one BMW, since Patrick drives an SUV.

When Nathan declined a vodka-laced Slurpee, I thought about declining too. Then he jingled his keys to explain, and I knew staying sober would make me look loyal in the worst way possible. But it's been much too long since someone's told me I'm charming when I'm drunk who wasn't also drunk, so I sip my drink slowly.

It's Shelby who comes to Nathan's rescue. "Drop it, Patrick. If you want to go to Last-Resort Paul's, go by yourself."

Patrick gives Shelby one of those extremely perverted smiles that are not at all subtle. "I'll stay for you, Shels."

"You've had too much of this," Shelby says flatly, not looking at him. She yanks the Slurpee out of his hand and gives it to Robert, who lets out a small hoot of joy as he dumps Patrick's Slurpee into his cup.

Shelby shoots me a smile. She got Patrick off her back, which was precisely what she wanted. Leila and Patrick are on the outs again, which means he's looking for someone to hook up with tonight. And since Shelby's hooked up with him before, he's playing the odds. Such a wasted effort. Part of the reason Shelby hooked up with him in the first place was because Patrick's probably the most attractive guy in our class. The other part is that she used to really like him. Her crush on him started in the third grade and, from what I can tell, ended that hot summer night when she hooked up with him in his parents' bedroom with all the lights on and a party raging on the other side of the door. Shelby's first time.

I wonder if Nathan's bored. If he wishes we were spending tonight how we spent last night. Or if he wishes our Saturday nights were more like how his used to be.

If he wishes we were playing Scrabble or that some of us were wearing paraphernalia from a fast-food restaurant.

"What would you normally be doing on a boring Saturday night?" Shelby's the one who asks him this. Everyone stops walking to listen.

"Maybe he's never had a dull night." Danica laughs.

Nathan shakes his head and returns his gaze to me. It almost seems like he's uncomfortable looking at anyone else. "It was all dull Friday nights," he says, smiling a little, like maybe he wants us to think he's joking.

"In that case"—Shelby's got a stupid grin on her face and the devil in her eyes—"the haunted barn. Or are you too scared, Robert?"

"Please," Robert says.

"No," Danica, Melissa, and I whine almost at the same time. "Not the haunted barn."

"Don't be such babies!" Shelby groans.

"It's forty minutes away," I argue, my eyes falling on Nathan so they get the point: we're not going to just ask Nathan Diggs to drive us all the way out to the haunted barn, a place you seriously have to be drunk to enjoy.

"I don't mind," Nathan says quickly.

"The haunted barn sucks. We're not going," Danica says.

"Even Dull Diggs is down to go," Shelby tells us. "Why are you all acting like such lame-asses?" Shelby puts her hands in her pockets and does *the move*, which isn't going to work on me but will probably work on the male members of the group.

"I'm not being a lame-ass; I just don't want to drive all the way out there."

"It's not like you have a curfew tonight. Everyone is staying with me except—"

Before she can give Nathan another awful nickname, I surrender. That's the only choice, really, when Shelby has her mind made up. "Fine. Let's just get it over with."

Nathan turns to Shelby. "So tell me about this . . . haunted barn. Is it as self-explanatory as it seems?"

Shelby's booming laugh drowns out mine. "Come on, Diggs." She tilts her head at the exit. "We'll take you places you've never been before."

We follow Shelby out to the parking lot and search for Patrick's SUV. Of course he's forgotten where he parked it.

"You'd better call shotgun," Nathan says in my ear. It surprises me that he thinks anyone would challenge the front seat when I'm the reason he's here. For now. When I do say "Shotgun!" once the car is in clear view, everyone ignores me—like this is no surprise. Nathan ignores me too, because he was probably kidding about it all along.

There is only one reason people go to the haunted barn: so they can talk about it the next week at school. So that instead of saying "we walked around the mall drinking until we got bored enough to see a movie, then passed out at Shelby's at a very unreasonable hour," we can say we did something out of town and dangerous.

ONE HOUR LATER the six of us stand on the hard dirt ground in front of the haunted barn, waiting to be haunted. Or freeze to death, whichever happens first.

"This is nice," Nathan says, eyeing the decrepit old barn.

It really does look like it could fall over at any moment, which would actually be more exciting than what we're really waiting for. The haunting. There's something that happens every once in a while. The barn comes to life. The two large doors in front, wide enough for things like tractors and multiple cows to fit through, open slowly, then shut all on their own. While this is happening, the regular-size doors on the right side of the barn are also opening and shutting on their own. My dad, forever the engineer, once told me that it's the barn's structure, the way the foundation was laid and the way the unsteady wood framing has shifted with time, that makes the doors do that. Mainly he told me so I would never go inside the barn. As if a possible encounter with a ghost wasn't enough of a reason to keep me out.

"Just be patient, Diggs," Shelby tells Nathan.

"We spend so much time waiting," Robert says. "It feels like this is all there is. It's like we don't have to be anywhere ever again."

Robert is drunk, but I get this. Saturday nights feel like this sometimes when they're slow. Like they're going to stretch out forever and ever, giving no real revelations, hitting no spikes, no climaxes, nothing new. Just a flat-line of waiting for what is bigger and better and beyond.

Melissa's voice is small, but full of concern. "My mom will worry if I don't come home."

"We have school on Monday," Danica says. "We do have *somewhere* to be."

"Fuck school," Robert replies.

"We need school," Melissa says, like she's worried that everything we say out here in the country, in the quiet, is going to be the truth somehow.

In the silence that follows, Nathan and I exchange a quick glance. We need school so we can leave. So we can find the bigger and better and beyond.

"Can you imagine how sad it would be," Robert says, "to have all the time in the world to just wait for something that might never happen?"

"So . . . there's a chance that *nothing* will happen with this barn?" The second the last syllable escapes Nathan's lips, the barn comes to life. This excites us more than it should. We're screaming and Patrick is running around in circles like a hyper dog. Nathan and Robert high-five. Melissa jumps up and down. Shelby is wearing that rare smile on her face where her mouth opens so wide, a bird could fly right into it. Danica is howling with laughter.

We're all so happy not to be waiting anymore. With the moonlight bouncing off the metal hinges of the barn, and the creaking of the doors opening and closing mingling with the chirping crickets, it's its own kind of spectacular.

Nathan walks close to me on the way back to the car. I feel a headache in place of where I should be feeling drunk and suddenly wish I hadn't dumped so much of my Slurpee in the garbage. We're almost to the car when Patrick and Robert yell to Nathan to come over and see something. Melissa shrieks at the ground. Danica's lip curls up in disgust. It's something gross, probably a dead rat, so Nathan goes. Shelby and I know better than to follow.

Nathan looks back at me, like he's checking to make sure my arm's not extended or I'm not scampering to keep up.

"That's funny," Shelby says, noticing. "I think he's trying to *girlfriend* you."

"Maybe." It just slips out.

"Doesn't he know you're not like that?"

She means this as a compliment. I laugh and shrug like this is the first time I've ever even considered this about Nathan—because why would I?

She laughs too, but she's studying me. I can tell because her eyes don't squint like they normally do when she's really, genuinely laughing. She's searching me for weaknesses—signs that I want him to be my boyfriend, that I'm going to say yes to him if he pursues it. She wants to know if I'm turning into the girl we hate right now but know we will become someday.

The girl we will become someday: the this-love-took-me-by-surprise-and-swept-me-away girl, or the I-tried-pushing-him-away-but-failed-because-he's-so-damn-persistent-and-I-can't-deny-my-feelings-any-longer girl, and the he-finally-rescued-me-from-my-confusion-and-comforted-all-my-doubts-about-love girl.

The girl we will become someday is just that—a future person. If we were showing symptoms of becoming her right now, it'd mean we were delusional.

The obvious secret that no one ever seems to remember when they're crying their eyes out over a boy who didn't want to be their boyfriend: relationships are supposed to be accidents. You don't find them. They find you. And there is no such thing as love in high school, so playing like there is—even entertaining the thought—is a waste of your time.

"I don't get him." This statement was meant to be casual with regard to Nathan, but saying this is like admitting that I've been trying to figure him out. Shelby is smiling and I know she's not fooled for a second. I try again with, "I think he was probably a giant nerd at his old high school"—throwing Nathan under the bus if it means I get to stay in the front seat.

"I have that theory too."

"You have theories about Nathan?"

Shelby raises her eyebrows.

Of course. She has theories about everybody. "So what are they?"

"Well, originally I thought his problem was that he's a virgin." She pauses to let me react. I don't know if she expects to me laugh or if she just wants me to feel more shame since I didn't have sex with him last night like I said I would. "I think he's always been good-looking the way Patrick has always been good-looking, but Patrick has always been cool, so people have always noticed that he's good-looking. With Nathan . . . it's like it's the first time people are aware he's hot and he doesn't know what to do now that people are noticing him."

I nod. It's not so far from the theories I've had about Nathan, I suppose. It might sound like Shelby's being passive-aggressive, and what she really means is that I was the first to have Nathan Diggs by default. But I know that's not what she means. One of us would have gotten him. Because we're evolved, we always get what we want. And Nathan is desirable. There's no denying that.

"He's like a lost puppy." She laughs, and I laugh with her.

I think of the way he kissed me the first day I met him, his hands getting tighter around my waist, his chest right up against mine. And the way he charmed my parents into smiles, turned my little brothers social, and transformed a tedious book into poetry. "He's not that lost, though."

"Right," Shelby says. "He's just never had a life before." She winks at me, so I take the compliment with a smile. I think she can see the ways Nathan and I are alike. The ways I could have ended up being just like him at his old school. All the things she's saved me from.

"So are you going to see Trip tomorrow?" Shelby asks, testing.

"I don't know."

"What would stop you?" she asks, more testing.

"Um, have you met Trip? He can be . . . a pain."

"Don't you miss him?" She smiles at me and gives a small thrusting motion with her hips. She laughs as I shake my head at her.

"These days I prefer Nathan."

"Yes, but Trip was your first. You guys had something special, even if it wasn't love."

This stings a little. Only Shelby would condemn you for falling in love, but also use it against you when you didn't. But this isn't something we're supposed to fight about, so I just smile and say, "Nathan's pretty damn good," and steal her move, wiggling my eyebrows up and down.

Shelby laughs. "Don't sell yourself short."

I playfully push her, keeping my hands on her shoulders and stepping forward as she steps back. I feel my anger dissolving with the little reminder that I'm not selling myself short with Nathan. I know that. Even Shelby must know that.

Melissa and Danica rush up to join us. The boys are still several paces back, bonding over the thing Melissa clarifies is a dead prairie dog. Danica rubs Melissa's back when she tells us, because prairie dogs are much cuter than rats and it's therefore more tragic to Melissa when one of them dies.

"Nathan told her it was the circle of life. It was actually really sweet." Danica changes the subject back to Nathan and I can't deny I'm glad.

"Do you know your Exit Strategy?" Shelby asks. Both Danica and Melissa match my expression—pure shock.

"It's a little early to be talking Exit Strategy, don't you think?" Danica asks.

Shelby turns to me. "You should be ready. You don't have the luxury of escaping him after graduation."

Melissa's voice is quiet, a baby voice, that indicates both shyness and inebriation. "But what if she doesn't want to escape him?"

The boys finally stop bonding, or whatever they were doing, and come over, ready to go.

"We should start calling him 'Designated Diggs,'"

Shelby says to me as we walk toward the car. She didn't come up with this on her own—she got it from a movie, but I don't remember which one.

"Did you just refer to me as Designated Diggs?" Nathan says, raising an eyebrow. He doesn't really look mad, though, just amused.

"Dude, don't piss off the DD," Patrick says, slinking up next to Shelby in the backseat, like he thinks he might still have a chance with her since she's letting him crash at her house. He should know better. The rule is, if he gets out of his assigned recliner in the corner of Shelby's room and tries to touch any of us while we're all squished in Shelby's bed, we scream at him and make him sleep in the living room.

We drop Robert off, and when we arrive at Shelby's everyone crawls out except for me. They're loud as they walk up the crooked path from the driveway, and Patrick still tries to stand as close to Shelby as possible, sealing his fate of sleeping alone in the living room. I know they're making jokes about Nathan and me because they all turn to look at us at the same time, laughing as they walk through the front door.

I offer to ride back to the mall with Nathan, so he can drop off Patrick's car and pick up his own, but it would be out of his way to come back to Shelby's. And besides, it's not like Nathan to deny me sleep at one a.m.

We kiss in the car until the bottom of the windshield

starts to fog, both of us gasping as my lips leave his. Because of how much I don't want to leave him, I have to be the first one to break away.

When I walk into Shelby's house, Danica and Melissa are sitting on the living room couch in front of the television. Blankets and pillows are piled next to them. They look confused and tired, like they don't know what to do except stare at the Fashion Network.

"What's going on . . ." My voice trails off as I glance down the hall and notice that Shelby's bedroom door is closed. Patrick is nowhere in sight. Never in a million years would I have guessed Shelby would give Patrick what he wanted tonight. Or ever again, for that matter. Shelby always laughs at Patrick, the way he's so obviously available after Leila asks him to be her boyfriend. He's boring to Shelby. He's too easy. It's not like when we were freshmen and all she wanted was Patrick Smith. She's had him now, and never really looked back.

For a second I try to make sense of it, but barely for a second. There's only one reason Shelby would ever hook up with Patrick, and it's simple. She's hooking up with Patrick because she wants to. I'm just not sure why she would want to.

CHAPTER
SIXTEEN

"Your car's making a funny noise. Should I check under your hood?" Trip smiles gleefully as he steps off his front porch to greet me Sunday afternoon. I made the decision to come after Shelby implied on Saturday night that I might not go because of Nathan.

Trip's in the blue flannel I've seen him in a hundred times. His jeans are dirty along the bottom. His hair flops as he comes toward me. The last time we saw each other, Thanksgiving weekend, he was too busy reuniting with his old friends and boasting about college parties, football games, and sorority girls to spend much time with me. We made out in my driveway for about five minutes, but that was it. He spent Christmas at his mom's house, four hours away, so I didn't see him at all over winter break, even though I heard he made a two-day stop at his father's house.

I shrug. "If you want." My car sounds the way it always sounds. It's just been a while since Trip's heard it.

His eyebrows twitch, and I can tell by that one gesture that he was hoping I would flirt back.

My lips are begging to smile. It's the pride thing again. Smiling is a knee-jerk reaction to seeing Trip Chapman, to having someone like Trip Chapman come toward you as if you're the only person he's ever wanted to see, so I can't help that. But that's all it is.

"What's up?" I ask him casually. As if it's just another day and it hasn't been almost three months since I've seen him—since I've kissed him. I take a deep breath. I never expected Trip to call after he left for college. I never expected him to see him again like this— even though State is only an hour away.

He blows past the moment and opens his arms to hug me. I allow myself to curl up into him.

"So, here you are." Trip always speaks slowly, but he never sounds stupid. After you spend some time around him, you realize that the delay actually serves as anticipation for whatever amazingly perfect statement is going to come out of his mouth next. Trip always, without fail, says exactly what you want to hear at the exact moment you want to hear it. Even if you yourself don't know what you want to be told, Trip will tell you. Right now he says, "It's been too long, Housing. I don't know why I waited so long. . . ."

I don't say anything; I let go of him.

"You used to be over here all the time last summer. Remember?"

I nod. It was *only* eight months ago. Even though I had a curfew and he had a summer job at the auto-body shop, we still managed to see each other every day. We never clarified what exactly we meant to each other, or if either of us was allowed to see other people. Bottom line: I was having fun. And I think he was too. When Trip left for State, he said, "See you later," but we both knew he probably wouldn't. I didn't even cry. There was a moment when my chest tightened and my mouth got dry, but I didn't cry. I slept for about two days straight after he left. That's it. I'd known exactly what to expect.

"Talk some sense into him, will ya, Aubrey?" Trip's father, Earl, is on the front porch. He kicks the wooden chair next to his with his foot, gesturing for me to sit. I've always liked Earl. There are three beer cans sitting on the ground beside him and he's nursing his fourth. There is one beer next to Trip's chair, still full and getting frosty with the cold.

"Are you thirsty, honey?" Earl asks as Trip picks up his beer and Earl notices I'm the only one without a can.

"No beer for me, thanks." I smile. Earl always offers, even though I'm four years shy of the legal drinking age, because it's the polite thing to do. Earl is young for a dad and he looks it, with his thick head of sandy hair and his handlebar mustache. People around town always refer to Earl, Zane, and Trip as the Chapman Boys. *Boys.* It's very accurate. Shelby used to call the Chapman house the frat house.

"Dad, Aubrey's cold. Look at her, she's shivering. I'm taking her inside." He grabs my hand and leads me through the front door.

"Have a nice chat," Earl calls to us.

"Oh, we *will*," Trip says back, but he smiles in a way that says we won't be talking at all.

I let go of Trip's hand once we're inside. *"So?"*

He doesn't answer me as we walk into the living room, where Zane is snoring loudly on the plaid couch while a basketball game blares on the television. I forgot how much I love it here, despite this being a frat house. It's buried in the woods along the outskirts of town, like a hunting cabin, and inside there are dark green rugs and all the lampshades are red plaid. Even with beer cans hanging out next to the usual clutter of old dishes and magazines, and throw pillows on the floor next to stray socks, it's still one of the coziest places I've ever been. The giant cedar table sitting crooked in the dining room always makes the house smell like the outdoors: rich and warm. There's a fire going in the wood-burning stove, too. I melt into the scene and wonder if maybe I really have missed Trip.

Trip walks slowly down the hall, looking back a few times to see if I'm following him. I am, of course, even though it's hard to rip myself away from the comfort of the living room. I flash back to last year: sitting on that plaid couch with Trip and Zane and Earl and Shelby, laughing at sitcoms, screaming at the television during football games, playing cards huddled around the coffee table; the nights when it was just Trip and me, making out, messing around, and listening above the crackling of the fire for signs that we were going to be interrupted.

Trip's room is comfortable too, even in its messy state. The plaid comforter hangs off the bed, because everything here is plaid and nothing stays where it's supposed to. The top of his dresser is cluttered with change and magazines and receipts, and the drawers hang open with clothes flowing out. It smells like Trip does on the weekends, like pizza and beer.

Trip smiles but stays quiet. The anticipation of waiting for him to speak becomes too much. I give him a light push on the chest.

He leans in my direction. "To tell you the truth, talking is the last thing I feel like doing right now." His eyes are soft and inviting. He's doing this on purpose, and it is such a Trip Chapman thing to do that I can't help but smirk. Distracting me by being sexy, distracting himself with sex.

I put my hands on my hips and the gesture disappoints him. He sits on his bed and slumps over. Naturally I join him, sitting next to him with my shoulder pressed up against his. His eyes stay glued to the floor.

Trip takes a deep breath. "I'm on academic probation this semester. If I don't get my grades up, I'm out." He's talking to the floor. "It's not a big deal, but . . . let's just say I'm already off to a lousy start."

"So what happened? You don't like college?"

"Oh, I like college." He gives me a smile that says I can't even imagine how much fun he's been having. "It's the classes that aren't my favorite."

I pinch the skin in between my eyes, then stop immediately when I realize it's the same thing my mom does when she's annoyed and disappointed and deep in thought for an appropriate punishment. "I don't . . . I don't know that I can help you."

He rolls his eyes and smiles. "Look at you, Housing. You're going to a good school next year. You obviously take this learning stuff seriously. You would never be stupid enough to fail."

I'm irritated right now, mainly because he referred to Barron as a "good" school. Barron is a great school. "Don't say you're stupid."

The way he's smiling, though, I know he doesn't

actually think he's stupid. Careless, maybe. "Old enough to know better, too young to care," Earl used to say to Zane and Trip anytime they did something reckless. He said it a lot.

"Study with me. Maybe even teach me how. You know, like, techniques or whatever. I could use some help writing essays, too."

"You know how to study." My voice fades as I stare at his face. He's wearing a sly smile. He's waiting for it to hit me that he graduated high school not because he finished his homework and studied hard, but because he got girls to do his homework and study for him. By *study*, of course, I mean *provide him with the answers*.

Girls were always waiting patiently, hoping to do things for him. They were everywhere. After football practice by his car, at his locker between classes. Even at his house, sipping beer with Earl and anticipating the moment when Trip or Zane would grace them with a wink, a smile, a kiss—and they would do anything for it.

Shelby and I used to laugh at these girls as we sat on Trip's couch, where we were more than welcome because Trip and Zane had invited us to hang out—not because we were doing their homework and waiting for them to give us something in return.

He smiles at me again, daring me to tell him no *again*. When Trip Chapman smiles at you, there are fireworks, and I can still hear them. But it's different now. The noises might be just as loud, but it's not as colorful, not as bright, not as enchanting. And without all that, fireworks are just explosions. They're just a racket.

"I need your help, Aubrey," Trip asks. "Will you help me?"

CHAPTER SEVENTEEN

Monday nights are the best. Yes, Mondays suck, but the dark cloud that is Monday has a silver lining in that Monday night is the night my friends and I always get together to watch our favorite show, *Mercy Rose*. It's about a group of teenagers in the small town of—you guessed it—Mercy Rose. It's a total soap opera loaded with scandal and betrayal, just the way we like it.

This Monday we're at my house because my parents are going on a date—*vile*, I know—but we always try to gather at the house that is parentless so we can curse freely, drink if we want, and shout obscenities every time our favorite character, Jude, takes off his shirt.

Danica, Melissa, and I are discussing whether or not we think Scarlet will die from her mysterious, possibly life-threatening disease, and who we think should get her current boyfriend, Jude, if she does, when Shelby arrives holding a package of Oreos.

"If they drag out Scarlet's death any longer, *I'm* going to die," Shelby says, plopping onto the couch next to me.

"Right!" we all agree. Enough is enough. Scarlet has been crying and coughing for the last three episodes.

"You girls actually *like* this show?" my mother says, having overheard.

"It's brilliant," we all say at nearly the same time. This makes even my mother laugh.

My father walks past her, holding up his keys. This is his way of saying he's ready to go.

"Enjoy *Macy Rows*! Good night, girls." He waves at us with one hand and uses the other to usher my mother out the door. He never gets the title of the show right. Sometimes I think he does it on purpose to make us laugh, which it always does.

The second we hear the garage door close, Gregory and Jason come bounding into the living room. They're scared of my friends, probably of girls in general, and my friends give them yet another reason to be afraid when they squeal, "Hi, boys!" and "Cute pj's!" Gregory and Jason put up with this for one reason—we have junk food and they want some.

"Are you surviving middle school?" Melissa asks Gregory. She's asked him this every time she's seen him since he started sixth grade this year. He always nods vigorously, and I almost wonder if he understands that middle school really does take *surviving*. It was a brutal time, even I'll admit. Awkward growth spurts, shiny noses, overactive sweat glands.

"Gregory is resilient," Shelby says. She's got my mother's large orange mixing bowls out and is filling them with chips and Oreos for my brothers. "Do you still have that scar?"

Gregory rolls his eyes slightly, but he's grinning as he pulls back the sleeve of his pajamas to show Shelby the long white scar traveling from his wrist to his elbow, from the day he broke his arm.

"Scars are permanent, Shelby," Jason says quietly, looking at the ground. He, too, is grinning a little, like he thinks Shelby is silly.

"You don't say," Shelby says. She hands them the bowl.

Now that they've gotten what they came for, they're off to their room. The deal I've made with them is this: they can do whatever they want in their room as long as they turn off the lights and pretend to be asleep when our parents come home. It's no mystery what they're doing. Not inviting girls over or smoking pot or even inventing dangerous games that could get them seriously injured, like who can jump the farthest off the bed. No, they're playing video games.

"It's starting!" Danica announces, even though we're all sitting right in front of the TV and can see for ourselves.

It's the same thing every week with us: we all lean forward and stop chewing whatever we're munching on during the opening recap—*"Last week on* Mercy Rose*"*—like we're afraid that the noise of the Oreos mashing in our mouths might cause us to miss something crucial that took place during last week's episode. We comment on each character during the opening credits. Sometimes we yell things like "Stupid whore!" and "Dumb bitch!" if a character is losing points for Team Girl—which Scarlet has been doing the past four episodes. Even if she's dying, that's no excuse. I'm thankful that my little brothers are too busy killing aliens to listen in on us as Scarlet's face flashes across the screen and Melissa and Shelby yell "Dirty slut!" at the same time.

We're predictable like this. And our consistency is comforting. Even with my rigorous schedule the past four years, I always made time for this. Our Monday nights.

I still don't know why Shelby wanted to hook up with Patrick on Saturday night. Shelby hasn't said anything about it and we haven't asked. Patrick was gone by the time we woke up Sunday morning, and Shelby refused to come out to breakfast with us. "I bet you're tired," Danica teased her, making the mattress move up and down with her knee. But Shelby just groaned and covered her head with her pillow.

"When do you start tutoring Trip?" Shelby asks during a commercial. Her head's resting on the pillow leaning against Melissa. Melissa chews nervously on a piece of licorice. She really thinks Scarlet's going to die this time.

"Next weekend." I don't take my eyes off the television. Partly because I don't want to miss it when the show starts up again. Partly because I don't want Shelby to think that talk of Trip deserves more attention than *Mercy Rose*. "Should be awesome."

We squeeze in a few more jokes about how the only way Trip will learn anything is if I remove an article of clothing every time he gets a correct answer. *Strip Psych 101!* We make a few jokes at Celine's expense because, despite being such a *loyal* girlfriend to Jared, Celine was always willing to do Trip's homework—though if you ask her, she'll spout off excuses about Trip needing a certain GPA to stay on the football team, and that as a cheerleader she cared first and foremost about winning games.

We have an extra hour to kill after the show's over, but we're too full of junk food to do anything but lie around on the couch. We laugh at Scarlet for being so unevolved, even on her deathbed, and wonder how many sit-ups Jude does to get his abs looking like *that*.

And I think that *this* right here is the one thing I'll never have at Barron.

PREDICTABILITY AND HIGH school boys are synonymous. On Tuesday Patrick waits for Leila by her locker before first period. Just like we knew he would.

Leila doesn't melt at his efforts right away—good for her—but she's sitting on his lap come lunchtime, probably thinking he's reconsidering that whole *relationship* thing. She knows nothing about what happened with Shelby, but she can't possibly assume Patrick was pining for her on a Saturday night, after *he* detached from her.

Nathan and I are becoming predictable too. In Drama, when Mrs. Seymour leaves the room and Melvin gives up finding any hidden talent, we sneak backstage to make out by the prop furniture. If we're not in the cafeteria at lunch, we're at the housing development and Nathan's kissing my neck and telling me I'm beautiful. I'm running my hands over his chest, his lips, through his hair, checking and double-checking to make sure he's real.

I don't hear from Trip the following week, and I start to think that maybe he didn't need my help after all. I feel relieved.

"IS THERE A reason Nathan Diggs asked me what your favorite restaurant is?" Shelby says, looking at her phone. *Mercy Rose* just ended, so we're all checking our phones. We're at Shelby's house this week, crisscrossed and leaning on one another on the overstuffed couch. "Oh," Shelby says, still staring at her phone. "He wants to surprise you on Valentine's Day." It's this Friday.

Danica stretches out her leg and pushes Shelby's shoulder with her foot. "Spoiler alert."

Shelby shrugs. "Well, Aubrey, what should I say? Where do you want to go on Valentine's Day? Certainly you don't want me to tell him to take you to Stimpy's." Which they all know is my *real* favorite place to eat. It's less of a restaurant and more of a diner . . . with a drive-thru.

"Solstice!" Melissa bolts upright. "He should totally take you to Solstice!"

"If he's going to drop that kind of cash, he might as well get a hotel room," Shelby says.

I put my hand over her phone. "Do not type that."

She laughs. "Oh, relax, I would never dream of suggesting something that would make you miss Celine's VD party."

Celine's parents always take a vacation around Valentine's Day, so Celine always throws a party. Celine's pretty ecstatic that this year Valentine's Day actually lands on a Friday. I'm really excited myself, since I don't have to work and can attend.

Celine's parties aren't like other parties, I've heard. Invitations are required, and if you show up without one, she won't let you in. She also doesn't let you in unless you dress up. Jared acts like a bouncer and actually turns people away. Shelby referred to it as the VD party last year and got uninvited. Jared still let her in, of course.

"Really, though," Shelby says, leaning toward me, "what's the hold-up?"

The hold-up. The truth is there is no hold-up. I want to have sex with Nathan; I want to so badly, sometimes I feel like running my nails up and down my thighs just to distract myself from the *wanting*. Sometimes I replay in my head over and over again the things we have done to each other with our one layer of separation, and before I know it an hour has gone by and I've been staring at the same page in my calculus book. When we're together there's no discussion about it, and to be honest, in some moments with him I think that we will, that we're *about to*, and when we end up doing other things, or having to stop because of parents or curfews, it never feels like something's lost.

Melissa pipes up at this. "Always leave them wanting more."

"But why deprive yourself?" Danica says.

"Don't pretend like you know anything about *deprivation*, Danica," Melissa says.

"And don't pretend you're not an expert on it."

"Whoa!" Shelby says. She's laughing and she's got her arms spread out like she's ready to hold Melissa and

Danica back in their respective corners.

This makes us all laugh. We're too evolved to really fight over something like this.

"You don't have to wait so long, Aubrey," Shelby says after our laughter has worn down. I know what she's referring to. It took Trip Chapman seven months and five days to get me into bed. Prom night. Such a cliché. Shelby's right. My situation with Nathan and my situation with Trip are completely different.

CHAPTER
EIGHTEEN

Nathan holds my face with both hands as he kisses me good night. It's almost eleven thirty, it's Wednesday, and there's definitely a chance that my mother is sitting in the kitchen waiting up for me. I grip his wrist so he won't pull away a second before he has to.

Tonight we removed the layer, went all the way, did everything two people could do under the sheets without their clothes. "Rounding home," Danica would say. "Hooking up to the max" is what Shelby would say. When I think about telling them, my cheeks get hot.

"I guess I should go inside," I say when we finally do stop kissing.

Nathan smiles. "Nah." He shakes his head.

I laugh at this, louder than Nathan expected, and he raise his eyebrows in surprise though he, too, is laughing.

Right before I reach the front door, I hear Nathan's horn and whirl around, startled. He's got his hands in the air and he's cringing a little. He must've honked it accidentally as he was leaning forward to watch me walk inside. We make eye contact again, and we both break out into the same enormous smile.

It's not hard to hold myself together when I walk in and see my mother sitting at the counter. She slides off the stool and comes toward me, tapping the place on her wrist where a watch would be if she weren't in her robe.

"Sorry," I tell her. She turns away from me, so that's the end of it. Really I'm thinking, *There's nothing you could do to make me sorry. Ground me forever; it'd have been worth it.*

I lie in bed, wide-awake. I let myself smile. I let myself squirm. I cover my face when I feel hot flashes of embarrassment—not the shameful kind, the kind that comes from thinking, *I can't believe that just happened.*

Nathan's hand on my back leading me into his room. His breath against my temple. His lips traveling down, stopping at my lips, edging my jawline, trailing along my collarbone. I squeeze my eyes shut because it's too wonderful.

It wasn't perfect "on paper," an expression my mother uses sometimes when she wants to point out how things can look versus how things really are. It didn't last very long, and I forgot to take off my socks. But I never expected my first time with Nathan to be good on paper. Like how the first time I rode my bike, I crashed into the mailbox, but I could still remember what it'd been like soaring through the air, and after the crash I knew what to do differently the next time. With Trip, the first time, it was too sweaty, and my whole body felt sore and sprained.

I stifle a giggle with my pillow. There's nothing about tonight that doesn't make me insanely happy.

It's my hands on his face, the roughness of his cheeks because he needed to shave. The way he held me so close and I could smell every speck of cologne, ounce of sweat, remnant of detergent, the fresh mint he'd just had, knowing we'd be spending the next few hours kissing. It's the way he said my name, the way his lips couldn't help but smile when he said it; the way his eyes got soft. How he asked if I was nervous and then answered for me, *Of course not.* And the way he whispered to me right at the beginning, saying something I couldn't understand, so I just nodded and he kissed me. My hands running through his hair, his breath tickling my ears, the weight of him. Lying with my head on his chest afterward while he traced small circles on my back.

This is why we don't write boys off, disregard them completely while they're in high school. It's these moments stacked up that make staying away from boys impossible.

They can make you really happy. You just can't count on them for it.

"WHO ARE THOSE for?" I ask Nathan as he walks toward me with a bouquet of pale pink roses on Friday after school. They're just slightly open, looking sleek and elegant.

"You don't know her," he says, holding them out for me.

No one has ever given me flowers, and I've never expected them to, so I've never really known my preference. At this moment I decide that pale pink roses are my absolute favorite.

"You like them, right?"

I must be beaming, because he smiles like I've answered him out loud with an enthusiastic *I love them!*

"Dinner tonight? Before Celine's party?" He steps closer to me to tug on a chunk of hair that never stays tucked behind my ear. "And if you're available after school . . ." He kisses me lightly on the mouth.

Of course, Nathan's not going to miss an opportunity to get laid on Valentine's Day. Now that we've *removed the layer,* he's no longer so apprehensive about his mother coming home early. And we've started referring to his BMW as his "bedroom on wheels." I love that he thinks he has to earn it with things like flowers and surprises. He tugs on the front strands of my hair again, something he does lately when he wants my attention. I've taken to pulling lightly on his sleeve when I want his. Shelby says we're like five-year-olds.

"Okay," I say, sticking my nose in the middle of the bouquet one more time.

"You can wear whatever you want, but I feel obligated to tell you I'll be wearing a tie," he adds before walking away down the hall. I can tell by the way he walks that he's proud of himself. He's caught me off guard and he likes it. *I* like it.

MY MOUTH DROPS open when Nathan shows up that night in a black suit carrying another bouquet. Red carnations this time. They end up in my mother's arms since I can't take them with me to dinner or to Celine's party. She promises to put them in water.

"Midnight," my mother reminds us as we leave.

I'd thought about staying the night at Shelby's to avoid my curfew, but I know that me being picked up by a boy and not coming home until morning is something my mother would turn down right away. It'd probably make her start to second-guess all the times I stayed over at Shelby's, if she hasn't started doing this already.

Ten minutes later Nathan and I are pulling into the parking lot at Solstice.

"It's not too late to go to Stimpy's," he says, grinning.

I just smile. I don't tell him that it doesn't really matter where we go.

CHAPTER
NINETEEN

Two hours later I'm squished in front of the mirror in the bathroom at Celine's with Shelby, Danica, and Melissa. We're fixing our hair and passing around Melissa's new lip gloss and my new perfume, because we are strict believers in that whole "What's mine is yours" friendship motto. We always complain about dressing up for Celine's VD party, but every year we have fun doing it. We're all in black, which is not an accident.

That's when Trip sends me a text.

HAPPY VALENTINES DAY. I'M NOT OUTSIDE :)

Last year, in an attempt to surprise me for Valentine's Day, Trip dropped by my house at four in the morning and woke up my entire family by mistakenly throwing rocks at my little brothers' window. Trip claimed that he "just needed to see me."

I think that's when my parents officially decided they did not like Trip Chapman and they were going to stop hiding it. My father told me he didn't he trust someone so good-looking and my mother said she thought he was manipulative.

The next text he sends says: THANK YOU FOR AGREEING TO HELP ME.

"Aww, that's really sweet," Melissa says. Her lips are stained red from her drink.

"Sweet of him to stay away. Yes." Shelby leans toward the mirror and runs the mascara wand over her eyelashes one more time for good measure.

"I don't know," Danica says. "I think *sweet* is Nathan taking her to Solstice." It reminds me of Sandra and her friends, and being thirteen and listening to them talk about the men they were dating, when money seemed to be the biggest factor, and they noticed it but pretended not to care about it.

When we emerge from the bathroom, the first thing I see is that Nathan isn't wearing his tie anymore. I've been obsessed with Nathan's tie since he picked me up, using it to pull him toward me, flipping it around my hands as I speak to him, tightening and loosening it around his neck. I can't help it. Ties are sexy. I had no idea. They're classy and mature—something every other boy has been missing.

Nathan's standing at the island in the kitchen, laughing as Robert, Patrick, and Jared get ready to take a shot of something brown.

". . . I have to take her home at midnight," I hear him say. A reason he's not joining them. When I asked Nathan if he had a curfew, he said no, he never has. The truth is he's probably never needed one.

Patrick guzzles down the shot, and before the liquor has settled in his stomach and his face is still puckering, he pats Nathan on the shoulder. "Dude, you should come back after you drop her off. You can crash at my place. Courtney will drive us." And it's true, Celine's little sister, Courtney McGillicutty, has a horrible case of acid reflux and doesn't drink. She's been offering people rides since she got her learner's permit. I suspect that's the only way Celine will be nice to her.

Shelby comes up behind me, handing me the same red drink that's stained Melissa's lips.

"Oh, look," she says, and the guys all turn to stare at her even though she was talking to me.

"This is the first new friend Robert and Patrick have made in years," she says like she pities them.

Robert holds up his empty glass. "Growth."

It's obvious from the way the corners of Nathan's mouth turn up, and how he glances at everyone around him who might be paying attention, that he's pleased that this news has been declared so publicly. I turn away from them and face Shelby.

"He used to be wearing a tie," I tell her, though I'm not sure why.

Nathan spends the next twenty minutes with Robert and Patrick. Every time I look over, they're laughing. Huddling together, sharing jokes, not wearing ties.

"He's a big boy, Aubrey." Shelby pats my shoulder. "He's becoming one of our friends—this should make you happy. I don't know why you're surprised."

I don't know why you're surprised you don't get to keep him to yourself forever is what she's really saying. And she's right. This is a good thing. Nathan is friends with Robert and Patrick—who basically go anywhere we go. He no longer needs me as his connection to *other people* at Lincoln High. That's fine. It was inevitable that this would happen, that Nathan would branch out on his own, without me. I have been preparing for this.

The truth: a little voice inside me keeps saying that it's really not going to change anything between us, that no matter how weird it is to see him having fun with guys like Robert and Patrick—guys I didn't think he had anything in common with—he's still going to keep me as his first choice.

I realize this type of thinking is dangerous.

"Um, when did Sam Perkins get hot?" Shelby asks

as we take a seat at Celine's dining room table. The rest of our friends join us. It's the best place to be, since it's within easy walking distance to the kitchen, where the drinks are, and we still have a full view of the living room.

"Sam Perkins has always been hot," Melissa confirms. This is only partly true. Sam Perkins has always been hot, but alas, he's a year younger than us so he was invisible. But now he's a junior and the new consensus is that because we're about to graduate—and once we graduate—we're not allowed to dip back into the high school pool; it's only fair that we have them now. Especially second semester of our senior year, when the junior boys have turned seventeen and are starting to get that very senior look about them.

"He's way hotter now that he doesn't have Nicole Maki's tongue down his throat," Danica notes. It's true. Sam must've noticed the increased attention he's been receiving from the senior girls and decided it was wise to end it with the one holding him back: his sophomore girlfriend, Nicole Maki.

"Maybe." Shelby shrugs and takes a sip of her drink.

"Hey, Aubrey." The way Celine says my name, smiling with glittering eyes, makes my stomach drop. "I hear you're tutoring Trip." Her eyes are still dancing when she not-so-casually glances at Nathan.

Nathan looks confused. Like he knows he should be

offended but has no idea why.

"You know better than anyone that he never had to study in high school," I say to Celine.

Shelby slowly turns away from Sam to look at me. She doesn't want to be too obvious, but I can see it on her face. She's pleased. This is the first time I've ever insulted Celine.

Celine's eyes slide to look at Jared, to make sure he didn't hear or understand my jab. He didn't, so she smiles, and I know I'm in for some kind of classic-Celine passive-aggressive insult.

Shelby always says something ten times ruder back when Celine tosses an underlying insult at her. Like when Celine told Shelby her skirt looked "vintage," then asked her with wide, innocent eyes and in a voice loud enough for everyone to hear, if she got it too small on purpose. Shelby had replied, "No, I got my skirt from the same place you shop. At Sluts Я Us." A clear insult. Not even a good one, but sometimes Shelby will stoop that low to make sure Celine knows she's being insulted. Because that's the thing about Shelby: she's in no way passive. But of course she came off as the bitch, not Celine.

Celine opens her mouth and is about to lay into me—I know she is—but Nathan speaks before she has the chance. "Who are we talking about?"

My friends must have radar, because they abandon their other conversations and lean in, giving us their full attention. They aren't going to give Celine the opportunity to answer this one. According to the theories, it shouldn't matter who Trip is, especially to Nathan. According to the theories, Nathan won't care. But Celine's still throwing Trip's name around like it's a threat. A threat to make me define Nathan the way she's stupidly decided to define Jared.

"Trip Chapman," Shelby says quickly. "He graduated last year. He's totally failing out of college and needs to borrow Aubrey's brain."

"He probably wants to borrow more than that." Leila chuckles and smiles a perverted smile.

"He wishes," Shelby says.

"Interesting that he chose you. To tutor him, I mean," Celine says. Passive-aggressive bitch—one point.

"Fuck off, Celine," Shelby snaps. "Everyone knows Aubrey's smart. She's going to Barron. I know it's a stretch for you to understand that Trip might be interested in actual help instead of just watching a cheerleader bend over his dining room table, but try to open your mind."

This works exactly the way Shelby intended it to. Celine turns away and starts talking to Jared, who, once again—and lucky for Celine—was too occupied in a different conversation to hear Shelby's insult.

Shelby gives me a look that says, *Can you believe her?* and I smile. I'm a little stunned, to be honest. Not that Shelby insulted Celine or defended me against any remarks that might make Nathan think I care about Trip—but that she acknowledged I was going to Barron. She told me she was happy for me after I got accepted but never really brought it up again.

"So Trip is your ex?" Nathan asks, trying to keep up with the banter.

"Not—no," I say, and I watch Nathan's face harden.

Robert Jules bursts out laughing. "Close, but no cigar."

Nathan nods. He chews on his lower lip the same way he does when he's trying to memorize a verb conjugation for Spanish class. He's not laughing with Robert.

I'm afraid for a moment that Nathan won't get it. That he won't understand why we need to be evolved like this, the same way he doesn't understand that he's good-looking.

"So you guys aren't into labels?" Nathan addresses all of us, not just me.

It makes it easier to answer him. "Not just labels. Any of it. We're not into any of it."

Nathan tilts his head as he stares at me.

In this moment, I look across the table at Shelby. She looks calm, bored, a little annoyed.

"Anyone who thinks their high school relationship is going to last longer than five seconds is delusional," Shelby says. She pointedly stares at Celine, who scowls.

"Especially when we're all about to graduate. Nothing is going to stay the same."

"Hey, I have no complaints, baby," Robert says, putting his hands in the air in surrender and then sliding his arm around Danica. She beams. In this moment, I'm almost positive Robert is thinking about how grateful he is for Evolved Danica, who hasn't asked him to define their relationship or forced him to answer the question plaguing Celine and Jared: what they're going to do next year when there isn't Lincoln High keeping them together.

Celine sits up. She's spunkier, less reserved now that Jared left the table to refill her drink. "I'll never understand: what do you guys have against love?"

Shelby and Danica answer at nearly the same time.

"Making," Shelby says.

"The physical act of," Danica says.

It seems like this isn't the first time they've been confronted about the theories and they've made these jokes before, at parties I missed.

"We're realisticists!" Melissa says. The entire top of her lip is red. She's slurring a little too.

"It's just common sense," Shelby says. "Relationships in high school are so unrealistic. Fun is realistic." Robert and Patrick nod along, laughing, and hooting a little. They agree with this statement and want everyone to know it. Shelby is playing this perfectly in accordance with the theories, and all the theories have worked on Nathan so far—why wouldn't they? There's nothing for me to be worried about. Logically, I know this.

"I believe the primates call it dating," Nathan says, laughing at his own joke. Everyone else laughs too.

You're welcome, Shelby mouths to me from across the table. She's smiling as she waves over Sam Perkins, who very obediently comes and stands next to Shelby's chair. He laughs with her for a little while before they decide to take shots together in the kitchen. Body shots—just a guess.

Patrick cracks open a beer. He nods to Nathan. "Have one, Diggs. Courtney can take Aubrey home."

"It's all right," Nathan says.

"I don't mind getting a ride from Courtney," I tell him.

He stares at me for a moment, like he's debating this. "I'll take you," he says.

"Oh, *great*," Celine says, leaning forward in her chair so she can see into the kitchen. "What the hell are Shelby and her latest victim doing?"

Nathan and Robert laugh at the words *latest victim*, and Patrick laughs because Nathan and Robert are laughing. We all look in the kitchen.

Shelby and Sam are facing each other with barely a foot in between them. They're each holding a full shot of tequila and a lime. Shelby rolls up the hem of her tank top and lowers her skirt half a centimeter, exposing three inches of her stomach. Sam starts to mimic her, rolling up his shirt, but Shelby shakes her head and tells him something. Sam nods, sets down his shot glass and lime, and takes off his shirt.

We can't help it. As girls in full view of a six-pack, Leila, Celine, Danica, Melissa, and I all gasp.

Next, Shelby whispers something in Sam's ear. His smile barely fits on his face. She grabs something else off the counter—a saltshaker. Shelby gives Sam a sly grin and kneels in front of him.

"What is she doing?" Nathan says in my ear, sounding both curious and worried. I don't answer because I don't know, but we all keep watching.

Shelby licks Sam's stomach, right above the place where his boxers stick out above his pants. She sprinkles salt over the spot she just licked. Now I get it. I know exactly what she's doing. She and Sam are taking body shots standing up. There's no room on the counter, and this is Shelby's glorious alternative. She says something else to Sam, her face still down by his stomach, and he nods vigorously, smiling as he looks down at her. He places the lime in his mouth, holding it between his teeth so the juicy part is exposed and ready for Shelby. Then she does it. She licks the salt of Sam's stomach, takes the shot, and slides up and off her knees, pressing against Sam as she sucks on the lime he's got in his mouth. This actually proves to be way sexier than the lying-down way. I wonder how long Shelby's had this trick up her sleeve.

"Wow." Robert laughs quietly, clearly impressed. All the boys look impressed, even Nathan. I can't really blame them.

"She's filthy." Melissa giggles.

"So maybe this really will turn into a VD party," mutters Celine.

When Nathan takes me home, Shelby and Sam are making out in the kitchen, Melissa's passed out in Celine's room, Danica is on Robert's lap, perched near an open window, smoking and laughing. Patrick calls to Nathan as we're walking out the door, "You should come back, man! The party's still going!"

"We'll see," Nathan says to him, raising his voice to be heard over the music.

We're quiet in the car. My leftovers have been sitting in the backseat for the past few hours and the car smells like ravioli. It's too cold to roll down the windows.

"Thanks for the ride," I tell him when we pull into my driveway. There's a layer of frost on the ground, making everything look sharp and slick.

"I wasn't going to not be the one to bring you home," he says. There's a slight edge to his voice. "Not when I was the one who took you out."

"Thanks," I say one more time.

I ignore that he won't look at me for more than just a

brief glance, and that his hands are still holding the steering wheel. I lean into him, putting my hands on his face and turning his head so I can kiss him. He kisses me back, without any hesitation.

When he whispers good night to me, he's smiling.

I want to ask him if tonight wasn't enough for him and he's going back to the party to drink with Patrick and watch Leila dance on the furniture, as she's known to do sometimes. And if tomorrow he'll be busy sleeping off a hangover or if he'll be over me by then, since he knows I'm evolved and won't punish him for it.

I blow him a kiss as I walk into my house right at twelve o'clock.

CHAPTER
TWENTY

Earl is slamming the door when I arrive at Trip's on Sunday evening. He called me last night asking me to come over today to help him with two tests he has next week.

"You have my permission to slap him, Aubrey," Earl says as he passes me. I've never seen Earl mad—he always leaves when he's angry.

The second I enter the house, I understand why Earl left.

"Brey!"

"Housing!"

Zane and Trip are sitting on the couch with the

television turned up way too loud. Neither of them is wearing a shirt. They look like they didn't shower today and the coffee table is buried in beer cans.

"You're drunk." I glare at him and feel the heat rising from my chest to my cheeks.

He smiles at me, like he thinks I might laugh it off. "Just a few beers," he says. His voice is deep with drunkenness and he's got that look in his eyes. The one that I used to find charming. All it says to me right now is that Trip finds himself charming.

"Just a few beers?" I repeat back, dumbing it down for them. "Like how many? One? Two? Nine?" I practically yell the last word; I can't help it.

Zane thinks this is really funny. So does Trip, but he's too busy giving me his bedroom eyes to really laugh.

"Zane had to spend all day with Jamie, so he needed to relax," Trip explains.

"Okay, fine. He doesn't have a test in Psych 101 tomorrow. He can drink as much as he wants!"

"I can still study." Trip raises his eyebrows. It might really be an attempt to keep his eyes open. "Trust me, Housing. I can do anything."

"Except pass college." I can't stop myself. I'm furious with him and it feels awful, like I want to cry or explode.

Don't ask for an apology from a boy, because you absolutely will not get a sincere one.

151

I turn to leave. It feels like more of a good-bye than when I watched his pickup pull out of my driveway before he left for college.

"Don't be mad, Housing. I'll make it up to you, I swear."

I pause at the door. My hand is shaking when I bring it to the knob. In getting wasted the night before his exam, the only one Trip is hurting is himself, but I feel hurt. I think of the way Earl stormed out of here, and I get it.

I turn the handle at the same time as someone else, and when the door opens I'm face-to-face with Chiffon.

At first she's taken aback—we both are—but a second later she's shaking her head at me. "Figures you'd be here." She opens the door and pushes past me, nearly knocking me over. Chiffon looks especially smug now that she's inside the house and sees that Shelby, Danica, and Melissa are nowhere to be found. I'm all alone. "Your fuck-buddy privileges never expire, do they?" she says.

Some combination of anger and humiliation ticks through me—because how can she say that to me, with all the bad choices she makes; the way she so easily gives herself over to boys like Zane Chapman, who won't even acknowledge his relationship with her in public.

She shakes her head at me, like she knows I'm coming up speechless, and the tiniest hint of a smile plays across her pale face.

Somehow Trip understands how brutal this is for me

right now, that I'm holding on to so much anger from his being drunk that being here with Chiffon stings extra hard. In a second he's up, pulling Zane with his right arm. Once Zane is on his feet, Trip pushes him toward Chiffon. Trip takes both my shoulders and ushers me into the dining room. Chiffon and Zane disappear down the hall.

"Sit down, Housing." Trip kicks aside a chair for me and I obey.

There's only the tiniest bit of satisfaction in knowing that Chiffon probably won't be enjoying herself dealing with a drunken Zane. Then again, I'm sitting next to my own drunken Chapman.

Trip keeps his hand on my shoulder. He bows his head, finally looking somewhat ashamed. He gets up to mute the television, glancing at me on his way into the living room to find the remote, like he's afraid I'm going to leave like Earl did. He's sitting in front of me before I can muster up the courage to go.

"This isn't working, Trip. I'm leaving."

I want him to say something. I want him to shut up. I want him to stop me. I want him to let me go. I need Trip to tell me what I want.

"Please." He closes his eyes. His hand reaches for me, knocks against the table, my knee, then finally finds my hand. He squeezes it. "Aubrey. Please. I really need your help."

I move my hand just slightly, but he lets go. His eyes

fly open. If he wasn't drunk he might look surprised. Trip leans back and his chair creaks. All the chairs around the Chapmans' cedar table are different, but they're all made of the same cedar. "Probably even from the same tree," Earl once told me.

"Maybe I'm just a lost cause." Trip laughs, small chuckles escaping from his lips as he rubs his hands over his eyes.

Maybe he's right. Maybe I feel bad for him because he used to be a god and now he's nothing but a mere mortal. Maybe it's like my mother said and he's manipulating me.

"Where's your book?"

Maybe I'm the lost cause.

Trip reaches into the beat-up backpack resting under the table—the same backpack he carried around all four years of high school—and slides his psychology book across the table. It looks so new and shiny, I wonder if he's ever even opened it.

"What time is your test tomorrow?" I have to know if I've agreed to a hopeless situation.

"Three." He looks optimistic because he knows the one thing he did right was fill his schedule with afternoon classes.

I pull out my flash cards and highlighter. Even though he's drunk, Trip can still write. Perhaps tomorrow he'll be coherent enough to memorize at least some of the material.

Thankfully, Trip knows which chapters he's being tested on. He brings his laptop to the table to show me where the teacher has posted the lecture notes online. We sit in silence for a good hour. I highlight the parts of the chapter that coincide with the lecture notes and Trip makes flash cards based on the highlights.

My phone rings around nine. It's not my mother, but I'm sure her phone call is just minutes away. It's Nathan.

"Hey," I say into the phone. It's a relief and a rush to hear him say "Hey" back. "Let me call you in fifteen minutes. I'm still tutoring." Nathan agrees to this, but there's impatience in his voice. I feel impatient too then. I flip through the book, happy that there are only a few more pages to go.

"So," Trip says, his voice slow and tired, "you're *tutoring* me? I thought you were helping me." He doesn't look up from the flash card he's writing. He's either upset or too tired for formalities like eye contact.

"What do you think it's called when someone helps someone else with schoolwork?"

Trip stops writing to smile at me, though only half of his face is cooperating. "I just mean . . ." He mimics me, raising his voice just slightly, just enough so I can tell it's unnatural. "*I'm still tutoring.* You didn't make it seem very friendly."

"Well, Trip."

"Well, Aubrey."

"We've never been very friendly." It's the truth. He's never been my friend. He's been my crush, then the boy I was kissing, the boy I was screwing, the boy I said good-bye to.

"We've always been friends." He looks genuinely offended. His pen rolls across the table and into the book when he sets it down, and I watch it. "You were my best friend."

"But we were—" It pains me to finish. "Together." It's the wrong word. It's the right word. It's the only word.

Trip isn't surprised by the word. Maybe even Trip Chapman understands that when one person gives over her virginity, the term *friendship* doesn't quite cut it. "Yeah. But isn't that what everyone wants? To be with their best friend?"

There was laughter, a lot of it, between Trip and me last year. I had a spot at the dinner table in the cedar chair with the tall back, and I knew where everything was in the kitchen. I knew how Trip liked his coffee and how many beers it took him to get drunk. I knew that he'd given up on pleasing his mother a long time ago; that no matter how much he fought with Zane, it took them all of two seconds to forgive each other, even after a bloody lip or a black eye. But he'd seen me naked. I'd seen him naked. He'd kissed me until my face was red and given me hickeys in places my mother would never find them.

Besides, it's impossible to be best friends with a high school boy.

I try to reason with him. "We were just having fun."

"Yeah. With each other."

"Fine," I say, handing him back his pen. "We were friends."

"We *are* friends," he corrects. His lips curve up at the word, but his eyes are still serious.

"We are friends."

He nods once, satisfied with my less-than-exuberant admission. He shouldn't be. I was lying to him.

I feel the rush of something again—a dull fury, an annoying sadness. I want to ask him how he could leave me like that if he really believed we were best friends. Best friends who were *together*. And why he came back only because he needed something from me.

Shelby's right; he just needs to borrow my brain.

"You know, you could stay tonight," Trip says, not looking up. He sounds like he desperately needs a drink of water. He also sounds like he's smiling. "Help me study in the morning."

Leila's right too. He wants to *borrow* more than just my brain.

"Trip—" But I'm overcome with a smile. It's so typical and so familiar. "I have school tomorrow, remember?" I've said this to him before, more than once last year when Trip wanted to drink tequila until sunrise, drive until we didn't recognize the street signs, or bury ourselves under his comforter until we couldn't tell up from down or left from right.

He smiles back at me. "I'm lucky to have you."

I don't correct him.

CHAPTER
TWENTY-ONE

"Isn't she off yet?" Shelby whines at Ms. Michel, who ignores her.

I give Shelby and Nathan a *Shut up, you're making it worse* look. Only Shelby really deserves it. The two of them are sitting at the round wooden table closest to the counter, sipping coffee and waiting almost patiently for me to finish my shift on Sunday so we can leave for the state basketball tournament. Every March, if our basketball team miraculously makes it to the state championship, the seniors are automatically excused from school. If the rumors are true, the parties during the tournament are life changing.

Now that we're about to leave I'm feeling nervous. It's really stupid. I should be excited. I've never gone on a road trip with my friends and stayed overnight. This freedom of hotels and fast food, and the luxury of spending time alone with Nathan without being in the backseat of a car—or in his room with the constant awareness that his tiny, stealthy mother might surprise us—should have me as thrilled as I was when my parents actually agreed to let me go.

"Oh no. Why do you look like that?" Shelby says. She's seen my face like this before. It's the face I make when I'm hiding something—usually nerves.

"What's wrong?" Nathan asks. He doesn't know this face of mine, and he never will.

Shelby gives me a pointed stare: *This isn't over.* She turns to Nathan. "Sometimes she forgets that she already got into Barron and it's okay for her to let loose and get crazy." Shelby makes my neurosis sound cool, a little prestigious, even. Only Shelby. It's the second time she's mentioned Barron out loud. Maybe in this case it was my only defense.

"I do that too. Forget to let loose." Only Nathan.

"Well, good." Shelby slides her sunglasses off her forehead and over her eyes. "Looks like I picked the fun car."

I watch Nathan smile at her. "You've never missed out on a day of fun in your whole life, have you?"

She purses her lips. He's got her figured out—this part of her, anyway. She won't give him a smile for it. "Nope," she says, enunciating that one word to make it seem bigger and bolder than it is.

"Never stressed? Not about tests? Or college? Or money?"

I cringe at the last two questions. I scrub the counter to give myself something to do. How could he? Someone who has as much money as he does—as his parents do—should never ask someone else about their supply of money. This unspoken social rule is why I don't tell Shelby when my father buys me a box of dark chocolate for no reason. Why I used to avoid talking about getting an A in geometry in front of Chiffon, and why I never say the word *virginity* in front of Melissa.

I wait for him to make it worse. To ask Shelby what college she's going to, and for Shelby to tell him she's not going. We have a really good community college. The problem is that once people enroll there, they never seem to leave. That's the joke, anyway. So Shelby never talks about next year and has definitely never mentioned enrolling in the community college. She's never told me what she's going to do.

"I don't believe in stress; I believe in living," Shelby tells Nathan. She smiles at the same time that he does. Her attitude is contagious. "Look at Aubrey," I hear her say.

I push away the hair that's fallen out of my pony-tail and is dangling in my face. I wipe my forehead. It's sweaty after so much scrubbing.

"Look at her," Shelby says again, smiling at me like she's fond of what she sees. "She's a mess of stress."

I smile for the simple fact that Shelby rhymed, and smile larger when Nathan adds, "You're a poet and you don't know it."

But Shelby's right. I need to get away more than ever.

WE'RE HALFWAY THERE when I receive a text message from Melissa telling me that she and Danica arrived ten minutes ago and have already been invited to three parties.

"Only three?" is Shelby's response.

"You think we'll have time for more than three?"

Shelby ignores this very *lost puppy* statement of Nathan's. "Brey, what's the name of that guy again? The one I'm excited to see?"

"Sam?" Nathan offers.

Shelby gives a small chuckle. She looks at Nathan like she's thinking about patting him on the head.

"Conrad Malone," I say.

"Ding, ding, ding—we have a winner!" Shelby leans forward from the backseat to high-five me.

"He was in the news," I explain to Nathan. "He plays for Victoria High. He's supposed to be the next big thing." Whatever that means.

"*My* next big thing," Shelby declares.

"Isn't Sam on the basketball team?" Nathan asks.

Shelby shakes her head. "It's all about the numbers, Diggs. Did you know there will be fifteen different high schools competing in the first round? Have you even added up how many new hot people we're going to meet tonight alone?"

Nathan smiles at her through the review mirror. "The mathematics of meeting hot people. Very nice."

When he glances at me, I turn away and stare out the window. I'm blushing and I don't want him to see. I'm blushing because I don't want to meet hot people. All I want is Nathan, and that is embarrassing. It's shameful, too, because I hope against hope that Nathan doesn't want to meet hot people either.

CHAPTER
TWENTY-TWO

We attend only one party after all, but it's the size of three parties. More people. A bigger house. A broader selection of alcohol. The first thing Shelby does is stand nonchalantly next to Conrad Malone, and he doesn't leave her side the rest of the night.

"He's the full meal deal," Shelby tells me on Tuesday before the evening tournament games start. She rattles off everything I already learned about him in the newspaper article. That he's been playing basketball since he was four. That he's going to Duke on a full ride. That despite his dedication to basketball, he's managed to maintain a perfect GPA. But what I'm most impressed with is how Shelby's whole face smiles when she talks about him, and how what she has to say about him extends beyond what we can all see for ourselves, how unbelievably attractive he is.

I yawn as the game starts and everyone stands up. If we lose this game, tonight will be our last night here.

To be honest, for me, that would be ideal. It's taken me only two nights to discover the truly epic part of basketball state championship week: the epic sleeping dilemma. We're all packed in rooms like sardines. So many people came knowing they could sleep anywhere, because even if we're from different schools, we're joined here for the same cause. It's never quiet, either. There's always music or laughter or cheering in the distance.

I reach down and grab Nathan's coffee where it's resting by his feet on the bleachers, and take a big drink. But it's not coffee. He winces at me, but I can tell that he wants to laugh. Robert notices and does start laughing, so Nathan lets himself go.

Melissa is jumping up and down, her mouth stained that very familiar cranberry red. Leila is holding her cup close to her, swaying and shouting, "B-E aggressive!" since this tournament excludes cheerleaders. Apparently the party has started.

I'm giggling with Shelby and whispering about

Conrad, whose team is playing on the other court, when Melissa announces in a high whine, "It's lame here—I want to leave!"

We follow her gaze to the left side of the bleachers, four rows back, to a set of cool blue eyes and strategically messy dishwater blond hair. Chiffon Dillon. She's weaving her way through the crowd with three guys I don't recognize and two of her girlfriends. Chiffon meets Shelby's stare and her eyes narrow.

Chiffon should know better.

"You've got to be kidding me," Shelby says.

"They just let *anybody* in, don't they?" Melissa shakes her head. She's on the verge of tears.

"It's okay." Robert reaches across Nathan, Shelby, and me, to squeeze Melissa's hand. He looks at Shelby, then Danica, then me, and back to Shelby. "You're not going to say anything, are you?"

Robert should know better.

"Hey, Chiffon," Shelby calls. "Chiffon!"

"Great." Robert takes a really long drink from his coffee cup.

Nathan's forehead is wrinkled.

Chiffon gives Shelby just a second of her attention, waving her hand in the air and widening her eyes as if to say, *What do you want?*

"Are you still fucking Zane?"

I don't know if it really matters that Chiffon can't

hear Shelby, when all of us can. Melissa's smiling, Danica's nodding, Leila's covering her mouth like she can't believe it.

"Are you still fucking Zane?" Shelby tries again.

Chiffon has turned her back completely now.

Shelby looks at me. "Is she?"

I feel my face grow hot and out of the corner of my eye I can see Nathan turning to stare at me, the way everyone within earshot is.

"You've been hanging at the Chapmans'; is she still hooking up with him?" Shelby asks.

"I don't know," I lie.

"He probably dumped her ass!" Melissa says.

"We'll find out, I guess." Shelby winks at her. "Hey, Chiffon." She walks up the bleachers toward Chiffon, slinking through the crowd. She holds her phone out in front of her and starts snapping photos of Chiffon when she's close enough. Chiffon's friends pull back a little and raise their hands trying to block Shelby's view of their faces. The boys with them frown in confusion. One of them seems to be saying, *What the hell?*

"Just thought Zane might like to know what you're up to." It's easy to hear Shelby's voice, the way she's shouting. Shelby leans forward, snapping more pictures. Chiffon slants toward her, too, then, as she says something to Shelby that we can't hear but know can't be very nice. The boys who are with Chiffon all go bug-eyed.

Chiffon's friends smirk and get the confidence to glare at Shelby. And Shelby turns to us, looking like she wants to laugh, shaking her head like, *Can you believe her?*

I thought after what she said to me at Trip's, I'd be glad to see Chiffon put in her place and embarrassed in front of boys she's with. But I wish more than anything that Melissa hadn't noticed her.

"Tell your new friends to smile," Shelby says to Chiffon. "Zane will want to get a good look at them."

Chiffon stretches her arm out, probably an attempt to knock Shelby's phone out of her hand, but right before she can reach Shelby, a boy in a purple Victoria High School T-shirt steps in front of her. The boy stumbles forward as Chiffon's hand hits him in the back, and the two drinks he's carrying sail through the air, covering Shelby in what looks like red wine or something mixed with cranberry juice. Her hair and the front of her shirt are all dripping red.

The boy apologizes profusely, but Shelby's face turns to stone and she looks around him at Chiffon. Chiffon is covering her mouth and her eyes are wide. I think for a second she's surprised, but then I see her friends. They're covering their mouths too, because they're laughing.

Shelby shakes her head. "Irrational behavior," she says, and her eyes light up. There must be a time-out or something, because there's a lull in the crowd. Shelby knows we can all hear her clearly. "It must be a side effect of your herpes medication."

If the boys with Chiffon were bug-eyed before, now their eyes are popping out of their skulls. Chiffon yells something back at Shelby, "Fuck you!" or "Fuck off!" and grabs Shelby by the arm. Shelby wiggles out of her grasp and pushes Chiffon away with her free hand.

I feel Nathan make a sudden movement beside me, and even without looking, I know he is jolting in the direction of the confrontation. The crowd keeps him from taking more than a step. When I do look at him, he's staring at Chiffon. But Chiffon is only in sight for a second. Her friends are pulling her away. The boys don't go with them.

Melissa squeals, "That was awesome!" as Shelby returns. "You got her to leave! Oh, your shirt!" She dabs Shelby's shirt with a paper napkin. Danica joins in, so I do too, even though we aren't making one bit of difference.

Nathan opens his mouth like he's going to speak, but he doesn't. Just runs two fingers over his lips, soothing them from whatever they were about to let slip out.

"What did she say to you?" Danica asks Shelby. She's standing a row below, facing us, with her back to the game.

"She's so crazy." Shelby rolls her eyes, gestures to her shirt, and pushes our hands away. Robert passes her a Big Gulp cup and she takes a long sip.

"What—what was that?" Nathan says. He's rubbing his chin.

"She's crazy," Shelby repeats, her voice dripping in irritation.

"So why go after her like that?"

Nathan doesn't understand; I was right.

Shelby laughs, like she doesn't hear the insult in Nathan's voice. "Relax. Jesus. Live a little, Diggs."

Nathan looks away, stops fidgeting, licks his lips. His expression is flat when he turns back to her. "Some living, Shelby."

I know Nathan well enough to know that doing this, saying this, to someone like Shelby terrifies him, but he's too mad. The alcohol probably makes him brave. I wish it would have this effect on me. I don't want him to be angry like this. I want him to understand what everyone else understands: What happens between us and Chiffon is just between us. No one else will get it. They shouldn't even try.

Shelby's smiling slightly, and she tilts her head a little. I'm familiar with the look. She's debating whether or not to humiliate Nathan. One quick jab, a Designated Diggs reference to remind everyone that her side is the one to be on. She picks at her thumbnail. This is the only thing that gives her away to me. He's making her a little nervous.

Melissa's the one to get mad about someone insulting

Shelby. And over Chiffon, especially. "She's crazy!" Melissa tells Nathan.

Danica's not paying attention to Nathan or Melissa. She hasn't taken her eyes off Shelby. "What did she say to you?" she asks again, leaning forward. "Right before she pushed that guy into you, what did she say?"

Nathan shakes his head at this. He doesn't think Chiffon pushed the guy in purple. He thinks it was an accident. He looks at me and I look to Shelby, because I don't know what to think.

Shelby rolls her eyes, but her previous enthusiasm is completely gone. "You know. The usual shit she says to me."

Danica's eyes widen for a second, a quick flash of anger pulsing through her.

Nathan looks back and forth between them, and I think that maybe now he'll see. This isn't something he can make sense of.

"Why is she crazy?" he asks, like he's skeptical we don't have an answer.

That's the problem, though. We don't. There isn't much to say about Chiffon that can't be explained by how we decided to treat her. I feel my cheeks flush, and my whole body goes hot. I'm so sure someone is going to tell Nathan that for everything horrible about Chiffon, there's something horrible about us. About me.

Robert offers an explanation. "She told Shelby she

wanted her to die." His voice is serious.

Now the way Nathan looks at Shelby is different; he's confused. "What?"

"Yeah!" Melissa says. She stomps her foot. "Chiffon is insane!"

"She's such a bitch," Robert says. He doesn't really know why we hate Chiffon; he understands that what she said to Shelby at Tommy Rizzo's barbecue last year was wrong. He sees Shelby, in front of him now, her shirt splattered red, the front strands of her blond hair turning pink. Nathan's expression softens too as he looks at Shelby.

Normally, Tommy Rizzo's house is a place Chiffon wouldn't exactly be welcome, but last year she took the risk and came with her group of girlfriends. That night, we decided to apologize to her. There was a little bit of a protest from Melissa. But Shelby had decided and so that was that. We all thought it was best that Shelby be the one to do it.

I was about five feet away from where it all went down, so I can only tell you what I was able to see. Shelby was wearing platform wedge sandals, and she was bad at walking in them. When she was almost directly in front of Chiffon, Shelby stumbled forward, bumping Chiffon into the barbecue and covering her white tank top with charcoal. Chiffon was gripping her arm after it happened—I don't know if she was bruised or burned—but her face didn't reveal that she was hurt. Chiffon's expression said only one thing: how much she hated Shelby. And then, if her glare wasn't enough, she said loudly, with gritted teeth, "I hope you die, bitch," and walked away.

Shelby just laughed, so we did too. What else can you do when someone tells your best friend to die?

Right now, with Nathan's sullen face, it doesn't feel funny. I'm still thrown by Robert's use of the word *bitch*. To Robert, girls are babes, not bitches.

But this is what Chiffon has turned into. Someone who told Shelby to die. Someone so obviously unevolved, there's no defense for her. That's why no one challenges Shelby when she says these things to Chiffon. They're afraid of being like Chiffon too, just like we are. It seems like a million years ago when she really was one of our best friends. We had slumber parties and passed notes in the hall. Chiffon's notes used to be so funny, we'd read them out loud after school. She loved movies, too, romantic comedies that made her cry happy tears. And she could run faster than all the boys, so they were always asking her to race them. But I don't think anyone remembers that part of her anymore. It's no different from what happens when Shelby and Celine fight—how everyone only remembers the mean comment Shelby made and not the subtle insult that caused it.

I think—just for a second because it's all I can

bear—Chiffon and Shelby are so alike.

Any fragments of frustration left in Nathan's face disappear and are replaced with worry. I do nothing to correct it. I don't tell him that that wasn't the first time one of us had mentioned someone she might have been hooking up with and used it against her, or announced to a roomful of people that she had an STD. No one says anything about all the times we didn't tell Chiffon we wanted her to die, but we treated her that way.

I watch Nathan stare at Shelby as she crosses the stadium to give a quick hello to Conrad before halftime. Conrad touches the stained front of Shelby's shirt and grabs a warm-up shirt off the back of one of the seats along the sideline, but she shakes her head, smiling. She blows kisses at him as he disappears into the locker room.

Nathan rubs his eyes. "I need a refill."

Robert returns moments later, with a full cup for Nathan. He promises Nathan it's stronger. Nathan lets me have a sip, and it's so potent it's hard to keep a straight face when I drink it. Nathan puts the cup down by our feet and doesn't pick it up for the rest of the game. I don't reach for it either, because the thing I trust about Nathan is that sometimes—most of the time, maybe—he knows better than I do.

At the party that night, Nathan pulls me into the hall-way, away from everyone. He tugs on my loose strands of hair. He takes my face in his hands, tilting it toward him. He smiles like the sight of me makes him feel better, calmer, but his face is still not all the way back to normal. For a second I contemplate telling Nathan the whole story, just so he'll stop feeling so bad, but the truth is I don't want him to know. I don't want him to know how I was before—unevolved—and I really don't want him to know that I am sometimes awful. He's not supposed to know—that's what Shelby would say. Because the reason Chiffon hates us is the same reason Nathan is here, holding my face and looking into my eyes like there's nothing he'd rather look at.

You've earned him, Shelby would say.

CHAPTER
TWENTY-THREE

On Tuesday, we lock everyone out of our room. We close the curtains and turn off most of the lights, and it's just the four of us, greasy takeout, gas station snacks, fuzzy pajamas, stacks of pillows, and reality television. It would be pleasant, but we all feel awful. Drained of energy, nauseous, and sleep-deprived. Epic parties breed epic hangovers, go figure.

It's not until six p.m. that we start to feel better. Shelby's the first.

"Conrad is an amazing kisser."

Danica groans, tossing and turning. She looks so uncomfortable, it makes me itchy.

"We've seen him in action on your face," Melissa says, her voice quiet and unenthused.

"I think I'm going to visit him at Duke next year," Shelby says casually. Her eyes are dancing, though, like she's picturing something really enchanting.

We're all someone else. Shelby's making plans. Melissa's relaxed, Danica's not. I don't know who I am until I stare at my phone, the screen blank from zero missed calls, and realize I am lonely.

"Duke is all the way in North Carolina," I tell her.

"I know that," she says. She has a dizzy smile on her face. Maybe it's the distance that has her making plans to visit a boy she's known only three days.

I still feel the pangs of loneliness. Loneliness and anger are cut from the same cloth, I decide. I don't like Shelby smiling like that when I feel like this. "It just seems a little weird that you want to visit him when you barely know him."

Shelby shakes her head like she can't fathom the words coming out of my mouth. She's still smiling. "Barron is on the way to Duke, you know."

"Is that your way of telling me you'll come visit us?" It just slips out: *us*.

Shelby's eyes widen, enough that I know she caught what I said. "Of course I'll come visit you." She doesn't say this like she's correcting me. She says this like it's a given, and maybe it is. But Barron is far. She'll have to spend ten hours driving or buy a plane ticket to visit me. Melissa will just be an hour away at State, and Danica is still waiting to hear if she got into the university. But even the university is only three hours away. I feel even lonelier thinking about the distance.

I squeeze my eyes shut and feel a pair of hands on my head. Shelby. She's sitting next to my pillow, combing the tangles out of my hair with her fingers.

"I love visiting places," she tells me, but I can't remember the last time Shelby went on vacation. "I love being the mysterious stranger."

I think of her breezing through Barron like a wild bird, flying against the current, but effortlessly—she'll be so foreign to everyone with her laidback life. For me, it will be a relief to have her there. I picture her at Duke, her hair getting a slight wave from the humidity, the sun making her skin golden. She'll pop in on Conrad, carefree and fresh, and he'll think he wants her to stay forever. But she won't. She'll come with no strings attached and leave that very same way.

"Conrad just assumed there'd be a victory party tonight for him even before they'd won. He's cocky like that." Shelby's sounding more like herself. She starts to braid my hair, small chunks at a time.

Melissa stares at us and sits up slightly, opening her mouth a little like she's about to whine for something she wants. Danica's breathing hard, completely relaxed and totally knocked out. I'm thinking about next year, and wondering if there's a way for me to be shiny and new at Barron, where we'll all be surrounded by only new things.

We're all back to ourselves again.

AT MIDNIGHT, WE'RE wide-awake. This is what happens when you sleep all day. We missed the basketball tournament games, but if we stay in tonight we'll be missing the last night of parties. Our team lost, so we are checking out at eleven a.m. tomorrow.

"I'm trying to make Robert give us a ride," Danica says, frantically texting.

"I'm trying to make Nathan," I say, though it's not really true. There's no way Robert or Nathan can drive right now.

"You can't make them do or not do anything," Melissa says, taking a big bite out of a Ben & Jerry's mini tub she got at the 7-Eleven down the street. "All you can really do is make them wear a condom."

This is probably the smartest thing I've ever heard Melissa say.

Shelby laughs. "Good advice coming from the only virgin in the senior class."

Melissa throws a pillow at Shelby. I can tell she put the weight of her whole body into the toss because she is now sitting forward on her knees. Before Shelby can hound Melissa, saying all the typical virgin catchphrases, like "Once it's gone, it's on," her phone beeps. It's a text from Conrad. The first one she's received tonight. Shelby giggles and flops onto her stomach.

It's really not funny to joke about Melissa's virginity. She probably would have lost it before any of us, if it hadn't been for what we now refer to as the Incident. When we were sophomores, a particularly promiscuous and not very bright senior chose to talk to her friends about the itching, burning, inflammatory redness that was taking place—ahem—down *there* during an assembly, and everyone heard. So when the boy Melissa had been consistently making out with and was planning on giving her virginity to that weekend came up with the phrase "If she's clean, we're all clean!" and Melissa was faced with the enormous sexual Lincoln High spiderweb that he was tangled in, she abruptly lost interest. Knowing that she could have potentially caught what turned out to be chlamydia had terrified Melissa to the point of abstinence.

Shelby keeps texting and laughing, smiling at her phone as if Conrad can see her through it. Danica snatches Shelby's phone and reads the next text from Conrad in a deep, breathy voice, "Send me a photo. I miss your face."

Shelby laughs as I help her part her nearly dry hair. Melissa brings her lip gloss. Danica holds up the phone and takes two pictures of Shelby sitting with her arms behind her back in a pink tank top, half smirking, half pouting. Shelby sends him the second picture and within seconds Conrad writes back: *WOW.*

The texts keep coming.

You're so fucking hot.

You sure you're not a model?

"You're too gorgeous for words." Danica reads this one out loud and rolls her eyes. This is a typical Shelby-is-too-beautiful-to-describe compliment. Danica's still holding the phone when it beeps again. She covers her mouth with her hand and says slowly, "Oh my God. . . ."

"What? What does it say?" we demand.

Shelby finally takes the phone out of Danica's hand. She shrieks when she reads it. Melissa and I have no choice but to peer over her shoulder.

NOW SEND ME SOME REAL PICTURES. CLOTHING OPTIONAL.

And we shriek too. Yes, Conrad and Shelby have had sex, but *this* somehow feels sexier. More dangerous. More scandalous. More mysterious.

Shelby grabs her lipstick and winks at us before she disappears into the bathroom holding her phone. We laugh harder, shriek louder, and bunch together so we're elbow to elbow because sometimes when we're this excited we just need to be close.

Conrad wants Shelby so badly, he's desperate to see as much of her as he possibly can without her being right there with him. He's surrounded by people at a party, but all he wants is her.

All of me wishes Nathan would message me with the same request.

I start brainstorming sexy poses to send to Nathan. The thought of Nathan opening a text and seeing me, barely dressed, is exhilarating. And if I surprised him with one, how would he keep himself from calling me that very second? How would he even be able to function for the rest of the party after that? The answer, of course, is that he wouldn't. I know exactly how to make his night.

When Shelby comes out of the bathroom, she's blushing.

"Oh my God, what did he say?" Whatever he said must have been good, because I've never seen Shelby so red-faced in my life.

"Nothing yet," she says, sitting next to me on the bed.

"What did you do for the pictures?" Melissa asks.

"Sorry, M," Shelby says, using Melissa's new nickname—something we've started teasing her about since she spent the weekend making out with a guy who went by L and never would tell us what the L stood for. "These photos are R-rated. FCEO." *For Conrad's eyes only.*

"I didn't ask to see them!" Melissa is mortified. "I asked what you did for them."

"They're just of me. Of all of me."

It's too much. I hit her with the closest pillow. Danica and Melissa are laughing, and Melissa is squealing so loud she covers her own ears. *Any second now Conrad's going to call*, I think. *If he doesn't try to knock down our door first.*

We scramble to get ready, spraying and drying and curling the final strands of our hair, searching for our shoes, and sliding on jeans. We have the address for the party Patrick, Robert, and Nathan are at. We don't know if they're at the same party as Conrad, but soon he's going to text Shelby back.

"Maybe they aren't sending right away," Melissa says.

There have been three commercial breaks on the television blaring in the background. Shelby's phone has stayed silent, and Shelby has been quiet too. Shelby shrugs. I stare at her phone. It's resting in her back pocket. It's right there, *on her,* and I don't know how she resists checking it for messages that might've slipped through without her knowing, or to see if the battery is dead or the photos aren't sending right away, like Melissa suggested.

"When did they break up?" Shelby asks about a celebrity couple being featured on TV. She sits down on the bed and leans slightly against the headboard but keeps her feet on the floor. I notice she's no longer wearing her boots.

"Last week," Melissa says at the same time I say, "Didn't you hear?" We sound too anxious, and we are. I debate making a joke about how Conrad must've needed some time alone with Shelby's photo. I debate calling him a horny bastard. But for some reason our usual behavior seems inappropriate. It feels like since Shelby hasn't acknowledged what's going on, we're not allowed to, either.

Danica's phone beeps and it makes me jump.

"Robert says they're going to a different party and he'll text us the address when he gets there," she says.

There's nowhere for us to go for now, so we all join Shelby on the bed. She slides her legs under the covers.

By the time we have the address thirty minutes later, we've all nestled back into bed.

"I feel like shit," Shelby says. She reaches for the Advil on the nightstand and takes two.

"Me too," says Melissa. Shelby tosses her the bottle.

I text Nathan to tell him we're not coming. This has somehow been decided even though none of us admit it. We stare at the television, the only noise in the room.

We all drift off to sleep eventually, but before I do, lying in the dark with the lights of the TV flashing and low-volume celebrity gossip still filling the room, something occurs to me. Really, when you think about it, sending a photo like that goes against the theories. They forbid us from doing things that require something in return. It's the first time Shelby's ever broken one of the rules.

CHAPTER
TWENTY-FOUR

We're quiet on the ride home. Shelby's asleep in the backseat. Nathan looks like he should be sleeping too. I offer to drive, but I'm just as tired and Nathan knows it.

Nathan's unusually quiet. He does look incredibly beat—his hair is a mess, his eyes tight, his breath slow. I try not to read into it. We're an hour from home and I can't help myself.

"Is everything all right?" I'm about to justify my question with an explanation—*you look so tired*—but Nathan's already distressed face gets worse, so I stay quiet and watch the trees rush by us out the window.

"You tell me," he says.

I turn my head so suddenly to look at him that my hair flies in my face and sticks to my lip gloss.

He doesn't appear mad. Just worried, sad, tired. He nods at the review mirror, at the reflection of Shelby leaning against the window using her jacket as a pillow.

"Is she okay?" Nathan asks in a whisper so quiet I can barely hear him above the hum of the tires reeling over the road.

I'm about to tell him that she's just worn out like everyone else, but he seems so genuinely concerned that I think he's referring to something else entirely. I'm afraid of what that could be. "Why?"

He glances at me, quickly, like he's checking for something. He chews on his bottom lip for a second, then shrugs. "She's just really quiet."

"This week was exhausting . . . ," I mutter. I might be completely off base in thinking that Nathan knows something I don't—a reason that Shelby might not be *okay*. But I don't think so. I want to say something about the pictures, ask Nathan if he saw them, or if the whole party saw them, or if our entire school will be receiving a dirty email later. Maybe it's a stretch to believe that because Conrad stopped texting after he got the photos, he did something bad to her; to believe that he would take what she gave him—FCEO—and share it. But Shelby didn't even want us, her best friends, to know how she felt about Conrad's lack of response and what that could mean, so I keep my mouth shut.

"She didn't say anything . . . to you . . . ?" He trails off, like maybe he's realizing something about Shelby and me and Danica and Melissa, and how we are with guys, how we deal with the way they treat us. When evolved girls do risky things, they own them, they aren't injured by them.

"If you were really as much of a gentleman as everyone says you are, you would just ask me about it." Shelby startles us. She sounds tired, but her voice is strong. "You should be asking *me* if I'm all right. Not Aubrey."

Nathan's mouth hangs open slightly. He looks guilty.

"Well, Diggs?" Shelby says, sitting upright, leaning forward. "You could at least tell me what you said to stop him from posting the pictures."

There's a secret between Nathan and Shelby, and even though it's not that hard a code to crack, I still feel anxious. We've been driving for over an hour, and Nathan's known something about Shelby and Shelby's known something about Nathan, and I didn't know anything.

Nathan's face gets serious and he doesn't look sorry anymore. "I told him my father was a judge and he would get in trouble. . . . I told him he would be arrested for distributing child pornography because you were only seventeen."

Shelby's quiet for a second. Eventually, she laughs. "That's it? I can't believe that worked."

"I told him it was a felony and he would go to jail for five years before they'd even consider letting him off for good behavior."

"Is that even true?" She laughs again, quieter this time.

"I—I don't know." Nathan keeps glancing at Shelby in the rearview mirror. His brow is furrowed, and for a second I stop fretting and picture Nathan threatening an arrest in the middle of a party. It's adorable that he lied for Shelby; even the lie he told is adorable—it's *so Nathan* to threaten someone with *the law*, made up or not.

She laughs again in disbelief. I smile because Shelby's happy and it's contagious. Nathan looks between us—a quick sideways glance at me and a peek in the rearview mirror at Shelby.

"You should be furious." He gives another lingering stare into the mirror. "*I'm* furious." He looks to me, then. Like I should be furious too. But I am whatever Shelby is. Shelby's leaning back against the window and frowning a little. She's no longer amused; she's bored with this now and also a little irritated. I'm relieved she's been so flippant with Nathan.

I wonder for a moment if he saw the pictures, and my stomach rocks.

"Oh, Diggs," Shelby says. She leans forward and puts her hand on his shoulders. She gives him a pat, then a squeeze. "You really are a good guy."

I watch the tension drain from Nathan's face. He gets the look, like he's grateful and completely at our mercy. At Shelby's mercy. It's because of the way Shelby said "good guy." She said it like it was a compliment, not an insult; it was missing its usual sting. Typically, *good guy* for Shelby is synonymous with *wet blanket* or *ugly*.

I lean against the cool window, waiting for the tension to drain out of me, too. Waiting to feel as carefree as Shelby, as relieved as Nathan. My phone vibrates in the cup holder—the place in Nathan's car that's mine, where I keep my phone or my drink or my spare change. It's Trip. He wants to know if I'll edit his Comparative Religions essay, which is due tomorrow at four o'clock. I tell him I will even though I'm beat. He messages back a smiley face and tells me to come by in a few hours; he's going to drive home from school.

Trip could really just email the essay. I don't tell him this, though. I just tell him I'll see him tonight.

IT'S NEARLY DUSK by the time I get to Trip's. I'm exhausted, but I'm here anyway.

"This is a stupid idea, Aubrey," my mother told me before I left. But I can manage.

No one's at Trip's when I arrive, but the front door is unlocked, as usual. I lie down on the couch and turn on the TV. I don't even register what show I'm watching before I fall asleep.

IT'S NOT CLEAR how much time has passed when I finally wake up to find Trip sitting on the edge of the couch looking down on me. It was growing late when I arrived, and it's definitely dark now.

"I guess you partied pretty hard, eh, Housing?" He gives me a weak smile.

"Atta girl!" I hear Zane shout from the dining room.

When I try to sit up, it's difficult. It feels like my head weighs a ton and my eyelids weigh even more. Trip notices that I'm struggling and slides one of the throw pillows that are strewn about the living room behind me so I have support. I manage a small smile of thanks. Nothing about the Chapmans' living room makes me want to wake up. The fire is crackling in the corner, providing the only light in the room other than the glow of the television, and I'm covered in a crocheted blanket that Trip's grandmother made him when he was seven.

"You had a good time," he concludes. "Even though you're back so soon?"

"I'm glad to be back." The confession leaks out of me like molasses.

An even bigger smile spreads across his face. "I have some stuff for you."

"Your homework?"

He shakes his head as he leans forward. "No, Aubrey. Something you'll actually like." He reaches into a paper grocery bag resting on the floor in front of him. I sit up slightly, getting curious. He pulls out a bottle of ginger ale and a package of salt-and-vinegar chips. This is the food Trip eats after a night of drinking.

"I don't have a hangover." I lie back down. I don't know why I feel so irritated by this mistake.

He shrugs. "I saw you asleep and thought I'd better get something for you just in case you were too sick to eat the steaks we're grilling for dinner."

I immediately recognize the deep scent of charcoal, barbecue sauce, and pepper wafting in the air and intermingling with the smell of burning wood from the fire.

"Think you can handle a steak?" Trip grins at me.

I feel oddly flattered as Trip helps me up and guides me over to my very own spot at the Chapman dinner table. It's a weird privilege to be included for dinner at the Chapmans'. They take dinner very seriously, clearing off the bills and dishes and empty beer cans that usually cover the dining room table. They even use silverware and make a salad.

"Veggies," Earl says, pointing proudly at the bowl of greens as he sets it on the table.

Zane pumps his fist against his chest like he's Popeye about to devour a can of spinach. "And vitamin C." He sets a carton of orange juice on the table and pumps his fist one more time.

"We're trying to be healthier," Trip explains. They've

got the right idea. Even though it's super weird that they're drinking orange juice with steak.

We laugh during dinner when Earl tells us a story about a naked couple he found today at the plant who'd been using the storage yard as a cheap motel. It feels so good to laugh. My whole body feels lighter. We laugh even harder as Zane, Trip, and I demand a full description of the couple and try to guess who they were. This town is small, so we've got a few good guesses.

"So how about that damn test?" Earl asks Trip when our plates are nearly empty.

"I thought it was an essay?" There's the strangest sense of panic that surges through me when I think I've been misled about another one of our study sessions. I keep thinking Trip will give me a reason to never come over here again.

Trip looks at me and smiles. "I've got both. But I made flash cards for the test already."

"Well, what are you waiting for?" Earl says. "Aubrey came all the way over here with a hangover." I glare at Trip for starting this rumor. "Go get them!" Earl's beaming, at me and at Trip.

We pass around the flashcards for Trip's quiz in French 101. It's the most entertaining study session I've ever been a part of by far. Especially hearing us try to pronounce the words. Trip has to correct us almost every time. "It's good for him!" Earl claims. Zane takes away

Trip's orange juice each time he reads him a flash card and only gives it back if Trip answers correctly. Halfway through the quizzing, Zane gets an idea to liven things up: Trip must follow up every one of his answers with "in bed."

"*Tourner à droite?*"

"To turn right—in bed."

"*Pratiquer?*"

"To practice—in bed."

"*Être pressé?*"

"To be in a hurry—in bed."

"*Sale?*"

"Soiled, dirty—in bed."

"*Pour réussir?*"

"To succeed—in bed."

I laugh harder than I have in days.

After the study session is over and all the dishes have been shoved into the dishwasher, Zane and Earl watch TV while I help Trip edit his essay at the table. It doesn't take long; the essay is only one page, after all, and Trip can revise on the spot with me looking over his shoulder. It probably won't count for much of his grade, but Trip needs all the points he can get. I wonder if he also missed Zane and Earl and their crazy dinners, and that's why he really came back tonight.

I curl up in the dark green recliner when we're finished. There's plenty of room on the couch, but Trip leans against the arm of the recliner, half sitting, half leaning. He rocks it slightly and when I glance in his direction, I notice he's staring at me.

I'm onto him. He's giving me the signal he used to give me last year when we were hanging out with a group of people in the living room and he wanted me to follow him into his bedroom. Now that he's got my attention, he leans forward in an exaggerated motion that signals he's about to get up and I'm supposed to follow him. That used to be all it took, just Trip leaning forward and staring at me, to get me to follow him into his bedroom.

And that's all it takes to make me follow him tonight. The second the chair rocks back as Trip's weight leaves it, I rock forward and stand up. I don't know why, really. I don't have any desire to be with Trip. I don't even want to kiss him.

The second we're in Trip's room, I know the real reason I wanted to be in here. I kick off my shoes and climb into his bed, burying myself in the flannel sheets and big plaid comforter that smells like cedar and pizza sauce —like Trip. It's so familiar, and I always used to be so happy here. I'm transported back to a time when I was deliriously infatuated, and to the moment when all my fantasies about Trip turned into an even better reality. It really is the best feeling in the world when everything that used to make you dizzy with desire becomes so wedged in your life that it changes from something you craved to something you belong in.

"You don't waste any time, do you, Housing?" Trip smiles and lies down next to me, over the sheets, keeping his shoes on. He's going to leave as soon as he finds out I'm not here to fool around with him, I think.

"Trip?" I ask, aching to keep my eyes open.

"Yeah?" I see his eyes slide closed for a moment too.

"Why did you stop calling me?" My eyes are closed and it's better like this. To ask him the hard question, the question I'm not allowed to ask, without having to look at him.

"You know why." There's a long pause before he continues. "But you're the first person I thought of—"

"When you were failing out?" My voice is weak, but there's still an edge to it.

I imagine him nodding when I hear him say, "Uh-hmm. You're always the first person I think of."

I want to ask him what he means. But everything feels foggy and thick, and all I want to do is give in to the comfort of his bed and lose myself there.

CHAPTER
TWENTY-FIVE

"Who do you think you are, Little Susie?" my mother shouts at me over the phone. I have the urge to call her a dork for saying that, for referencing that ridiculous old song that she hums along to in the kitchen, "Wake Up Little Susie," about a girl and boy who fall asleep together by mistake. But calling her names will only hurt my cause.

"I'm sorry, Mom, it was an accident! I swear!"

I'm standing in Trip's dining room staring out the window, waiting for Melissa to pull into the driveway with clothes and deodorant and makeup, while my mother tells me over the phone again how worried she was and how mad she is. I don't point out that she knew exactly where I was and that if she was as worried as she claimed to be in the voice mail she left me last night, she could have just come over and gotten me.

I don't dare go home this morning. If my mother were to see me like this, with bed head and smelling like cedar and Trip's aftershave, it would only make things worse for me.

Melissa's white car tears through the trees and pulls up the gravel driveway.

"Okay, Mom, I have to go. Can we talk about this tonight?"

"Come straight home after school. I mean it. This isn't over!"

Melissa storms inside, and I'm so quick to greet her we practically bump into each other. Shelby's with her, but she's in no rush. She hasn't even made it to the porch when Melissa and I scurry into the bathroom. Melissa's brought a hair dryer, which she blows at me in the Chapmans' tiny bathroom while I attempt to change into the clothing she's brought. I've managed to shower this morning. It would have been nice if the Chapmans used conditioner.

Shelby doesn't join us in the bathroom. We can hear her in hallway teasing Zane, speaking to him through the crack in his door.

"Zane, get up and entertain me."

"I've missed you."

"Do you sleep in the nude?"

"Zaaannnnee, are you dreaming about me?"

"Where's your little girlfriend?"

When I'm finally fit to be seen—wearing a pair of Shelby's jeans, which are just a little too long, and one of Melissa's long-sleeve tees, with dryish hair and a made-up face—we find Shelby in the living room chatting with Trip, hunched over the coffee table as he eats cereal.

He smiles when he sees me. "Is the fire out?"

Only Shelby laughs, since Melissa and I took this whole getting-me-to-school-looking-normal-and-not-as-if-I've-just-slept-over-at-Trip-Chapman's-house mission very seriously.

Trip was a zombie when I woke up this morning. At seven a.m. Less than an hour before the first bell. I screamed and ran around the room, called Melissa, jumped in the shower, then finally called my mother. Trip, still fully clothed with his shoes on, mumbled something like "Oh, shit," but fell right back asleep.

"Are you going to be okay?" Trip asks me, leaning around Shelby so he can see me.

It's not fair, the way Trip's looking at me right now. Like he cares about me, like he's waiting for me to tell him I'm okay so he'll be okay too. The first thing I loved about Trip was this—the way he seemed so exposed, like I was unknotting him slowly and he was unraveling, but happy to do so because I would be the one to hold the pieces of him.

What's even more unfair is that aside from that, he's wearing a thin white undershirt that shows off the shape of his chest and the definition in his arms. His hair is messy, and everything about his face is alluring.

"I'll be fine," I tell him, but my voice catches.

"Stop drooling—we're taking her away now." Shelby says this to Trip, but I flinch like she's talking to me.

"Come on." Melissa turns the doorknob. She's pulling on my arm with her other hand.

"Yoooouuuu," Shelby sings, pinching my waist as we walk down Trip's driveway. "You couldn't help yourself, could you?"

"I told you, nothing happened."

"I believe you." Melissa nods at me.

Shelby climbs into the front passenger seat of my car. Melissa frowns. She might be jealous that Shelby's not riding with her. Or she might be worried for me, because if Shelby thinks I've hooked up with Trip, she's never going to let up.

"Seriously, Shelby," I tell her.

"Okay, okay. You didn't hook up with him. Why the hell not?"

I pretend to concentrate on pulling out of the driveway and onto the road. Then on switching lanes.

The answer I have is not the one I'm supposed to have.

"Oh, come on," she says, as if I said "Nathan Diggs" out loud.

"It wasn't like that," I try to explain. "It's not like Trip and I were . . ." *Going back to the way we were* is how I want to finish the sentence. I can't bring myself to.

"Don't sound so sad about it."

But I am sad about it. I feel the loneliness again. For passing out in Trip's bed and knowing that's the closest I'll ever be to him again. For being fine with it. For being fine with never again getting what I used to want more than anything, because now I have something else, someone else, I want more. Even though, in the grand scheme of things, it doesn't matter.

"We just fell asleep." This makes me feel better. This makes me feel worse.

At school, I'm teased. My story is hilarious to Robert, especially the part about me being so scared to go home that I'm wearing Shelby's and Melissa's clothes. Celine cringes with jealousy, so at least there's that. I can't look at Nathan. There's no reason for him to be mad—for him to be anything—about what didn't happen between Trip and me.

"My mom called me Little Susie," I tell them at lunch.

The only one who gets the joke is Nathan. He laughs, and I lean into him, but not for long. He's laughing at something else now, and leaning away from me, talking about something to do with the tournament parties;

something that makes Robert's eyes grow wide; something that has them high-fiving.

"Let's leave," I say to Nathan, tugging on his sleeve.

"Okay, hang on."

I think he's going to cut them off to tell them where he's going. To brag, maybe.

There's an anxiousness spreading through me. I want us to drive to our housing development and lie together in the backseat. He can tell me what's so funny and I can tell him again that nothing happened last night.

It's all I can think about as I watch him with Patrick and Robert. The three of them laughing more at jokes I'll never get.

Sometimes I forget that Nathan is just another guy. He kissed me before he ever told me the entire truth about himself. And the theories worked on him just like they do on everyone.

So I don't remind him we were supposed to leave. I sit next to him in the cafeteria and laugh about last weekend like it was epic.

I'M GROUNDED THAT week, including the weekend, and I get a special *talking-to* from my mother about how I should not be having sex, especially not with Trip. At least I don't have to lie to her about what happened that night.

On Saturday morning I wake up to a series of this-is-what-you-missed drunken text messages. They used to make me feel special, but it feels bad to be receiving them again.

Some of them are from Nathan. One says **ROBERT AND PATRICK ARE CRAZY,** as if I didn't know. Another says, **GOOD NIGTT.** I assume this was supposed to say "Good night." I wonder how drunk and crazy Nathan got with Robert and Patrick while I wasn't there.

The final text message is from Shelby. **NATHAN DIGGS FINALLY CAME ALIVE TONIGHT.**

CHAPTER
TWENTY-SIX

My lips were stained red the entire summer after fifth grade thanks to all the cherry Popsicles in Shelby's freezer. We wore bikinis every day that summer, sitting in Shelby's backyard trying to get tan, running lemon juice over our hair even though only Shelby's hair ever got any lighter from the sun.

Shelby's sister, Sienna, had her first boyfriend that summer. His name was Josh and Sienna said his name a lot. Josh was never a *he* or a *him* or a *boyfriend*; he was always Josh.

Shelby could spot the lovesickness early. The desperation of it, the wrongness of it. But I thought it was sweet.

Josh was always touching Sienna. His hand forever on her shoulder, on the small of her back, tickling her palms, tracing hearts into the back of her neck. And he always had secrets to tell her. She always had things to whisper back.

Sandra was dating too, but her dates were always *hes* or *hims* or *dates*; they didn't have names. And she never let them touch her. She never had much to say to them. All they got was her rehearsed smile followed by the words *Good night*.

This was back when Sandra worked as a secretary for the environmental division at the plant and always had one of the other secretaries, Peggy Lawson, over. They would spend hours at the dining room table with magazines and lemonade talking about men and how there were no good ones left.

"Enjoy it while you're young," Peggy used to say to Sienna.

Sandra would sigh and say, "Ah, young love." And even though it always sounded like she was joking, she and Peggy never laughed.

Then one night Shelby and I were lying in the front yard on an unzipped and unfolded sleeping bag watching the stars, talking about boys like we knew what we were saying, when Josh's car pulled up. Sienna rushed out of the car and Josh chased her. He caught her when she was halfway up the walkway. Sienna was crying. Josh was holding her shoulders, then putting his hand under her chin so she would look at him. I couldn't tell what they were fighting about, what Sienna was crying about. Not exactly. But there was another name bouncing around amid their yelling, Sienna's sharp tears, Josh's defensiveness. Hilary. That's all I can remember about the fight itself, that it wasn't just about Sienna and Josh, it was also about someone named Hilary.

Sienna stopped crying eventually and let Josh hold her face between his hands and wipe away her tears while he whispered something to her that made her kiss him passionately. Shelby rolled her eyes and flopped back down. I watched a little longer as Josh kissed Sienna, leaning over her, almost overpowering her. She would have tipped backward if her hands weren't balled into fists gripping his shirt.

Shelby had seen it all along. Something wasn't right about this love. I could see it now. It was too early, too soon, too much—so fast and furious and eager that it was swallowing Sienna.

For Sandra love was slow. It had contingencies. Money and homeownership and chewing with your mouth closed and keeping your nails clean. *Nonsmoker. Nonalcoholic. Savings account. Employed.* All words that Sandra and Peggy said about men before they said the word *love*. Factors and rules and checklists. Love was less about feelings than it was about so many other things.

Things I couldn't understand but knew were important too.

I remember wondering if there was a balance—a way to have the rules and the love, if they could ever coexist.

CHAPTER
TWENTY-SEVEN

There's music, but I hear the clinking of glass over everything else. Patrick gave us real martini glasses to drink out of. They're tinted blue and so glamorous. It's spring break, our last one during high school, and everything deserves a toast. I don't know why Patrick has trusted us with these precious, breakable, beautiful things.

Then all I can hear is Shelby's laughter, loud and unforgiving.

"Open your eyes, Aubrey." It's Nathan's voice, so I open them. His hand is on the side of my face.

"Can you play? Do you need to lie down?" Melissa's

face comes into focus and I realize it's not so bad with my eyes open.

"Maybe you take it easy for a while, baby." Robert. I see his hand reaching for mine, removing the martini glass.

I look at Nathan. He's smiling, so I smile too.

"She's good," I hear Shelby say. "She just needed a minute."

She's right. Once my eyes are open and I'm walking down the hallway holding Nathan's hand, everything feels fine. I don't feel dizzy from that shot I took with Nathan anymore. Now I feel like dancing, like singing, like I could do anything. I squeeze Nathan's hand and he squeezes back.

"I feel like I'm flying," I tell him, and he laughs and nods like he's flying too. He's flying with me.

But then we're sitting. Shelby's got the empty bottle we were passing around taking shots from earlier. She holds it above her head, she twirls it, she drops it, she laughs. I'm surrounded by people sitting in a circle— Nathan and Patrick and Robert and Danica and Shelby and Melissa and Sam and Leila and the Riz and Celine and Jared and two junior girls who cheer with Leila and Celine and two junior boys who play basketball with Sam. A circle, with the bottle in the middle.

"I don't want to go first!" Melissa cries out. Tommy is rubbing up next to her greedily, his hands on her shoulders, pushing her toward the center of the circle.

I feel laughter, so much of it, bubble out of my lips. I can't believe we're playing the game we thought we were too old to play in middle school. We're about to graduate high school; we're so close to the real world but still too far away to touch it, and that makes us so, so young.

Danica's smoking, sharing her cigarette with the boy next to her. I wait for Patrick to tell her to put it out, his mother will kill him, but he takes a drag himself. Robert spills on the beige rug when he's refilling Leila's drink. I stare up at the walls towering around us so high, the ceiling stretching up and to a point. The ceiling looks a million miles away. I hear laugher and shouting and glasses clinking together. *This room is barely big enough to contain us and everything that we are*, I think.

When I stop staring at the ceiling, everyone's looking at me. The bottle picked me. My name is being called; I can hear it coming from every direction. Before I can ask what's going on, Tommy Rizzo is in front of me. He puts his hands behind my head, and then he's kissing me. All I taste is Wintermint. I'm kissing him back. I'm laughing in his mouth. I was never supposed to get to kiss Tommy Rizzo again.

When he pulls away, there are hands patting my back and so much noise I want to cover my ears. Nathan presses his face into my shoulder. I think he's trying to snuggle with me, but I realize he's only leaning forward because he's laughing so hard and this is where he's landed.

He straightens up and whispers in my ear. "Your turn."

I fumble with the bottle until it finally spins, whirling around so fast it makes me dizzy to watch. So instead I watch Nathan. Nathan watches the bottle, his eyes moving, spiraling, leaping. If it lands on him, everything I'm wishing for in this moment will come true.

But everyone starts chanting Sam's name, and when I look back to the group I see the bottle is pointed at Sam. My eyes find Shelby next because Shelby's kissed Sam so many times before, and now I'm going to kiss him. She's smiling that rare smile, showing all her teeth, and laughing, gripping Melissa's arm to keep from toppling over as she bounces on her knees.

We meet in the middle and Sam's kiss is soft, exactly what I would expect from him. All I can think about are *the numbers*. How Shelby used to be the only one of us who kissed Sam, and now I'm kissing him, and Melissa or Danica or Leila could kiss him next. All I can think about is Nathan's head against my shoulder, his breath in my ear, the first time he kissed me—how all his kisses belonged to me, and now, any second now, that's not going to be true anymore.

The bottle lands on Shelby next. She falls into Sam and he's not as gentle with her. I wonder if that's the last time she'll ever let Sam kiss her.

She grips the bottle tightly and smiles wickedly at all

of us before she spins. This time the bottle is all I can watch. I don't even blink as I watch it spin furiously with a blur of moving shapes behind it. It stops on Nathan.

Seconds turn into minutes, minutes turn into hours, that's how long it takes for Nathan and Shelby to meet in the middle. I have the slightest urge to push him—so this can be over. There's no rule that I have to watch, but I'm scared. I don't want to be caught looking away. And I'm afraid that if I don't watch, Nathan and Shelby will have one more thing between them that I don't know about.

So I watch as they face each other, both on their knees. They can't seem to stop laughing; Shelby's red and I can't decide if it's from the alcohol or Nathan or both. Nathan rubs under his chin, fidgeting, stalling.

Just do it, just do it, just do it!—this is all that's screaming through my mind.

And then they do. A moment ago they were staring at each other, red and laughing and fidgeting, and now they're kissing. Shelby's holding on to his shoulders. Nathan's hands are gripping her waist. The seconds are still minutes and the minutes are still hours and their lips are still together. Their entire bodies are suctioned together. There is not even enough space to stick a pin between Nathan and Shelby.

I can breathe when they stop, and I try my very best to laugh and clap and hoot the way everyone else is. Shelby fans herself and winks at me or maybe at Nathan, I can't tell. Nathan's laughing, and his lips are red and wet. *Used.*

But we're supposed to be like this. We're supposed to be reckless and careless and wild. And none of it is supposed to hurt. If we've kissed too many people, smoked too many cigarettes, had too much to drink, laughed too hard, offended too many people—we've done it right. We haven't wasted any time. And Nathan and I have a lot of catching up to do.

He looks at me before he spins the bottle, his eyes wide and amused. He's in awe. He's drunk. He's happy. We're going to Barron next year, and these are the last moments of freedom carved out for just us—before summer jobs and Barron college courses will take over. Soon everything we do will matter on a greater, grander, larger scale. This is our last chance to be like this. Nathan Diggs seems to have just figured out what that means to him.

THAT NIGHT I can't sleep. I'm next to Nathan in one of the rooms in Patrick's ridiculously large house, in a bed so big we could spend the whole night ignoring each other if we wanted. But my back is pressed against Nathan's chest and his arms are around me. It's so quiet I can hear him breathe, crisp and clear. It's really dark in here too, thick curtains allowing for no light to get through.

"Hey, Aubrey?" he whispers. His breath tickles my ear. "Are you awake?"

"I'm awake," I whisper back. In here, our whispers sound loud.

"Remember when I told you I was going to stay, that I wasn't going back home for spring break?"

I nod. My head rubs against his arm so I know he felt it.

"I think—I think I'm going to go."

"You're going to leave?" I turn to face him even though it's impossible to see him.

"Yeah," he says. "I don't know when I'll get the chance again, to see everyone. After graduation, or before I leave for Barron."

"You just decided tonight?" I don't know why I want to know, why it's important. It just is.

There's a pause before he speaks. "Yeah."

I open my mouth, thinking the right words will come out, but nothing does. I don't want to tell him I'll miss him even though I will. I don't want to tell him that I'm scared of what he'll do with all the people he's known forever, now that he doesn't know when he'll get to see them again—now that he knows his time is running out and he doesn't want to spend every one of these hurried, blissful seconds with me.

WHEN I WAKE up, I'm cold. Nathan's not beside me anymore. The room is still dark, but I think it's morning because there's light peeking out from under the door and I feel well rested. Nathan could be downstairs with Patrick and Robert, laughing while Leila and Danica cook breakfast and Shelby and Melissa sit on the couch wearing sunglasses and complaining about not having enough sugar for their coffee.

Or he could have left. He could already be on an airplane and a million miles away.

My chest stings with something I'm becoming way too familiar with. I take a deep breath and close my eyes and remind myself that it's going to be okay.

I've managed to keep him for three months, but in no way does that mean I get to keep him forever. That's the whole idea, isn't it?

This is what the theories prepare us for. This is why, when he's finally gone for good, it won't hurt as much. It doesn't matter that I'll be at Barron with him next year. That was never what would keep Nathan and me together, and I know that. If anything, it's what's going to make everything—trusting the theories, letting Nathan go—sharper and harder. But I know I can do it. I picture my pain separated into fragments. Instead of getting pierced with a giant knife that has the potential to kill, I'll just be stabbed occasionally with razor blades. So when he finally leaves me for good, and the last cut is inflicted, I'll be used to the pain.

CHAPTER
TWENTY-EIGHT

Shelby and I go to the park on Friday. It's the place we go every day during spring break even though it's crowded with little kids with kites and mothers with large hats. We're the only ones who stayed in town, and I'm glad. I never have to work during spring break, but usually I go somewhere with my family. Last year it was Washington, DC. This year my parents asked my brothers and me how we felt about skipping a spring break trip and we all favored it. Gregory and Jason missed playing their video games every day while we were in DC. And I missed Shelby.

It's getting warmer. Shelby and I can sometimes go

the entire afternoon wearing just our T-shirts.

"Patrick or Robert?" Shelby rips up the grass and lets it slide between her fingers. I'm doing the same thing. All around us smells like fresh-cut grass and lush dirt.

"Robert." We've played "Who would you rather?" a million times. Our answers are always different, depending on the day, the hour, the second—who made the winning point of the basketball game, who just broke up with his girlfriend, who would make Celine more jealous. "Jared or Sam?"

"Jared. Nathan or Trip?"

I throw a handful of grass at her. She turns away just in time and the pieces stick to the side of her head, tangled in her hair.

"Don't tell me you didn't see that coming."

And I can't—Nathan or Trip—it's been coming, creeping up with the grace and concealment of a herd of elephants. If Shelby and I aren't at the park sitting in the sun, or in Shelby's room watching movies, or in my living room eating junk food, we're at the Chapmans'. Our "spring break hideaway," Shelby calls it. State has the same spring break as Lincoln High, and Trip didn't go away either.

"Remember the rules of the game," she says quickly before I can answer. "It's only for a night. Just sex, no consequences. Like it never happened. Just one night you can erase."

Right now, with my legs stretched out in front of me and the low afternoon sun shining in my eyes, having only communicated with Nathan via text but still hearing from him every night, a night of *just sex*, something I can erase, forget—a night that will blot out quicker than any of the other moments we've vowed to smear away—doesn't sound like anything I want from Nathan. It sounds like exactly what I would get from Trip.

I answer her honestly, even if I give her the wrong answer. "Nathan."

Her smile is small and close-lipped and her eyes are hidden behind sunglasses. I can't tell if I've surprised her.

"So Nathan's that good, huh?" Her smile tilts sideways and I throw grass at her, two handfuls, because I can't be as blasé about sex as I wish I could. Talking about it embarrasses and delights me—and the delight is embarrassing. And now I'm laughing way too hard to feel anything but happiness.

I don't like the idea of Shelby staying and me leaving in the fall, but I like the idea of coming back—to this. To my best friend, with her loud laugh and rare smile, to our once-in-a-lifetime friendship—where everything will always be this easy and we'll always be this close.

And sometimes I love that Shelby will be here next year, right where I left her. She'll be my lifeline when I come home just like she was my lifeline all four years at Lincoln. When Danica, Melissa, and I come back for Thanksgiving or Christmas or summer, Shelby will remind us of where we came from and what we're capable of. We're always the strongest when we're with Shelby.

I HELP TRIP with his English essay that evening. In college the professors don't let up on homework over spring break. And in this case it's a good thing, because Trip really needs a whole extra week to finish his research paper and make it good.

I lie on the couch with my feet in Trip's lap, reading his paper and marking it with my red pen. The TV's on mute, but there's a basketball game on. He taps my feet, a nervous tic I'm used to.

"You have some sentences in here that are bullshit."

Trip leans back into the couch. "Bullshit like the grammar is bullshit, or bullshit like I made that up bullshit."

"You know what kind."

Trip smiles. He looks caught. No one should look that good when they're guilty. I hate him for it. "Nothing gets past you, Housing."

I toss the paper at him but keep the compliment.

There's a voice in my head when I'm around Trip. It's been there ever since I saw that first text message from him in January. *Resist, resist, resist.* He's a vortex that I don't want to be sucked into, a place where I'll be disappointed, where the answer to what everyone assumes—that Trip Chapman's had me exactly the way he wanted me—is yes. It's a place I don't want to go. Nothing else matters as much as me not going there. Not even Nathan.

"What about the sentences in the third paragraph?" he says. He lightly pushes my feet off him so he can sit close and show me what part of his essay he's talking about.

"Those, I liked," I admit. "You put the facts together really well. It's your conclusion that needed help. And your intro. Lucky for you, those are my strong suits."

Trip smiles at me; I can feel it without even looking at him.

"You're good at the things I'm not good at. And vice versa," he says. "We make a good team." He pats my knee so I'll look at him, and I do. "Admit it, Housing."

I shrug.

"And there is one thing we're both really good at," Trip says lowering his voice, leaning closer to me. "And that makes us a great team."

"Stop it." I put a little extra malice in my voice. I have to. My smile is so big.

Trip leans away, but I know he's still studying me.

"I have to go." I get up casually, so he won't know I'm in a hurry to get away from him.

"Now?"

"Yeah, now," I tell him instead of good-bye.

I MEET SHELBY later that night in her bedroom for bad television and too many Oreos. I tell her about Trip. I confess that it's not that easy.

"Just kiss him then." She smiles and pinches my side so I'll laugh, so I won't be so serious.

"I don't want to kiss him. I just think about it sometimes."

"Really, Aubrey. Just kiss him. Who cares?"

And I realize that the answer to that question might be no one. I realize it might just be me alone, worried about what going back to kissing Trip Chapman would mean.

But I can't be sure. And Nathan returns tomorrow.

CHAPTER TWENTY-NINE

Nathan is darker than when he left. When we meet him at the mall, he tells Shelby and me that he played a lot of baseball during his spring break because "it didn't rain once." He looks fresher somehow too. He looks new again.

We round the corner on our way to the movie theater and run into Chiffon. She's with Zane. And Trip.

"The pharmacy's that way, Chiffon," Shelby says.

"Easy." Nathan keeps his voice low. He puts a hand on her shoulder like he's going to hold her back. I watch his fingers pulse, giving her shoulder a quick squeeze. I remember everything Nathan sees when he looks at Chiffon. And what he doesn't see.

Zane frowns and puts his hand on the small of Chiffon's back, and they walk in the opposite direction. Just days ago Zane and Shelby were sitting across from each other at the Chapman dinner table having roast beef and apple juice. I wonder if Chiffon knows, if she cares, if it worries her.

"I thought he knew better than to be seen with her in public," Shelby says to Trip. I can feel the prickling of his eyes on me subside, and I know it's safe, that he's looking at Shelby, so I look at him. His hair is still too long, the T-shirt he's wearing too faded and worn.

"Change your tampon once in a while, will you?" Trip says to her.

Nathan laughs the kind of sudden laughter that sneaks up on you and flows out without your consent.

"Why don't you change yours, Trip?" It's a lame comeback, especially for Shelby, so Trip sneers at her, raising his lip slightly. "It reminds me of Elvis when you do that," I told Trip once. I found it hilarious that he could never look mean, even if he tried.

Trip's eyes find me again and I have no choice but to let them. "You look *nice*, Housing." The way he says *nice*—like he's saying something more than just that four-letter word people use to be polite—makes something in my chest flutter. It's not polite the way Trip says it.

"Thanks." I feel like crawling into a hole. Trip doesn't understand the rumors that have survived his legacy at

Lincoln High. He's looking at me as though I'm something he likes, and the air is filled with the white noise of everything that Trip has had.

Nathan's staring at Trip. Something flashes across his eyes—recognition. Nathan looks to the ground suddenly, like he's been caught. But I feel like I've been caught. I watch him clench and relax his jaw four times.

Trip and Shelby are bickering about something; I know the mocking pitch of her tone and the sluggish voice Trip uses when he wants to be funny. Nathan won't look at me. *I'm dressed nice for you*, I want to say. *Because you were coming back today. That's why I'm wearing green and my hair is curled at the ends.*

"Aubrey?"

Whenever Trip says my name, it's all I can hear. It takes up all the space around me.

"We're going to miss our movie," I say. And after a quick wave instead of a real good-bye, when we're walking away from Trip, I touch Nathan's arm and he reaches it across my waist. I'm happy, but there's still an inkling of something—a tingling in my chest—impossible to ignore, like a black dot just the size of a pin on a whitewashed canvas.

Shelby goes ahead to get our seats. Nathan and I stand in line for popcorn.

I don't ask Nathan, "What's wrong?" or "What are you feeling?" I say, "How long do you think it would take to eat a seven-pound burrito?" Because it's not supposed to be like this with us. There's not supposed to be any tension. I know better.

He gets what I'm talking about: El Burro—the infamous taco cart set up on the outskirts of Barron's campus. Open all night long. The seven-pound burrito is their specialty.

"Who wants to eat a seven-pound burrito?" Nathan says. He doesn't turn to look at me, but I can see the skin crease around the corner of his left eye and know he's making a face. "A seven-pound burrito is an impulse purchase. One of those things that seems like a good idea at first but just ends up giving you indigestion."

"At least it's cheap." Only four dollars.

"This is what you want to talk about right now? El Burro?" His voice is low, unsure. Defensive. It's there in his words, in the way he's standing. He manages to keep his head down, but he still stares forward, looking hard at the menu on the wall above the counter even though we already know what we're getting.

"Yes," I tell him.

He slides against me then, our shoulders pressing into each other. I don't know if he's doing this on purpose or if he just took a step to the side and this is where he landed, but I'm so glad he's here. There's more I want to say to him, but the theories are what's kept him here this long; they were what he wanted, what he still wants.

"It's going to be weird next year," he says. I don't say anything, I just wait. "Having access to things like seven-pound burritos and all."

I laugh a little—the way Nathan's jokes always makes me laugh, but I call him out too. I can't help it. "You don't seem excited."

I can't hear him sigh, but I feel it, the rising and falling of his shoulder against mine. "It's all coming up so fast."

I forget that Nathan didn't choose Barron. He didn't find the pamphlet when he was ten and decide that if a perfect GPA was going to count for something, it was going to count for that. He was born into Barron sweat-shirts and framed Barron diplomas on the walls, drinking hot chocolate out of worn Barron mugs. He didn't study to reach a goal; he studied to keep up. And since coming to Lincoln High he stopped pushing forward. He's sitting down while time just hurtles at him, because he finally can.

"Can you come over tomorrow?" he asks. "Or do you have to *tutor*?"

I ignore the snide way he said the word *tutor*, and when he looks at me, I know he didn't mean it. "I don't have to do anything."

"Just you?"

I'm nodding before I even open my mouth. "Yes."

CHAPTER
THIRTY

Life seems simple and small when you think about how so many things can be divided up into before and after. How something happens and like the flipping of a switch—that quick, that easy—everything changes. I used to think this would only matter with big things, like the death of someone close to you. A car accident. Surviving cancer. Seeing your parents cry. Graduating high school. Getting married. But it can be anything. There's before we learned about the theories, and after. Before, when Chiffon was our best friend, and after, when she was our enemy. Before, when kissing Trip was the most important thing, and after, when not kissing him was the most important.

I stare at Nathan while he scrubs the front of his car. Everything about Nathan's house is clean. The paint is white, the grass is short and even, the driveway doesn't have cracks. And now his car will match. He's much too concentrated on getting the bugs off the bumper to notice I'm staring.

There's another *after* looming on the horizon: after I've lost him.

"I don't feel like going to school tomorrow," Nathan announces. He stands up and runs the sponge over the hood even though he's already cleaned it.

We say things like this. What we want and don't want. Saying it out loud makes it viable, attainable. It's all very brave. Only Shelby means these things when she says them. "So what should we do instead?" I play along.

His smile makes him transparent. For all the ways Nathan is extraordinary, sometimes I'm so glad when he's typical.

"Italian food? Right now . . . ," I say, smiling at him in a way that says I'm not referring to eating out at all. He comes over to me and I wait patiently, making him walk the entire length of the driveway to get to me. His hands are cold from the water, but I don't care. He smells like chemicals and I don't care about that, either. I just let him kiss me. I put my fingers around his wrists so I can feel his pulse.

"Let's go." He laughs at his boldness, at the excitement of maybe getting exactly what he wants exactly when he wants it.

We climb into his car, leaving the bucket of soap and sponge on the ground. I worry for a second that we've left the hose on, but Nathan is so calm, I know he turned it off. This is just one more thing I really, really like about him. His ability to be careless without being reckless. It almost feels safe. My fingers dance on the back of his neck as we drive to the housing development.

My phone rings the special Shelby ring, three notes scaling up, right as we pull into our favorite spot. Nathan recognizes it and waits for me to answer.

"She'll understand," I tell him. He kisses me along my neck. My phone beeps. And a few seconds later it beeps again.

Nathan stops. "What does she want?" He's as curious as I am, so I lift my phone out of the cup holder and open the message where Nathan can see it.

The message is not from Shelby, though; it's from Trip.

ZANE JUST BOUGHT SO MANY PEACHES.

"Peaches are my favorite," I explain without being asked. I should have waited to be asked. The message that came right before Trip's is from Shelby, so I open it right away.

COME TO THE PARK.

"We should go," Nathan says, kissing me on the cheek.

"Right now?" This is a stupid thing to ask because when Shelby sends a message, immediacy is implicit.

Nathan shrugs. Shrugging away the housing development and my hand against his leg. He leans toward me, but only to pull his phone out of his back pocket. "Robert's there too," he confirms, staring at a message on the screen.

I don't know where I am. After Nathan saw Trip. After Nathan became friends with Robert and Patrick. After he learned that everything he'd heard about Shelby being the daring one, the beautiful one, the more alive one, was all true. After he learned that Trip knew my favorite fruit and he didn't.

But we're driving to the park. Nathan's calm excitement bursts once we arrive and see everyone we could possibly want to see on a Sunday afternoon. There's a volleyball net set up. And Doritos. And cherry Slurpees. The girls are in sunglasses and the boys take off their shirts. All the markings of spring and senior year. Nathan, Robert, and Patrick make jokes no one else gets and take turns trying to scare us by spiking the ball too hard. Jared rubs sunscreen on Celine's back, even though the sun's disappearing and the sky is slowly fading into an evening glow. Another telltale sign of spring.

I feel unprepared. I'm in a borrowed pair of sunglasses telling Tommy Rizzo for the millionth time that no, I'm not taking off my top; my navy bra absolutely does not look like a bathing suit—when I start to feel it. The cool awareness that I'm floating in the after, and that in the place I've come from before there was someone with me. Nathan.

We make out in the car before he takes me home. He tastes like cherries and processed cheese, and his cologne is dulled by the smell of sweat and grass. He smells like spring. And spring is when we all get ready to leave. Like the days before Trip's graduation, when he told me it felt like everything anyone did was for the last time, and I could sense it—the urgency in Trip and all his friends. Summer is the dead point after spring good-byes, when full-time jobs and hot weather and the last nights of sleeping in your own bed interfere with the days and the people you spend them with. Only some people make it into your summer and fewer make it into your fall. We really leave in spring.

Nathan smiles and waves as I climb out of his car, and I wonder if he knows what's going on. Or if he's so caught up in last moments that he doesn't even notice that this, right now, is one of them.

CHAPTER
THIRTY-ONE

I've been through the Detach before. Text messages that once filled up your inbox stop coming. The person who used to linger at your locker before school is no longer there. The spot that used to be saved for you in the cafeteria is gone, just like your ride to the party on Saturday night. On both sides of the Detach, it's the same. With Tommy Rizzo, I stopped answering his calls and searching him out in the hallway. In August, Trip told me he'd see me soon and didn't call again until Thanksgiving.

Girls are finally flirting with Nathan Diggs and he's finally flirting back. Leila touches his arm at lunch. Mary Ann, a junior on the swim team, stops by his locker before practice. He sits sandwiched between Celine and another cheerleader during the senior assembly. Nathan doesn't tell me if he's craving Italian food because all we do is drink Slurpees with everyone at the park. We don't make out in Drama because now Robert sits with us. We study together in Nathan's room, but his mom is home, and even if she wasn't, Nathan's phone doesn't stop beeping long enough for him to read aloud to me.

Nathan is free and open and enjoying it, and it's obvious. I don't know if he'll really take advantage of his situation or just relish that there's a situation for him to take advantage of in the first place.

He might want Shelby because she makes him laugh or Danica because she practically ignores him, or Melissa because she's so pretty and so innocent. He might want Mary Ann because she's aggressive. Or Celine because he's never been very fond of Jared. Or one of the girls who blush just hearing his name, because it would be easy. I was the first girl he met here—the first evolved girl he'd *ever* met—but his time is running out, and now there are others who want to know him before he leaves.

When you're the first, you don't get to be the last, too. Not usually.

IT'S NATHAN'S FIRST Friday night as a free agent and I'm missing it. I'm glad. I'm tortured.

THERE'S NOT ENOUGH coffee to serve or doughnuts to glaze the next morning to distract me from all the things I don't know about last night. No one comes in for coffee. My phone is quiet. Usually this means everyone is still asleep. Usually.

It's assumption—even if you're the one doing the assuming—that will screw you every time.

"You can leave early," Ms. Michel tells me around eleven thirty. There are still a few hours left on my shift.

"Why?" I don't stop working. I keep moving, twisting dough dusted with cinnamon and powdered sugar to be baked for the lunch crowd.

She looks me up and down and I realize that I'm also dusted with cinnamon and powdered sugar. A real mess.

"I'll stay in the back," I offer.

She shakes her head, pats me on the back. "No, no, go on. You have a friend in the café waiting."

When I walk out from the back kitchen, I'm looking for Nathan. I find Trip instead.

"What are you doing here?"

Trip smiles, giving me a look like the answer should be obvious. Then he takes a bite out of the chocolate doughnut he's holding and I think maybe the food is the reason, not me—though I know better.

The door chimes behind us as we walk out. It's hotter than ever today. Trip helps me peel off my jacket, holding the neck so I can wiggle my arms out.

"Do you have a test next week or something?"

"No, Housing." He shakes his head. He doesn't give me my jacket back when I hold my hand out for it. He keeps it tucked over his arm. "I just came to see you."

"Okay." The word is hard and abrupt when it comes out.

"Everything all right?"

"I'm fine."

"Come on." He puts his arm around my back and turns me toward the street, where his blue-and-white pickup is sitting curbside. He opens the door for me, a formality since his truck is too old to have automatic locks and he'd have to lean all the way across the bench seat to unlock the passenger door for me if he got in first.

I do as he says. I slide in, careful not to scratch myself on the loose spring that has worked its way through the faded blue leather of the bench seat. Without meaning to, I think of Nathan's BMW. How the spring in Trip's truck is an obvious warning to those who sit there—*you will get hurt if you're not careful*—and the BMW is supposed to be safe.

"Take a load off." He nods at the dashboard. I slink down into the seat and put my feet up on the dash, just like I used to.

"You work too hard, Housing."

"You don't work hard enough."

"You should relax more. I can see the tension on you—it's everywhere. You're covered in it."

"That's not tension, it's cinnamon." I tilt my neck back and close my eyes.

"Atta girl."

I can't help but smile. It feels good, smiling, closing my eyes, putting my feet up. Sitting next to Trip in a place I used to love. Trip makes me feel safe, the way I felt around him last year—a way I don't always get to feel around him or anyone anymore. It's because of the theories. Trip wasn't with me because I needed him to be, or because I asked him to be, or because he thought I would cry if he wasn't. He was with me because he pure and simple wanted to be.

"Why'd you come all the way down here to see me?" There's a simple answer or there's a complicated one. I want the truth.

He hesitates for too long, so I sit up slightly and stare at him—telling him with just a look that I know there's more and I want him to tell me.

He picks at a loose piece of leather hanging off the steering wheel. "There's a seminar tomorrow. My Comparative Religions professor is speaking. It's at a church, starts at ten. He's offering extra credit to all his students that go."

"So you're leaving early?" I lean my head against the seat and turn so I'm facing him. "Tonight?" Trip usually keeps himself here until Sunday night to avoid the temptations of the weekend that, for Trip, leak over into failed quizzes and sloppy essays.

He nods. "Later tonight. You should come over for dinner. We're making hamburgers."

I picture hamburgers and chips and peaches. It's tempting, I'll admit, but not tempting enough. "I'm going to a party tonight."

"Of course you are."

"You'll be back next weekend?" It's so easy and casual coming out of my mouth, but my chest tightens. Trip wasn't supposed to come back—ever. I was never supposed to be sitting in his car with my feet on the dash and my body tilted toward his like this ever again.

He smiles and gives the faintest nod. I think he's about to say something, but he stops himself. He leans closer to me, just a little, but enough that I can smell the cedar on him. His hand reaches for me, moving slowly toward my face.

I close my eyes. He's going to touch me, let his fingers run over my lips, and under my chin, and then he's going to kiss me and I don't know if I want to stop him.

I don't feel his fingers against my cheek; I feel the slightest bit of pressure at the crown of my head. My eyes open slowly. Trip takes the loose strands of my hair and tucks them behind my ear. There's cinnamon and powdered sugar in my hair and I see the tiniest bit of white powder on his fingers when he pulls his hand away. Trip just tucked away those lonely strands of hair that used to be Nathan's, the pieces of me he used to tug when he wanted something, or push behind my ear over and over again while he stared at me.

Trip leans away. "Sorry," he says, so quietly I almost don't think he really meant for me to hear him.

I'm sorry too. But only because I miss Nathan. I'm glad Trip didn't kiss me, and that also makes me sorry. Everything was so much easier when that was all I wanted.

CHAPTER THIRTY-TWO

It's not really a party Robert's having, but there are enough people around the fire pit in his backyard that when I walk up the stairs to use the bathroom I'm surprised to hear Nathan and Shelby—I hadn't even noticed they were gone. And even though everyone watches Shelby, and I am no different, and I've been waiting since I arrived a few hours ago for Nathan to touch me or look at me the way he used to, somehow I lost track of them. Or maybe they're hiding. They made their escape and brushed leaves over their path as they left.

I'm not proud as I lean against the wall outside the kitchen, listening to them. Robert's house is a split-level.

The entryway leads both upstairs and downstairs. If they leave the kitchen I can escape down the hall, maybe even down the stairs, without them seeing me. I'm really not proud I've come up with an Exit Strategy, but I have to know—I *need* to know—what Shelby and Nathan are talking about alone together in the quiet part of the house.

Shelby is sitting on the counter and letting her legs dangle—I know this because I can hear the soft tapping of her heels hitting the cupboards below.

"That was my favorite part of the movie too. Of course. When the guy gets the girl." Nathan's on the punch line of a joke I missed.

The way he's talking to her bothers me, but I also have this stupid desire to laugh at him. It's like Nathan is trying to find something relatable in Shelby—like when he asked her about stress and college and money. Soon he'll discover that it's better that you can't relate. That Shelby lives in this other world that's brighter, more colorful, bolder, more daring, more dangerous, and that being around Shelby means you get to feel like you're somewhere else, somewhere better.

"I lied to you," he says. His voice is lower now, less excited. "I've never been on a motorcycle." I remember the first day he met Shelby, when she accused him of wearing a leather jacket because he rode a motorcycle. Apparently Nathan remembers it too.

"You never told me you had," Shelby says.

"You assumed. I didn't correct you."

"And now do you feel absolved?"

"I don't like lying."

Shelby makes a *tsk* noise, snapping her tongue. "It's been months and you're just coming clean. What else do you need to come clean about?"

"If you're referring to the photos, I wasn't lying when I said I didn't look at them." I never heard Nathan say this—and I would have remembered.

"Again, with the photos."

"I'm sorry—I just . . ." I imagine Nathan rubbing the top of his hand along the bottom of his chin to get through the silence.

"Go ahead." Shelby sounds a little bored, a little annoyed. Exactly the way she's supposed to sound. "Just say it."

Nathan hesitates. "I just don't know how you could be so—"

"What?" She lets out a quick laugh, but her voice is sharp. "Careless? Stupid?"

He doesn't hesitate. "All of the above."

There's a long space of silence, but somehow I know Shelby's not insulted, or pissed. I think she likes his honesty. "What's the most dangerous thing you've ever done?" she finally says.

He's quiet again, which means he knows and doesn't want to say. I think the most dangerous thing Nathan

Diggs has ever done is snap at Shelby Chesterfield. Or accuse her of being unfair to Chiffon. Or tell her how to react to her own naked-photo scandal. Then I have another thought.

"Was it Aubrey?" And once again, Shelby's mind is tangled with mine.

"I don't know," he says, his voice a little muffled. "What about you?"

There's another long silence and I picture Shelby smiling at him and shaking her head because she'll never tell.

"Okay," Nathan says. "I think the better question is: What are you most afraid of?"

Nothing, I think. *Shelby's not afraid of anything.*

She's quiet while she must be waiting for him to realize this. Then she says, "The truth?"

"Please, yes. If you don't mind." There's a smile in his voice. I hate that I can hear it.

"You'll think it's stupid."

"I promise to pretend I don't."

"A zombie apocalypse. Or a dinosaur apocalypse. Any apocalypse, really."

It's just the kind of thing that would make Nathan laugh, and he does. He also sighs. "Come on, Shelby." That's all he says; that's all it takes.

"I'm having dinner with my dad next weekend. He says he has something to give me," Shelby says, and I'm shocked. Shelby's dad left when she was four and Sienna was ten. That's really all I know about him, except that the only way he ever gets in touch with Shelby or Sienna is by showing up unannounced. Neither of them are ever pleased to see him when he does this. Sandra doesn't ever see him or talk about him, not even about why he left. I'd always assumed he just left because he felt like it, because he's a horrible man and he did what he wanted without caring who he hurt or left behind, and that Sandra, Sienna, and Shelby were better off without him. "He gave Sienna money when she graduated, but not as much as he'd told her he was giving her. Half of what he promised. I'm afraid he's going to lie to me; I'm afraid he already has." She takes a deep breath. "I only see him for big events." She laughs a little, one jilted chuckle. "The last time I saw him, it was my sixteenth birthday. It was so horrible I couldn't concentrate on my driver's test and failed."

"Does it help at all to prepare for the worst?"

"I am prepared for the worst. But to be honest, I want his gift. I *need* his gift. And if he's been lying to me, then I'll have nothing next year. Everyone will be gone, and I'll be stuck."

"There are other ways to—"

"I know there are other ways to get out of here, but all of them require money, don't they?"

"Where would you go?"

"I don't know." She sounds mildly annoyed. I'm

annoyed too. Nathan doesn't understand that *getting out of here* doesn't always mean leaving, it can simply mean changing.

"Remember when you told me you liked it here? Was that the truth?"

Another secret, from another conversation. More that they know about each other that I never knew.

"I do like it here," she snaps. "But I still don't want . . ." She clears her throat, like she's trying to cover that her voice cut out.

I could finish the sentence for her. Everything is going to be different next year, and if nothing changes for you, then you're left behind. I never thought of Shelby as being left behind just because she wasn't going away to college. Shelby is always one step ahead, and I knew she would be next year too, somehow, even though I didn't know about the money.

"I don't think you should worry," Nathan says. "There are always options."

"I guess." Shelby sucks in a deep breath.

My phone vibrates against my side. It's Trip. I press ignore, but he just calls back. I ignore him again. That doesn't work and the vibrations keep going. I ease down the hallway and into an empty bedroom, closing the door gently behind me.

"Trip, what?" I whisper into the phone.

"Aubrey, I need your help."

CHAPTER THIRTY-THREE

I'm quiet when I leave the bedroom. The entire upstairs is silent, including the kitchen. My heartbeat feels loud. It's beating so fast and heavy that it's echoing in my chest, my ears. There are a lot of reasons Nathan and Shelby could have stopped talking, but there's only one reason I believe right now.

I have to see if it's true. When I reach the steps, I turn my neck, glancing back toward the kitchen. It looks empty. But I barely get a peek before I'm falling, tumbling down the stairs. I land on my back in the entryway, having rolled down the last step.

I blink a few times. Robert is staring down at me. He

helps me up and dusts off my shoulder, which I realize is symbolic, as my shoulder didn't really need dusting. My left ankle feels like it's on fire.

"Are you okay?" a voice from behind me says.

I turn around, gripping Robert's extended forearm so I don't fall. Nathan and Shelby are at the top of the stairs looking down at us. "Are you okay?" Nathan repeats.

"Yeah," I tell them. Then I tell things only to Robert because it's easier that way. "I—I was just leaving. Trip needs—" I realize how ridiculous it would be to finish. To say, *Trip's car broke down and I have to go get him so he can make it to church tomorrow for extra credit.* "I just—I have to go." I give all of them a pathetic wave and turn to leave.

"Where is she going?" I hear Shelby say to Robert or Nathan, to someone who's not me.

Robert's the one who answers. "Who is: Trip Chapman."

It's hard, and I have to ball my hands into fists to do it, but I walk on my ankle like pain isn't shooting at it from all directions. I ignore the pain. I'm lucky it's my left ankle so I can still drive.

Trip is right where he said he was going to be on the side of the road, almost to the highway. Halfway to his destination.

"What's the matter?" he asks me as I lift my hood with too much force.

"Think it might be time for a new car?" I snatch the

jumper cables out of his hands and hook them to the battery and the engine block without looking at him.

"It overheated," he says. "Now it just needs a jump and it'll be good as new."

I know exactly how to jump Trip's truck, exactly where the negative and positive terminals of my battery are without looking at the labels and how it takes all of three minutes before Trip can restart his truck.

Trip smiles when his truck starts. I stay in my car. The cars need to run together for a few seconds longer. Trip doesn't even need to signal me; I know when to turn off my car. He walks toward me with a victorious smile on his face.

"Thanks again, Housing," Trip says, placing his hands on the car door. He leans over and peers at me through the open window.

"Yeah, sure." I move to start my car even though it's still too soon to know if Trip's truck will stay running.

"Wait a second." Trip reaches across me and puts his hand on mine, over the keys. "What's the matter?"

I release the keys and let them fall into Trip's hand. He opens the door for me, so I climb out.

"What's wrong?"

I haven't said anything; I've hardly moved except to get out of the car. I'm not looking at him. I don't acknowledge when Trip puts his hand on my shoulder and rubs it. I squeeze my eyes closed. I wish I was someplace else, someplace where I could be alone with all my feelings. I wish I looked indifferent right now so Trip would just let me leave. I wish I felt indifferent.

"Aubrey?"

When I face him, he looks worried, confused. All the things that I am.

"My ankle hurts," I say.

"Your *ankle*?" Trip steps back, his hand falls from my shoulder. "Why are you lying to me?"

But my ankle really does hurt, so now I'm angry. My ankle hurts and it's Trip's fault. Nathan is alone in the quiet part of the house with Shelby and I'm not there, and it's Trip's fault. Trip and his stupid old truck. "Why did you call me? Why didn't you ask Earl or Zane, or anyone else, to come help you?"

Trip takes another step back from me. "Earl is working the night shift and Zane was drinking when I left." He looks to the ground, pops his jaw. "And there wasn't anyone else I wanted to call."

Last year I would hold my hand up to Trip's jaw while he popped it. I would laugh at the way it felt under my palm. It stings that I can remember things like that so easily.

"My ankle really does hurt." It's important that he knows I have a legitimate reason to feel as awful as I do. And that it's his fault.

"I'm sorry," he says quietly.

"And it's because of you—"

"I'm sorry," he says again, a little louder this time, so I raise my voice too.

"It's because I fell on my way to help you—"

"I'm sorry!" he yells. He walks toward me, his voice completely unsteady. "I'm sorry for everything, okay? I'm sorry you had to leave your party. I'm sorry you hurt your ankle." He hesitates when a large semi truck drives past and it's too loud to hear anything else. He looks away, but only for a second. "I'm sorry I left last year and stopped calling you like you meant nothing to me."

Now I'm the one who has to look away. I wasn't supposed to be nothing, and yet, that's also exactly what I was supposed to be. I was supposed to be better than all the other girls because I didn't need him to call me after he left. I didn't need to mean anything to him.

"Can I take a look?" He gestures to my ankle. I nod, and lean against the car as Trip kneels in the dirt. He slips off my shoe, sets my foot in his lap, and gently touches it. "Tell me when it hurts."

Trip puts light pressure on the inside of my ankle, right under the bone, staring up at me like he's afraid and concerned and sorry. For a second I feel it—the one thing it's important never to feel, the emotion that violates the theories in the worst possible way: hope. They can detach and leave, and then come back. And be sorry for leaving. There's hope in that and it's wrong, and I can't let it fool me.

"It hurts."

Trip frowns. "And how about here?" He touches the other side of my foot.

I shake my head.

He stands up, not even bothering to brush the dirt off his jeans. "Let's go back, put some ice on your ankle."

"I drove all the way out here so you could make it to school tonight, and you want to go back?"

Trip shrugs. "I can always leave in the morning."

"No."

"No?" There's the faintest smile on his face at this response. But when I don't smile back, Trip stops smiling altogether. "Come on, Aubrey. You're hurt."

I'm pushing him away and he's pushing back. I've seen this a hundred times. When Chiffon ignored Ronnie; when Melissa stopped texting Todd; when Shelby stopped asking Sam to do body shots. All the times when pulling away from Trip's kisses only made him want to kiss me more. Trip is still completely at the mercy of the theories, that's all this is. Would he be here, offering to take care of me, if I had agreed with him the night he said we made a great team; if I had let him kiss me in his room the day he asked me for help; if I'd had sex with him the night we fell asleep in his bed; if he'd thought I expected him to call me after he'd left for college? No. The answer is always no.

That's why I leave Trip standing next to his pickup on the side of the road. That's why I don't go back to the party. That's why I turn off my phone.

CHAPTER
THIRTY-FOUR

Melissa says everything without saying anything at all. She comes over on Sunday afternoon. "Because your phone is off," she says. "And to study." This is a lie, because Melissa can't study around other people, not even in a library. She studies at home alone at her desk with noise-cancellation headphones on.

I don't make her pretend. I turn on the television in my room, even though I really do have a test tomorrow. Studying doesn't feel as important as showing Melissa that I'm okay. She won't tell me the real reason she came over here, which means there is a reason. I probably don't want to know.

"So. You and Trip Chapman. Again," she says. She smiles. "I think it's sweet."

I nod. For the briefest moment, I debate telling her the truth.

I wonder if everyone else thinks it's sweet. Or if they think it's lame, me with Trip. No different from last year. "You're a repeat offender," Shelby would say.

"Boys are so predictable," Melissa says as she stares at the television. "It almost makes them reliable." She laughs, shaking her head.

Nathan has always been predictable, but it took me until now, these past few weeks, to really see it. He met my parents so he could see me topless in his BMW. He invited me to his hometown so he could make out with me during Drama. He acted surprised by the theories, but they still worked on him. He lied to me about Barron the very first day I met him. That should have been my first clue he would turn out to be perfectly predictable.

"Where are Shelby and Danica?" I ask her.

Melissa shrugs. But she never was good at keeping secrets. Or lying. "With Robert and Nathan. I think."

I stare at the television like I'm actually interested in what the too-excited girl is saying about peasant skirts. I give Melissa a slight nod.

That's the last we talk about Trip or Nathan. It's a relief, but it's also like having an elephant in the room. I want to ask exactly what happened between Nathan and Shelby. But I can't bring myself to ask Melissa about something that's not supposed to matter. Because really, it doesn't matter.

This is what I remind myself for the next hour of television and fashion talk with Melissa, and when I close my eyes to go to sleep that night.

IT'S NOT SO bad at school. Mary Ann is by Nathan's locker. Leila squeezes his arm when she passes him in the halls. Robert is his favorite person at Lincoln High. The junior girls laugh too loudly at his jokes and follow him around. Nathan asks me to study after school on Wednesday, but the location he chooses isn't his car or his room. He asks me to meet him in the library.

I arrive thirty minutes early to grab us the table in the back. The one that's blocked off by bookshelves and a corked wall displaying the Book of the Month. My English teacher allowed me to leave class early since the place I'm going is the library.

When I get there, the table is already occupied. Shelby and Nathan sit with their chairs pressed together, with Nathan's laptop on the table in front of them. Nathan says something quietly, and Shelby covers her mouth. Her whole body shakes as she tries to contain her laughter, and Nathan smiles, saying "Shh," but he looks like he wants to laugh too.

They're sitting so close. They're talking so close.

They're laughing so close. I wait for them to kiss, that's how close they are. A boy has never been that close to Shelby Chesterfield and not kissed her. I step behind the corked wall.

It takes me a few seconds to realize that they aren't going to kiss. They don't even seem to be debating it. They're just talking.

For some reason that's worse. The pit in my stomach deepens. I have no idea what Nathan and Shelby could possibly be talking about with such vigor and ease. They have more to say to each other than I could have ever imagined. They even have their own secrets.

I step forward, and the second I do Shelby spots me. She waves me over. I put on my best smile as I walk toward them.

Nathan leans back, away from Shelby. "I thought we weren't meeting until after school." He speaks too quickly. Shelby and I exchange a glance. It makes me feel powerful. Shelby is still on my side.

I've been here before, I remind myself. We all have. Trip and Shelby kissed at a party five weeks before he kissed me at Dion's. Patrick followed Shelby into her bedroom and stalked Leila's locker the next day. I stopped calling Tommy Rizzo and now he's hitting on Melissa. It's all about the numbers. It's *only* about the numbers. This is no different. No. Different.

"You're so punctual," Shelby says because I haven't said anything. She gestures to the chair across from her. I sit down in the chair across from Nathan, though their chairs are pressed so close together it's like I'm sitting across from both of them.

"What are you guys doing?" I nod at the open laptop in front of them.

"Nathan's trying help me figure out what to do next year." She stops talking to lick her lips, the only sign I get from her that the thing she's about to say next will be something that's going to surprise me. "He's got a few outrageous ideas as to what I should do with the money from my dad."

The lick of the lips wasn't just a warning of surprise. It was a signal to play along. Because Shelby and I are supposed to know everything about each other. She doesn't want Nathan to know she told him a secret. She doesn't want him to know how special she's made him.

"What money?" I ask. "What are you talking about?"

Nathan glances between us. Shelby blinks at me, but she's quick to put on a smile. "Oh, you remember. You remember how he gave Sienna some money after she graduated?" She continues before I have a chance to answer. "Anyway, I saw him the other day and he gave me a check."

Nathan's staring at the screen. He's holding his pencil

like any second he's going to start taking notes, but his notebook is closed. He clears his throat.

Shelby ignores him. I try to ignore him also.

"So, what are you going to do with it?" I ask her.

Shelby goes off, chattering, moving her hands. I briefly hear the words *IRA*, and *CD*, and *interest rate*, as well as *moving costs* and *out-of-state community college*. She's ending all her sentences with "or something," which she does whenever she doesn't really know quite what she's talking about or wants to downplay what's actually important to her.

I'm staring at Nathan. He's staring at the screen. He's helping her. He's got his fingers all over her future. Like he cares about it. Like it matters to him. He's investing in it like he'll be in it.

"Sounds complicated," I say when Shelby stops talking.

"It's not that complicated," Nathan says, looking at me finally.

But I can't look back at him for very long. "As it turns out," I tell Shelby, because it's easier, "I actually have more to study than I thought. So I'm just going to go."

"You don't have to go," Nathan says. "I can help you with the overload. You know that."

But I'm already standing up, already turning to leave.

"You better stop her now," I hear Shelby say to

Nathan. "Because I'm not going to study. Not tonight. No way."

I glance back. Their eyes are locked, their mouths are smiling. It's like I've already left, the way he's looking at Shelby, the way he's no longer nervous. So I just leave.

CHAPTER
THIRTY-FIVE

I can't stop remembering the first day I met Nathan. I try really hard not to think about it, but it's embedded in my mind, and it's always showing up now that I know it's about to be a distant memory. I wish I could forget.

I was really nervous.

I was really excited.

I was really happy.

My strawberry milkshake was full. It was so good, and I knew that at seven p.m. I should have been hungry enough to drink it. But I couldn't. Just like I could barely finish the slice of pizza after we left the Drama room. I was full of something else. Butterflies, nerves, excitement—Sandra used to call it "love stomach"—but whatever it was, I liked it.

Nathan couldn't finish his milkshake either. Even though strawberry is his favorite.

We hadn't known each other seven hours before but were now sandwiched in the back of his BMW breathing on each other with strawberry-flavored breath. This made everything seem brighter and better and more exciting.

He touched my arm during lunch, a quick gesture after I'd made him laugh. Now his hands were on my knees because we were so close and my legs were tilted toward him, and it seemed like a natural place for his hands to rest. I leaned into him. I touched his arm, his chest, his hand, anytime I felt like it, but I never could leave my hands on him for too long.

I wasn't thinking about the theories. I was thinking about Nathan's hand on my leg. The way he made jokes about school and never once commented on the weather. How sometimes his hands were shaking when they touched me. How his lower lip was always tucked and hidden by his top lip right before he started laughing.

Soon all I could think about was kissing.

Nathan's hand brushed past my face, past my cheek, and he froze, letting his thumb linger over my lips.

"Can I—" His voice caught. He lowered his eyes and smiled. "Can I kiss you?"

I couldn't speak, though everything about me was screaming, *YES!* I was desperate for a kiss, but I was terrified to kiss him. There was nothing I wanted more, and that was the terrifying part.

His eyes studied mine. His hand stayed on my face. He moved closer. "I really want to kiss you, and you seem like the kind of girl that needs to be asked."

"I'm not," I blurted out.

He smiled at this, and I smiled because he was going to kiss me, and for a second I wondered if we would ever stop smiling and actually kiss. But we did, and it was the best kiss of my life. I think it will always be the best kiss of my life.

I trusted him, without having any reason to. I don't think that will ever happen again. I won't ever be that stupid again. I won't ever let someone have everything because I'm so sure they deserve it. You have to be careful. People can often seem the most deserving before you really know them.

CHAPTER
THIRTY-SIX

Friday after school, Shelby tells us she'll see us later. She promises to meet us wherever we end up. But the place we end up is Sam's party, and Shelby is nowhere to be found.

Nathan is nowhere to be found either.

Shelby's absence is obvious. It's like this party isn't real yet. It's missing Shelby's laugh, and Shelby's restlessness, and Shelby's jokes about the things we never knew could be so funny.

I hear "Where's Shelby?" more than once. I always walk away, out of earshot, before I ever hear an answer.

My ankle has just started to feel better, but now the

burning is in my chest and my head, and I want to run around screaming or curl up into a ball on the floor. I want to vomit or go to sleep or do jumping jacks. I want to crawl out of my skin.

Shelby and Nathan. Alone in the quiet part of the house. Telling secrets. Sitting shoulder to shoulder. I wonder if he had sex with her last weekend, or after school, or if tonight will be their first time. I wonder if he asked before he kissed her or if he knew he didn't have to.

I decide to erase it. I pour myself a drink, all vodka with just a splash of orange juice. It burns as it goes down, but I don't care. At least this pain is justified. There's a logical reason for it.

Everything's supposed to be funnier when you're drinking, but tonight it's not. I have to pretend to be happy, carefree, charismatic; as if Shelby was here, as if Nathan was watching. Because they *all* have to see how okay I am.

It's only eleven o'clock, or at least I think that's what the clock says; it might say one, and I'm just seeing double. I'm beyond wasted. I'm more drunk and stupid than I've ever been or ever wanted to be. Everything's fuzzy. Everyone's too loud. Nothing is flat. I have to lean against the wall, and even the wall feels like it's tilting. I close my eyes and the wall tips me back.

When I open my eyes I see him. He's standing in the

kitchen holding a keg cup and talking to Patrick. I try to focus on the people moving around him to see if I can find Shelby, but it's too hard. Everything's blurry and spinning. And when I blink again, he's gone. Patrick's talking to Leila.

I don't know what's real anymore. But I can see the front door—bright white, opening and closing as people walk through it, in and out. I move toward it. I want to get as far away as I can from where Nathan might be. I don't know how I make it outside and down the street. The trees are reaching for me, the sidewalk is sliding beneath my feet. And when I can't walk any farther, I stop at a gas station. I don't need gas, but water sounds good. I press against the cool glass doors. They don't open. Inside is dark, but I try again anyway.

The failure weighs a ton. All I want is water. I can't go back; I'm not sure which way I came from. So I sit on the ground. It's cold and hard and there are cigarette butts around me and an old white Styrofoam coffee cup, but it feels so good to sit. A shiver runs through me, and the parking lot in front of me is sloping. I close my eyes and fumble for my phone.

I have to get out of here. I can't do it on my own. I need help. I have to call someone.

Of course, there's only one someone I can call.

"Aubrey?" Trip's voice is crisp on the phone. I want to bathe in the clarity of it.

I open my mouth to talk and a groan comes out. That's when I realize I'm crying. My face is wet.

"What's wrong?"

My tears are making it impossible for me to open my eyes. I can't breathe and for a second I think I'm going to drown in my own tears and snot.

"Where are you?" His voice is soft. I want to lie down on it.

"The gas station by Stimpy's." This is where I am. This is where I'm going to die. I cry so hard my head starts to hurt.

"Are you alone?"

My crying answers for me.

"All right, just hang tight, okay?"

But I can't stop crying, so I can't answer him.

"Aubrey. Listen to me, okay? It's going to be all right. Do you understand?"

"Okay," I say. If Trip thinks I'll be all right, then maybe I will be. I lie down on the cold, dirty cement.

My breath starts to come easier. I'm going to be rescued. The world won't be spinning if I'm in bed. And Trip's bed seems like the best place to be right now. I squeeze my phone with both hands and hold it against my chest. It vibrates in my hands, so I turn it over to stare at it. The screen is bright, and the words are fuzzy, but if I put it really close to my face I can read it.

Two text messages. From Melissa and Danica.

WHERE ARE YOU?

And: **WHERE THE FUCK DID YOU GO?** Because Danica curses in all her text messages.

My phone fumbles in my hands, and the buttons are so small, but I manage. I type **TRIP** and press send.

My phone buzzes again. *Nathan Diggs.* His name is on my screen.

I'M AT SAM'S. ARE YOU STILL HERE?

I want to tell him that he's stupid. That it doesn't matter where I am. And especially not where I am in relation to where he is. But there's too much to say and the buttons are too small and the screen is too bright. I do the next best thing. I throw the phone. I watch it skid a few feet away from me in the parking lot after cracking against the pavement. It's probably broken. Just like Nathan and me. *Good.*

I don't feel like crying anymore. I don't want to know if Nathan's on my phone. It doesn't matter where he is or what he wants.

A truck pulls into the parking lot and it makes me jump. I've lost track of time. I don't know how long I've been lying here. Hours, maybe.

It's not Trip's blue-and-white truck that pulls up. It's Zane's black truck. But it's not Zane who climbs out and walks over to me. It's Chiffon.

"You're not Trip," I say. My tongue feels heavy and dry in my mouth. If it were possible, I would spit it out.

"No shit, Sherlock." She grabs my purse off the curb. She shakes her head and mumbles something that sounds mean as she walks over to my phone, picks it up, and slips it into my purse. She holds out her hand for me.

"Where's Trip?" I raise my hand limply to meet hers. My hand weighs 189 pounds.

"He's at school. Remember? An hour away." Her voice is annoyed, angry. She shoves her hand into mine and uses her other hand to steady me. "He called Zane to come get you, but since Zane has Billy this weekend, I thought I'd do him a favor."

I'm standing now, and somehow walking without falling toward the car. Chiffon struggles to open the truck door while holding me up, so I try to stand on my own. I can't do it. The truck moves, the ground tilts. I grab onto Chiffon. She stumbles a little.

It takes me three tries to get into the truck, even with Chiffon's hands pushing and pulling me onto the seat. I feel like a liability, a burden—which is ironic because I've always gone out of my way to *not* be either. I want to tell this to Chiffon, but she's talking to someone on her phone.

"Yeah, I got her." She's buckling my seat belt. She's rolling down the window. Her phone is sandwiched between her shoulder and ear. "Not good. Plastered. . . .Well, her phone was in the middle of the parking lot so I doubt she could answer it. . . . How am I supposed to know how

it got there? The girl is wasted. . . . Yeah, she'll live."
She eyes me carefully. It can't be very pretty. I've got my
head leaning against the door, practically hanging out
the window. I couldn't change position even if I wanted
to. "Okay. Okay. Okay! Christ, Trip. I get it." She slams
her phone down on the dash and mutters, "I can't decide
if you or Trip is the bigger pain in the ass right now."

I mean to laugh at this, but the cool wind feels so
good against my face that I close my eyes and imagine
I'm flying.

And then I'm falling. Chiffon is telling me to walk.
I'm standing. There's gravel under my feet and it's so loud
when I step on it. It's impossible to walk on.

Dive-bomb! I hear Shelby's voice in my head and a
small giggle comes out. The gravel is in my hands. Chiffon is cursing. My knees hurt. But I know this gravel.
This is the gravel in the Chapmans' driveway. Chiffon's
arms are pulling me up, sliding around my waist, moving me forward.

I wish Shelby were taking care of me. I wish Melissa
and Danica were here too. This would all be funny if
Shelby were here. Danica would be telling everyone to
relax and offering cigarettes. Melissa would be just as
drunk as me, so I wouldn't be alone. Shelby would sing,
"Hey, lush, have fun, it's the weekend," as she put me to
bed.

Chiffon walks me to Trip's room and helps me into

his bed. I want to thank her. But when I try to talk, all I can do is moan.

"Go to sleep, Aubrey," she says. And that's exactly what I do.

When I wake up, I can't tell how much time has passed. Probably not a lot, because Trip's room is still dark and usually the sun peeks through his blinds and lights up his entire room. I don't know what time it is, or how long I've been asleep, but my head is pounding, my stomach is turning, and I know for certain that if I don't make it to the bathroom, Trip's bed is going to be covered in vomit.

I launch myself through the door, which is thankfully not completely closed, and down the hallway into the tiny bathroom. And again, I'm lost in a timeless space, curled up on the cool tile of the bathroom floor or bent over the toilet. I'm sweaty, and freezing, and my brain feels like it wants to break out of my skull.

"Aubrey." I feel cold hands on me, rubbing my back.

He stays with me the rest of the night. He brings me a fleece blanket for my shivers. He rubs my back when I throw up, and feeds me water and ginger ale and crackers. He leans against the bathtub and lets me lean against him when I'm not perched over the toilet. The night is a blur of sickness and dizziness, with just bits of relief and warmth when I'm lying against Trip and his arms are around me.

CHAPTER THIRTY-SEVEN

Sleeping is the only thing I know how to do. I remember Trip waking me up to drink water and another time to call my mom. I told her I would be staying at Shelby's all day watching movies. I was too out of it to decipher whether or not she believed me.

When I open my eyes on my own, Trip's room is dim, except for the lamp on Trip's side of the bed. My head hurts, but I'm not nauseous anymore, and that makes me want to jump for joy. But I don't want to push my luck. I'm buried under the covers wearing one of Trip's white undershirts and a red pair of his boxers. He's lying on his back next to me, propped up by pillows, making flash cards, in a very similar outfit.

Trip puts his hand behind my head like he's spotting me when I move to sit up.

"That was bad, huh?" My voice is hoarse.

"You poisoned yourself, Housing." Once, last year, my mother insisted that drinking hard liquor was like poisoning your body. It was always a joke after Shelby found out and told everyone. *Pick your poison.* I'm glad my mother's not here to see how right she can be sometimes. I think about drinking straight from the bottle, like I've been doing all semester, and I'm sure I'm going to lose it again. I cover my mouth, but I'm lucky and nothing comes up.

"So who were you trying to keep up with?" He's smiling, but his voice is kind of serious.

I sink back down into the pillow, shaking my head. I try to laugh about this, at my own ridiculousness. Self-deprecation can be funny. But all I can do is cry. I cover my face. It's no use trying to stop what's pouring out of me right now.

I remember everything. Nathan is hooking up with Shelby. He's allowed to do whatever he wants and this is what he wants, this is who he wants. Trip pulls me into him and hugs me.

"Hey, come here. You're okay."

I'm getting snot and tears on his shirt, but he doesn't seem to mind. His hand runs over the back of my head, smoothing my hair. I have the slightest urge to push him away. I don't deserve this kindness from him, not when just last week I left him on the side of the road.

I don't deserve this kindness from anyone, because I did this to myself.

There's a knock on the door and Chiffon sticks her head in. "Dinner's ready," she says. "Can she eat?"

"We'll be out in a second," Trip tells her.

I sit up. My entire face is wet and I can't breathe out of my nose. In a way I feel better, knowing Chiffon saw me like this.

"Dinner?" I ask.

Trip stands up. He nods and smiles but doesn't say anything. He lets it sink in that I've slept the entire day.

"Better get cleaned up." He takes off his shirt and tosses it at me. I finish wiping down my face with it. I even blow my nose on it. Somehow I know that's allowed. "Here." Trip hands me a pair of sweatpants. They're mine. I don't remember leaving them here, but here they are. He throws me one of his sweatshirts. It swallows me whole and I'm tempted to go back to sleep, but I am really hungry.

I watch Trip slide on jeans, put on a new T-shirt, slip a sweatshirt over his head. I don't think I've ever watched him dress. I wonder where we made the turn in our relationship—to dressing each other instead of undressing each other.

Earl, Zane, Trip, and Chiffon are having chili, Caesar

salad, and orange juice. Trip made me a microwave pizza.

"The grease will help," he promises me.

Billy's having something lumpy and cream-colored, though most of it is on his face. Billy is starting to look like an actual person. He has a few teeth now. And because Zane shaves his head, Billy actually has more hair.

Billy screeches when we all move to sit at the table and he's still stuck in his high chair. The noise makes me jump.

"He does that sometimes," Trip says.

I catch Chiffon laughing quietly at this, but she won't look at me. We're sitting at the same table, and all I have to do is tell her thank you, but they seem like the emptiest words right now. I wonder if seeing me too drunk to walk and covered in my own snot was justice enough.

Through some spell of luck, my phone still works. Between last night and this evening I've missed five calls from Melissa. Two from Danica. Two from Shelby. Nine from Nathan. There's only one text message. It's from my mother, asking if I plan on coming home at all today or if I've officially moved out. Even though I've already spoken to her, I text her to let her know I won't be home until late. I still have to pick up my car at Leila's—the place I left it before we rode with Patrick to Sam's—but I'm not in the mood to see anyone.

There's a sharp ringing. It's the ringing of another phone, but it startles me and makes me drop my phone again.

"That thing's taking quite the beating," Earl notes.

Billy starts chattering and wiggling and being loud about it. Like he knows the ring, or maybe at this age he just likes anything noisy. Zane leaves the room, phone in hand, and comes back a few minutes later. We all wait for him because at dinner the Chapmans are more polite than they are all day.

"That was Jamie. She's on her way to get Billy." Zane turns to Chiffon. "So you gotta go."

She freezes for a second and her cheeks turn pink. "Oh, okay."

"Come on, Zane. We're just about to eat," Trip says.

Earl shakes his head, muttering to himself, glancing at the door like he's pissed enough to leave.

Zane's really kicking her out. Zane's ex-girlfriend is coming over to pick Billy up and he's making Chiffon leave. It's awkward and awful.

Chiffon puts on the fakest smile I've ever seen. "I just have to get—" Her plate slides forward when she stands and knocks over her glass of orange juice.

"I'll get your stuff." Zane disappears down the hall. He has to feel bad, guilty, *something*, about what's going on.

"Shit, shit," Chiffon curses under her breath. Everyone has their hand in the mess, dabbing up the juice.

Zane returns with Chiffon's Windbreaker and a backpack overflowing with clothes. I try not to stare as she walks to the door with her head down. She won't even look at Zane.

"I'll call you tomorrow, babe," Zane says to her before she shuts the door.

"Goddamn it, Zane." Earl pushes his chili away from him.

"What?" Zane shrugs, but there's a thick layer of defensiveness in his voice. "Chiffon knows how it is. She knows it's easier not to have to deal with Jamie."

I wonder how many times Zane has said that to himself, that it's not a big deal, the way he's treating Chiffon, only inviting her into certain parts of his life and pushing her out of others. And not sticking up for her. Never sticking up for her.

And last night she helped me so Zane wouldn't have to—or maybe because Zane wouldn't have helped. I never thanked her.

There's an urgency that takes over, a ringing in my ears and a squeezing in my chest. I follow her outside.

"Wait!" I'm not wearing shoes and I have to step off the porch and onto the gravel to reach her, but I don't care.

"What, Aubrey?" There's strength in her voice to make up for the red around her eyes, the quiver in her lip.

I mean to tell her thank you, but what comes out is "I'm sorry."

Her cold stare turns malicious. She rolls her eyes and

a tear falls down, but she hits it away. "I really don't want your pity."

"It's not pity." Everything seems so backward in this moment, that Chiffon would think I pity her when last night I was the one who was so drunk I couldn't walk. "I just—I don't know how to thank you for coming to get me last night, and—" I feel my chest tighten more, but I manage to finish. "I just . . . I'm sorry." She deserves better than Zane, just like she deserved better friends in tenth grade. "For everything."

Chiffon licks her lips and looks away. I think for a second that she really will cry in front of me. "I'm sorry too." Her voice is harsh and her eyes match, but even in their severity they can't hide the sadness. "I'm sorry you and Shelby and Melissa and Danica thought that Ronnie Adams was more important than me."

Melissa's voice is in my head telling me to scream at Chiffon and correct her: Ronnie Adams was more important to you than *we* were, and that's why we got rid of you.

"Ronnie Adams is no one," I say. "We didn't know what we were doing. We didn't know anything about boys back then. We didn't know how to deal with their crap." Even I can hear the hollowness in my explanation.

"But you sure knew how to deal with me."

I shake my head, suddenly feeling as though I might cry too. "No," I tell her. "No, we shouldn't have said those things to you, we shouldn't have . . ." I stop because the list is too long. I can't name all the things we shouldn't have done to Chiffon. I can't even validate our past offenses against her by pointing out that she still did relatively well for herself. She was still invited to parties even though she was sometimes laughed at or whispered about when she got there. She still had real friends, even though her old ones lingered in the halls like ghosts, always taunting her, punishing her for the boy who liked her when she was fifteen.

Because the bottom line, the conclusion, won't change no matter what I say. Her reputation dwindled while ours thrived; it plummeted so that ours could skyrocket.

"You guys were very wrong about me," she tells me. She's opening the door to her car. This is what she wants me to know before she goes.

I nod but have the strongest urge to ask her why she's with Zane. *If everything we'd presumed to know about you was so wrong, why are you with someone like Zane and letting him treat you like you don't matter?* But before I can even take a breath to form the question, I realize I already know the answer. I'm a part of the answer.

We both jump a little when we hear the front door open and the screen door slam. Chiffon gets in her car quickly this time, and I know Zane has just come outside. He looks baffled, maybe irritated, that Chiffon is still here. Trip just looks confused. He glances down at my feet, my white socks covered in dirt and pebbles.

Chiffon barrels out of the Chapmans' driveway and doesn't look back.

"Your pizza's getting cold," Trip says, opening the door for me and reaching out his hand. It's all so typical and so wrong. I'm invited in and Chiffon is asked to leave.

I wonder where I'd be right now if I'd been the one Ronnie Adams was enamored with instead of Chiffon, and I was the one who broke Melissa's heart. I take Trip's hand and let him guide me back into the warm house, back to my spot next to him at the dinner table. If I'd never evolved, I wouldn't be here. Not like this.

If I'd never evolved, I wouldn't be able to make sense of Nathan's decision to detach from me. I'd think it was unacceptable. I'd probably be fighting for him right now.

Immediately I miss Shelby, because Shelby's the one with all the answers. If I can't lean on the events of the past or the boys of the future, I want to at least be able to lean on my friends and the theories.

"Please be nice to Jamie when she gets here," Zane says. It takes me a second to realize he's talking to me.

CHAPTER
THIRTY-EIGHT

Guilt is a funny emotion. It's an emotion I never expected to feel toward Trip, but now I'm swimming in it so deep, I don't know how I'll ever see above the surface.

"Thanks for being there for me last night," I say to Trip as he drives me to get my car at Leila's after dinner. I'm glad that's where I left it and I don't have to go back to Sam's. It'd be like returning to the scene of the crime. I stare out the window when I thank him because it comes out sounding so cheesy.

"I'm not even going to ask why in your drunken stupor you wanted me to come get you. I'm just glad you did."

If possible, his reply is even cheesier.

"Okay. *Right*," I say. So he knows I'm not fooled.

"I'm serious, Housing," he says. "I've missed that . . . you needing me."

I whip my head around to stare at him. "I never needed you." It's so absurd. What with the theories and making him constantly pursue me last year—how could he possibly think that I ever *needed* him?

Trip smiles and his eyebrows hike up slightly. "Yes, you did, Aubrey."

There's a dip in my stomach.

"We needed each other," he says, readjusting himself and leaning back so he's closer to me.

I want to scoot closer too, and tilt my head so it's resting on his shoulder, the way I used to. But I don't. We just sit there barely touching for the rest of the drive.

When we arrive at Leila's, Trip waits for me to get in my car before he drives away, honking as he leaves. I'm about to put my car in reverse when I notice Shelby in my rearview mirror. She's walking toward me from Leila's open front door. Hanging out at Leila's on Saturday night isn't unusual; I should have known she might be here. I roll down my window and take a deep breath.

"Trip Chapman, huh?" she says, smiling. She looks just like my best friend. Talks like her, too. I feel a smile creep across my face. It's not scary to see Shelby. Even after I'm nearly positive she's been with Nathan. But if it wasn't her, it would have been someone else.

"You know . . ." I rub my head. "It's just . . . whatever . . ."

"Oh, I *know*. I'm a pro at the *whatevers*." She glances at her feet, shaking her head.

"Do you need a ride?" I ask.

"No," she says. "I've got a ride coming. I heard honking and thought it was him."

The BMW horn and the horn on Trip's old pickup sound nothing alike. Still, I've got a hunch. "Nathan?" I'm glad my voice is steady. I'm going to get through this, and the right way this time. I've known this day was coming, after all.

She nods quickly, waves her hand. *Whatever*. "I'm glad you're here, though. No one could get ahold of you. Not last night or today. Now I know why."

"The thing with Trip . . . it's nothing, really. We're not—"

But Shelby doesn't need an explanation and she doesn't want one. She interrupts me, asking how many weeks until the series finale of *Mercy Rose*. It's in three weeks, so that's what I tell her.

There's still something sad about sitting here talking to her about the parts of our lives that don't directly involve us, and skimming over Nathan's name. But there's comfort in knowing we can talk like this. Like nothing has changed between us. No matter what happens, we don't have to be hurt, we don't have to wage a war. No one has to know what I did last night, how I handled myself. I can earn back all the points I lost.

We get to keep each other and that's really the most important thing.

The theories weren't created so we could keep boys. Forever was never an option with them. The theories exist so that we could have them in the first place. So they would be happy to stay, and free of the burdens of commitment, defining the relationship, and answering the question *What does all this mean?* And we would be happy too, because we would be spared from expectations and disappointment and heartbreak, and all those things that no girl wants to feel.

So it might seem at times like the theories were for them, but they weren't. They were for us.

AS IT TURNS out, I'm a pro at *whatevers* too. I flirt with Tommy Rizzo. I let myself warm to the idea of tasting his Wintermint breath again. I tease Sam about our kiss during spin the bottle. I don't correct Robert whenever he says something implying that I have a thriving sexual relationship with Trip Chapman.

A game. That's all life is; that's all it feels like. Everyone waiting for their turn to spin the bottle or for the bottle to finally choose them. "Who would you rather?" is real. We can be erased, that's real too.

Nathan and Shelby are happy. She looks natural sitting in the front seat of his car with her hair blowing in the spring breeze and a smirk on her face. Nathan's always alive, laughing at her inappropriate jokes, smiling and nodding whenever she asks for a ride to *anywhere but here.*

Nathan Diggs has been Shelby's *whatever* for two weeks. I haven't been alone with him for two weeks. Robert sits in between us during Drama. If we talk in the hall, we're part of someone else's conversation. Lunch is like that too. We don't make plans to study. He doesn't offer to drive me anywhere. There's no reason for us to be alone, so we're not.

Not until Friday during Drama, when we're alone together in the middle of the improv circle. We're surrounded by the class, and Melvin, but in the scene taking place, it's just us. We're forced to talk. Just the two of us, pretending to be other people.

Nathan tagged himself in the scene with me. I'm a patient, he's the doctor.

"Tell me where you're hurt." He mimes using a stethoscope on me. Only he doesn't touch me; he lets his hand hover over my heart.

I look to the improv circle. Certainly any one of these girls wants to tag me out to play doctor with Nathan Diggs.

I lean away from him and his stethoscope pantomime.

"Maybe you could tell me exactly what's wrong," Doctor Nathan says. He runs his fingers over his upper lip like he's stroking a mustache. The class laughs.

"I have smallpox. The really contagious kind. Everyone in this office has been compromised."

Nathan presses his lips together like he wants to laugh. It's stupid, but this makes me feel like crying. That he can still do these things he used to do all the time, like laugh at me when I had no idea I was being funny. But he's not doing it because of me, he's just doing it because it's something *he does*.

"Smallpox hasn't been around since the seventies," Doctor Nathan says.

"That's not true," I say, but because Nathan said it, I know that it probably is.

"You must be feverish." His hand slowly comes toward my forehead, toward those stupid strands of hair that he always used to pull on.

I jerk away from him and watch his eyes get large. He makes it easy to forget the theories, the way things are. "Don't touch me." It just tumbles out. I hear my own voice echo back at me and realize I've probably said this very loudly.

Nathan leans forward slightly. "I wasn't going to," he says softly, just to me. His hands are folded together and pressed against his chest, like he's keeping them as far from me as he can without removing them from my sight.

Everyone is silent. Nathan's eyes dart around the circle, at all the faces watching us. I feel hot and dizzy, and right when I think I'm really going to collapse, someone hits me in the arm. It's Robert, tagging me out of the circle.

I'm vaguely aware of an improv scene going on behind me as I walk away from the circle, away from the stage. But I don't even turn around to make sure Mrs. Seymour hasn't returned to class, or to check if Melvin is watching. I just keep walking until I'm outside and the sunlight is blinding me. Then I run as fast as I can to my car.

CHAPTER
THIRTY-NINE

I stay late after school to ask Ms. Martinez some questions about our physics assignment. Studying has been tough lately. Concentrating is hard. Life is a game with exhausting strategies.

Nathan is by my locker, pacing in the quiet, empty hall when I leave the physics lab. He sees me coming and leans against the locker next to mine.

"Hey." My voice is perfectly indifferent and perfectly friendly even though Nathan's not smiling.

"Why weren't you at lunch?" he asks the floor.

"I was studying. Didn't anyone tell you?" I rarely do things without Shelby, Danica, or Melissa being aware of them and Nathan knows that. After I left Drama early I went to the French Roll to study and eat lunch, but where I went didn't stay a secret for long.

Nathan shakes his head. "I didn't ask." He moves over slightly. Just enough so I can open my locker.

"So now you've asked," I say, fumbling in my locker to grab the books I didn't feel like carting to the physics lab but will need to bring home. I don't expect him to stay now that his question has been answered, but when I close my locker he's still standing there, staring at the ground.

"So what happened today? During improv?"

I shake my head and shrug, like I don't know what he's talking about.

"It kinda seems like you hate me," he says.

"I don't." I'm not lying. *Hate* is too strong and too rigid a word to peg on a guy in high school. Like *loyalty*. Or *commitment*. Or *boyfriend material*.

Nathan finally looks at me.

"You're not angry with me?"

You should be furious. I'm furious. We're back in the car, driving down the highway, only I'm the one he's staring at through the review mirror; I'm the one who doesn't make sense to him.

"I thought you might . . ." He scratches under his chin, as if that's enough to finish the sentence. When he realizes that I'm about to leave, he talks quickly. "When you left the auditorium, I—I went after you. But you were already gone. I thought you might've wanted to talk."

I feel hot prickles of anger. He shouldn't be pressing this. He should just believe me and leave, and be grateful to do so. He doesn't walk away, so I do.

"Wait." He steps in front of me. "What if *I* want to talk?"

"There's nothing to talk about."

He shakes his head. "Aubrey—"

"Stop." Nathan is wasting his breath if he thinks he has to talk to bring himself absolution—it's been his since the day he stumbled late into Lincoln High and I was the one to notice him. I don't want to know his excuses, his reasoning. That's the beauty of all of this—we don't have to know the specifics of why someone decided they didn't want us anymore. He opens his mouth to speak again, but I only let him get out the first syllable of my name. "It's nothing," I tell him.

"Then why did you freak out?"

"I didn't—"

"Come on, Aubrey. You freaked out. Everyone saw you."

I make another attempt to leave. He steps in front of me again.

"Look," he says, his voice is soft. "Are you upset about Shelby and—"

"Shelby and *you?* No, I'm not upset about that."

"Then why won't you just talk to me about it? Why do you keep running away?"

"Because there's nothing to say!"

I move away from him and he grabs my arm. It makes me want to scream, the reminder of how his touch can feel gentle and strong all at the same time.

"Aubrey . . . I never wanted us to have nothing to say to each other. . . . Just because Shelby and I—" This is what he says to me. He's holding on to my arm to make me listen to *this*. I yank my arm out of his grip and it works—he doesn't finish. "You don't understand," he says instead.

He's so wrong. I understand perfectly.

I don't raise my voice. I just shrug. I hope he can see that I mean it when I tell him, "It doesn't matter to me what you do. I don't care that you're hooking up with Shelby."

He shakes his head. "I'm not—"

It's the question I'm not supposed to ask, but here I am with the perfect opportunity to ask it. I take it. "You're not hooking up with her?"

Nathan stares at the ground. He nods. "No, I did."

I can't speak. *Did*. It's all I can think about it. *Did*. He used to. He *did*. He's not anymore.

"You can't really be mad about that though, can you?" he says.

"I'm not mad about it."

"Okay." His tone is mocking. He shrugs. "I feel like I've messed up."

"You didn't do anything wrong," I tell him again.

"It feels like I did. Even though you were doing the same thing."

He stares at me now, for the first time looking me directly in the eyes. He's desperate, but I'm not sure which answer he's more desperate for: that it's okay he started hooking up with Shelby because I'd been doing the same thing with Trip; or that I was never hooking up with Trip and he's really the only person I've wanted since I met him. Neither answer will make it better or worse for him.

"I wasn't." He doesn't really deserve the truth, but I still give it to him. There's no reason to lie, according to the theories. He felt like he was doing something wrong—something that would hurt me—but he did it anyway.

He doesn't look relieved or disappointed. He seems confused.

"Trip is my best friend," I explain. Trip. Shelby. All my best friends are intimidating. They're extraordinary. When I think about it like that, it makes me feel weak. But maybe I'm strong in my own way, to have kept people like that in my life. I try to tell myself that I'm strong while I'm standing across from Nathan and he's giving me the look he gave me on the first day of school.

I'm all yours.

He scratches the back of his head and stares down the hall behind him like he's thinking about making a quick getaway. I know he won't go anywhere, though, not now. He opens his mouth a few times. He's got something to say but he just can't find the words, or he's not brave enough to use them.

"What do you want from me?" I finally ask.

His lips stay sealed and he just shakes his head, looking to his feet like he wishes he had something to kick.

But he doesn't have to answer. I know exactly how he feels. When nothing is defined it's freeing, but it can also be unsatisfying.

There's a pull to stay, to wait for him to sort out whatever it is he wants to say—but I don't give in to it. I go. Exactly like I'm supposed to. The theories can still protect me. They have to. Nothing else will.

Nathan grabs my arm and turns me around so I'm facing him. His face is barely six inches away from mine. I don't pull away and soon both his hands are on me, gripping my shoulders.

And then I do exactly what I'm not supposed to do. Nathan Diggs is kissing me and I'm kissing him back.

CHAPTER FORTY

This is who Nathan Diggs is now. Impulsive. Confident. He knows that when he kisses someone they'll kiss him back. Nathan Diggs can kiss whoever he wants, and he wants me.

The sheets on Nathan's bed are cool against my skin, Nathan is hot against it. I want to laugh, I want to scream, but I don't wind up doing either. I just let myself go.

And then I do it again the next day.

Maybe Nathan's back here with me because Shelby's bored with him. Maybe he only likes me because I don't make him apologize or ask him to explain what happened between him and Shelby. But that's not what he tells me.

"I'm happiest when I'm with you."

I spend the entire weekend with Nathan, not with my friends. They all know where I am. "Huddled up in the love shack," Shelby says. But it doesn't matter to them, and of course, it really doesn't matter to Shelby.

Shelby and Nathan are still friendly Monday at school. They walk to second period together, just the two of them, because they both have classes in the science wing. At lunch, they banter back and forth, trading sarcasm for wit. She rides with us on the way to the park, throwing out snarky comments from the backseat that make Nathan laugh so hard he spits out his Coke. They act like they always do, except they don't hook up. They don't share secrets. Whatever was between them is gone. Erased.

It's the theories, basic and simple. They're the reason I was the first girl Nathan wanted the moment he stepped foot into Lincoln High. They're the reason I got to keep him for months. And now he's back.

Nathan tugs on my hair during Drama. He grabs my hand after lunch and holds it until I have to turn right and he has to turn left. He pulls me in for a kiss after school even though we're both going to the same place. He does all the things I thought he was done doing.

And then he does them again, and again, all week long. And I let him.

WE'RE WALKING UP the steps to Robert's house when Nathan tells me he's sorry. He's sorry for things he was never supposed to be sorry for.

I hold his hand tighter and tell him to stop apologizing. He doesn't listen.

"I wish I could take it back," he says, tilting his head like he's going to kiss me. But he lingers. He waits for me to close the gap. "I want to be with you," he whispers.

I kiss him, but I don't say anything. All I can think about is girl points and how many I'll be losing if I say *I want to be with you, too*, the way he seems so badly to want me to. How many other girls will be in this position in the future if I tell Nathan I forgive him for the all the things he doesn't have to be sorry for; when he tells me these things like he's waiting to be let off the hook. But there was never supposed to be *a hook*, there was never supposed to be a restriction. There was supposed to be nothing we could have done that would hurt each other. Did he know that all his apologies would fall to the floor and we'd be back like this again—the same way Patrick weaves in and out of Leila's life? The preferred way. The way Nathan wiggled out of my favor and into Shelby's. I think that maybe this *is* what he planned all along— coming back to me—and we'll be here a hundred more times. Apart and together, apart and together, in a cycle. Never really moving on, always trusting that stupid, lingering hope that if he detaches, a few weeks later I'll find him pacing in front of my dorm room. And him always knowing he can come back, easily, just by kissing me, just by telling me I make him happy, just by offering me an apology. Will the things he says to me always expire when he meets another funny, too-beautiful-to-describe girl who has secrets?

It's just like Shelby said.

You should be ready. You don't have the luxury of escaping him after graduation.

We could detach and exit but never really be free of each other. And I wonder if I've just made myself available to it, and if we'll be back here again, and again.

And maybe it's stupid, the rules shouldn't be any different for Nathan just because of Barron—I know that—but I can't seem to forget that this is all fleeting and temporary. When Nathan kisses me, I try to forget that he's going to stop one day. When we ride in his car, just the two of us, with the windows down and the music low, I try to pretend that no one else has ridden here.

And as I kiss him in the dark of Robert's driveway, I tell myself that next year doesn't matter, and concentrate on his hands on my back, his lips against mine, the way I'm leaning into him with my whole weight and he's got me. But the theories are still there, in the forefront of my thoughts, reminding me that all of this with Nathan is either for the moment or a lie, and only time will tell how well Nathan Diggs can fake sincerity.

CHAPTER
FORTY-ONE

We all gather at Shelby's on Monday for the season finale of *Mercy Rose*. We're sitting on Shelby's bed, painting our toenails and eating junk food, waiting to see if Scarlet will just die already, and waiting for Jude to admit his true feelings for Scarlet's sister.

We're celebrating, too, because Danica got her acceptance letter from the university. Robert's going to State. The theories are necessary here. I don't ask her how she feels about it.

"I can't believe it," Melissa says during a commercial.

"What?" I ask.

Shelby takes the opening. "That Tommy Rizzo

hasn't had his way with you yet?"

My mouth flies open. "The Riz, Melissa?"

Danica laughs. "Melissa's been shacking up with the Riz almost as much as you've been shacking up with Nathan."

"Although technically *shacking up* involves more than just *oral* exams." Shelby's made Melissa's face turn red. She leans into me as she laughs. "Right, Aubrey?"

It makes me feel rotten when I remember that she really does know what it's like to be *shacked up* with Nathan Diggs.

"That's not what I was going to say!" Melissa says. "I was going to say that we're all leaving each other. And that's sad."

But Melissa is still red, and Shelby is still snickering at her dirty joke. Danica jerks to cover Shelby's mouth when the show comes on, knocking the popcorn bowl, making kernels fly everywhere. And now it's a battle, between laughing like we want to and giving our undivided attention to the show.

My phone beeps. I ignore it. It's Nathan, I know, because it's nearly nine, and Nathan always calls at nearly nine. That brief moment when he's done with dinner and homework, before he heads up to bed to read or watch TV. That window of his time that belongs to me. But right now I belong to Shelby, Danica, and Melissa.

Shelby's phone beeps next. She taps her fingers over

the screen and then she does the unthinkable. She peeks at it, even though Jude is yelling and Scarlet is crying, and we've been waiting all season for this blowup to happen. Shelby's face is expressionless and she doesn't look at us. It's as if she doesn't know that reading a text during *Mercy Rose*, not even waiting for a commercial, wouldn't make us all curious. Then she does something I never thought I'd see any of us do, and returns the text.

Melissa breathes out when the commercials start— a deep and neurotic sigh of relief. "Who was that?" she asks in a small, worried voice, like maybe she thinks something is terribly wrong—a family crisis: Shelby's grandmother dead; Sienna in jail—because why else would Shelby answer a text message during the last ten minutes of the season finale?

Now Shelby's eyes stay glued to the television. "No one," she says. She shakes her head, gives the television a smirk. "Fucking Patrick."

"Lame," Danica says, but her voice is vacant.

Shelby would never return a text from Patrick in the middle of our show—I know we all must be thinking it. And Patrick's been attached to Leila for the past month, barely even noticing Shelby. Sam would have been a more believable answer, I think. And that's when I realize it: Shelby's lying.

"I can't believe you ate all the Oreos," I say quickly to Melissa, who's still clutching the empty Oreos container to her chest the way she has been through most of the show. I don't want anyone to ask Shelby what Patrick wanted. I don't want her to know that I'm onto her.

"I can't help it," Melissa says, shaking her head, taking a quick swipe at her face like she's afraid she's got Oreos smeared across it. "I'm a stress eater."

"You're such a mental case," Shelby says, smiling. The words are wrapped and padded with love, the way so much of what Shelby says is.

I hate myself for not believing her about the text. For thinking that what she's hiding will hurt me. The thought that's looming, deepening inside me, I push away: the last time Shelby had secrets, Nathan had them too.

CHAPTER FORTY-TWO

Nathan isn't at school. He told me when I spoke to him after I got home from Shelby's that he felt like he was coming down with something. That's why he couldn't talk longer than two minutes. That's why he probably won't answer his phone today. *I'll most likely be asleep*, he said.

Doubt is ugly. It's consuming and fluid and chameleonlike. It's as if my feelings are actually stinking up the air, making it cloudy.

Sienna brought Shelby to school today, and Shelby never takes rides from Sienna unless it's a Friday night and she's desperate to get somewhere. But no one else seems to notice. No one asks her about it, so I don't either.

Leila and Patrick cling to each other, but not too much—not the way Patrick clings to her when he's wandered away and is desperate to gain her affection again. He doesn't even acknowledge Shelby except to steal a few fries from her plate when she's not looking.

I feel ridiculous and I wish I could shake whatever it is that's plaguing me, forcing me to theorize and accuse. It's lonely, thinking the worst about other people, stacking up all the things that are wrong. But I can't stop. I'm alone in this pit of assumption, and at this rate I'm going to keep finding ways to dig myself deeper and deeper, until I'm alone in the dark with the truth looming above me, shaking its head: *You should have known better.*

At lunch, Robert tells us all to go to the park after school, but Shelby declines. "I'm doing this thing for my mom."

"What?" Melissa asks. "Does Sandra need our help too?"

Shelby waves a hand. "We're picking out a present for my grandma. Dishes, maybe. Something for her kitchen."

The first thought that pops into my head: This is a smart lie. None of us would dream about tagging along for a shopping trip involving kitchen supplies.

"Sienna's going too." Shelby must've thrown this in for good measure.

The murkiness is getting thicker, pressing down harder, blurring everything.

Shelby gets up from the table to bus her tray. She leaves her purse on the floor, leaning slightly against my foot. My eyes follow her. Some seniors on the basketball team stop her on her way back from the trash. She does the move—hands in pockets, chest up—and I know she won't be back right away. I bend forward, reaching into her unclasped purse. It's almost too easy, to fold my fingers over her phone. Next, I feel my way past a wallet, a pack of cigarettes, a lighter, a tube of lip gloss, until I find her gum. I take a piece and pop it in my mouth for everyone to see while I slide Shelby's phone from my hand into my purse, which is resting between my feet under the table.

"I have to get something from my car," I say, groaning my way through the sentence. No one will want to go with me all the way out to the parking lot.

My breath picks up as I shove out the doors of the school. I start to run. Doing this makes me insane, I know that. It makes me a bitch, too, but it's better than being alone with all these dark thoughts.

I shut myself in my car and look around. I'm truly alone with this awful thing I'm about to do. I press the screen and go straight to the text messages. Shelby has not received a text from Patrick since Saturday. There are recent texts from Nathan. Several. Not only from last night at nearly nine, but also from today. Just thirty minutes ago.

ARE YOU OKAY? Nathan wrote right before lunch.

R U? Shelby's response.

NOT REALLY. Nathan.

I scroll down to read Nathan's texts from last night.

> **GOT YOUR MESSAGE. WE CAN MEET AT MY HOUSE AFTER SCHOOL. NO ONE WILL BE HERE. THIS WILL MAKE YOU FEEL BETTER EITHER WAY.**

Shelby answers with: **FINE. SEE U TOMORROW.**

The rest of their texts from earlier in the month are the kind I would expect between Nathan and Shelby.

> **WE'RE ALL AT THE PARK WHERE ARE YOU?**
> **DID YOU BRING MONEY FOR THE VODKA?**
> **MELISSA NEEDS SOMEONE TO CARRY HER.**
> **PATRICK CAN'T REMEMBER WHERE HE LEFT HIS CAR.**
> **DID MR. TINSKLEY NOTICE I CUT SECOND PERIOD?**

I'm careful not to scroll up too far, afraid of what I'll see if I allow myself to stumble onto the texts from when they were hooking up.

I take a deep breath. I don't have very much time left before Shelby might come back to the table. The rest, whatever Nathan and Shelby said to each other when they were hooking up, is in my hand. Just a few more flicks of the finger, to expose what could hurt me.

Of course, I do it. I hate myself for being so predictable. I hate myself for having no control. I hate myself for caring.

But what I hate the most is that Shelby and Nathan still have secrets.

MEET ME HERE.

LET'S LEAVE FOR LUNCH, I CAN'T WAIT.

I'LL CALL YOU IN FIFTEEN.

I'M OUTSIDE YOUR HOUSE.

WE'LL GO TO THE PARTY LATE.

WHAT TIME SHOULD I PICK YOU UP?

ARE YOU READY YET? HURRY UP!

The texts aren't scary. They're vague, which is worse. It's a choice I have now, to let my mind run away with them: *It must've been the Tuesday after the Detach when they left for lunch; was it Sam's party they decided to go late to? Could the night he was waiting outside her house have been the first time they "hooked up to the max"?* And that's the easiest thing to do, to assume the worst. To soak up all those moments that hurt and weren't supposed to—that weren't supposed to matter at all but somehow in the emptiness of the parking lot, alone in my car, they seem like all that matters.

Nathan and Shelby have arranged a meeting, and she's been lying to me. There were no texts from *fucking Patrick.* The pain is reaching up and pulling me further and further down again. I grip the steering wheel. My keys are in my lap. It would be so easy to drive away, to go home and bury myself under the covers.

Or going to Nathan's might offer the quickest relief. It would be best if I arrive and he's actually very sick. And then he could tell me he's only meeting Shelby to discuss her money or her options for community college. That's the thought I hold on to as I pry my fingers off the steering wheel and hustle back to school.

I need to remember the theories. Despite what I've allowed myself to believe about Nathan, the theories are still relevant. Without them, I've turned into a crazy and clingy girl with no regard for girl points or reality—a girl Nathan would never want. A girl Shelby Chesterfield would never be friends with.

When I get back to the cafeteria, Shelby is still with the basketball players. She's got Jimmy "Treetop" Mulinski by the wrist and is swinging his arm back and forth, like it's her own human yo-yo. Aaron "Red Beard" Billson leans down to say something to her and she lets go of Jimmy's arm to push Aaron against his chest, letting her hand linger, while Sam stands laughing with them, waiting for his turn to be touched.

"Maybe the text last night was from one of them," Danica says, and it startles me. I hadn't realized she'd come up beside me.

"Maybe."

304

I feel the girl points slipping away at our assumptions. But how many does Shelby lose for lying to us?

I return to my seat at the cafeteria, even though most everyone has abandoned the table in favor of mingling. I'm confident as I slip the phone back into her purse that no one notices.

CHAPTER FORTY-THREE

It's hard to conceal suspicion, practically impossible not to let it grow and get out of hand and smother you. There's still an hour of school left when I leave. I don't even worry about how I'm going to cover my tracks.

I turn into Nathan's driveway, and the second I'm out of my car he's walking through the front door like he saw me pull up, like he was sitting by the window. His face is confused. He does look like shit. There are bags under his eyes, and he hasn't shaved. But he's fully dressed and his hair is damp so I know he felt well enough to shower. Something about him looks put-together. Something about him seems torn apart. Like when a rug is laid down to cover a stain but is still really out of place in the room.

"Hi," he says, his voice timid, hesitant. He tries for a smile as he shuts the front door.

"How are you doing?" My hands feel empty, like they should be carrying soup or Kleenex. He's standing on his porch to greet me, but he's waiting for me to come up to him. In the dark places of my mind, I think he met me out here to keep me from coming in.

I walk up the stairs. There's a moment when I reach out and he reaches out, but we both stop and smile awkwardly, because if Nathan's really sick, we shouldn't be touching.

"I came to see how you were doing," I say.

He nods, but I'm not sure what he's saying yes to. "I'll be honest," he says. "I've been better."

I nod back because I don't know what else to do.

He's squinting at me, chewing his lip, scratching his unshaven jaw. In the silence, that's the only sound, the tough prickling of his whiskers against his hand.

"Have you talked to Shelby?" he asks me. His hand bobs up and down in front of me twice, waiting for my answer. It's the gesture of a person ready to lecture. Or explain.

"Yes," I say quietly.

Nathan lets out a sigh.

He looks caught. He clears his throat, then slides down so he's sitting on the top step. He rests his head in his hands. His fingers both massage at his scalp and pull at his hair. It's the first time I think he actually might be sick.

I sit down next to him, concern creeping up on me. Why does he look like this? I'm about to ask, but he starts talking first.

"So are you okay? Are you mad? What—what do you think?" He's rambling. But his head is still down, so I can't look him in the eyes.

"I think . . . I wish I knew what was going on."

At this, his head pops up. His eyes dart back and forth so quickly I can't catch their gaze even if I try.

"Is she coming over here?" I'm so full of questions I could burst. This is the first one to claw its way out and I feel the others pushing behind it.

He doesn't ask how I know that, or why I'm here when I'm supposed to be in AP Physics. He just nods. "You can stay if you like," he says. "But I wouldn't recommend it."

A spark of anger courses through me. "Why not? Would you just tell me what's going on? Please."

I regret saying *please*, a begging word. But it seems to be what breaks him. He presses his balled-up hand against his lips.

"Can you come back in two hours?" he finally says.

"Why?" School will be out in a little less than an hour. It will take Shelby at least ten minutes to get to

Nathan's. The time that follows, when he doesn't want me here while she's here, doesn't make sense. None of it makes any sense.

He turns so he's facing me. "Please." His right hand skims past my wrist as he reaches for me, but he doesn't grab hold. "You're just too early. I'll have answers, if you just . . . wait."

"What answers? What am I waiting for?"

"Just trust me," he says. It's those words that drive me down the steps. But leaving is what he wants. Leaving is saying that I trust him. I want to cling to the theories right now—*I don't need to have any confidence in him; it doesn't matter what he's hiding in the grand scheme of things because he's a high school boy and whatever we have together isn't lasting anyway*—but I'm surrounded by lies, and it feels like I'm grasping at nothing.

"Trust you with what?" I yell at him. What else am I supposed to give him? Two hours *for what*? Shelby, *for what*?

He breathes out and looks away. He shakes his head. I think if he were talking, he'd be warning me, *Don't do this, Aubrey*, but part of me wonders if maybe he's thinking, *Don't make me do this*, and the way I feel isn't what he's concerned with at all.

When he looks at me his eyes are dreary. "We weren't going to say anything to you unless . . ." He shakes his head.

"Unless I found out on my own?"

"No." He's still shaking his head, faster now. "Unless there's actually something to tell."

"You guys have too many secrets."

"What secrets?" He looks genuinely baffled, and I can't tell if it's an act. "I promise, there's nothing else we're hiding—"

"Just tell me, then." My voice is shaky and high, but I can't help it. "I don't think anything could be worse than *this*." The not knowing. The assuming.

He covers half his face, a palm fitted over his mouth, fingers padding into his cheeks, and tells me in a muffled voice, "Shelby might be pregnant."

I feel like I'm underwater, like the walls are closing in, like I'm at the part of the roller coaster that I hate, the part right before the drop, when you just keep going up and up and you crave nothing but that release of safely free-falling back to the ground. I'm aware of Nathan coming down the steps toward me, telling me that Shelby is only seven days late, so they didn't want anyone else to know until they were sure there was something to tell.

I feel his hands on me, his fingers around my arms right above my elbows. *He's never touched me like this before*, I think, and it occurs to me that it's really possible now that he might never touch me like this again. I feel like I'm losing something. I'm not even sure what it is, but I feel everything slipping away from me—there's no controlling all the secrets Nathan and Shelby have. There's no stopping how what they do together could affect me, or even themselves. There's no controlling anything. Everything I want to grab onto for comfort— every theory that promises that Nathan and Shelby could be together and it wouldn't hurt me—is dissolving right in front of me. It's the worst feeling I've ever had.

It's worse than loneliness. It's desertion.

"Shit," Nathan says quietly. "I just—it might be nothing, but—" The second he sees my face his lips snap closed.

It might be nothing or it might be everything.

"How . . ." is all I can say, and it barely qualifies as a word. It comes out like a croak. All I can think about is: how could this have happened when Nathan is always so careful and Shelby is a *condom advocate*, and I've done my part by pushing aside those horrible feelings about them being together, the razor slices that made me drink too much vodka and throw my phone across the parking lot?

Nathan runs his fingers over his lips. I remember the last time I saw him do this. At the party during the basketball tournament right before he said something to Shelby he thought he might regret. He doesn't want to tell me how careless he was. Nathan made me feel like the reckless one once. I remember how good it felt—powerful; brave, even. I don't have to wonder if Nathan felt like this with Shelby. I know he did.

"It might be nothing." He repeats what must be the mantra holding him together. It does nothing to keep me from unraveling.

I want to ask what it means if she is, what happens next, but all I can see of their future has to do with Zane and Jamie, the way they control each other's lives but aren't really a part of them, and how it's nearly impossible for anyone else to be in their lives either.

Nathan shakes his head, like he can read my mind and doesn't want us to go there yet. But I don't know how to go back. He looks stronger now that I'm falling apart. It's true what they say about strength thriving off weakness. I wait for something to happen. I wait to throw up, to faint, to cry. But instead I scream.

"How could you do this to me?" My voice is so loud and high and helpless that I barely recognize it.

Nathan and Shelby. It was never supposed to hurt me.

I want to make it worse for him. For putting me through this. For putting me through those few weeks when he was with Shelby, and for letting the past resurface after we perfected ways to bury it. I know I could leave this entire situation and be free of it. I could be free of him, too. But it's so clear to me in this instant: I never wanted to be free of him. And now I might not have a choice.

"I—I'm sorry," he says. "I'm sorry, I'm sorry, I'm sorry." I think he'll say it forever.

I close my eyes, but I can still feel it when he moves closer to me. I remember when having Nathan so close was exhilarating. It used to be comforting, too. When I open my eyes, I stare at him, hoping that maybe I'll be able to feel some of that again.

"It's probably nothing," he says, quietly this time. "I read that usually it's just stress. That's probably all it is. Because finals are coming up, and we're about to graduate, and . . . I'll call you in a few hours, after we know."

I don't believe in stress; I believe in living. I wonder if Nathan remembers—I'm positive he does. But Nathan couldn't even bring himself to come to school. He's even been researching it; brainstorming alternatives, forming his own theories to make himself feel better. It's already more than nothing.

"Why does she have to come *over here*?" The thought of them together in this makes my stomach turn, my vision blur. "If it might be nothing, if it might just be stress, she should just find out on her own. She doesn't need you."

Nathan's quiet for a while. He licks his lips before he says, "She doesn't want to go through this alone."

"She said that to you?" It's a deafening rage I'm feeling; it's something I've never felt toward Shelby before.

Nathan shakes his head.

"Then why are you doing this with her? Are you afraid she'll stop seeing you as the *good guy*?"

Something like shock passes over Nathan's face. "That's not why."

"Then what the hell, Nathan? Why are you doing this to me?"

He finally yells back. "Because I care—I'm sorry—I can't help it! She didn't ask me to be with her when she took the test. I told her I would be. Because it's the right thing to do."

"It's nice that you care about her," I say. I'm crying, barely. It's most obvious in my voice. Tears sting my eyes, but they don't fall. "Because she doesn't care about you at all."

He takes a deep breath. His face is hard, accusing. "I don't know about that, Aubrey. You're supposed to care about her, too, aren't you? And neither one of you is supposed to care about me. But obviously that's not the case."

"She doesn't care!" I'm astounded that he can't see it—that if he does, he's choosing to ignore it. I'm the one who cares. Shelby's the one who created the theories, all the ways to camouflage our feelings and all the reasons it was vital that we did. "She's never cared."

Nathan speaks before I have the chance to keep going. "Did you know she called Patrick twenty-seven times after they hooked up for the first time, left him twenty-seven voice mails?"

He waits for me to respond, but I stay completely still.

"She even went to his house in the middle of the

night, and for about a week showed up at Robert's anytime Patrick was over there, until . . ." He shakes his head.

I can't help it; I think of Shelby and Conrad, and that night after the tournament when she gave him something precious and he stopped giving her anything at all.

I want to tell him it's not true. But Nathan never lies. Not even when he should.

"She told you that?"

"Of course she didn't." His eyes close, like he can't even look at me. "Patrick told me."

Patrick and Shelby. Two summers ago. Right before junior year. Right around the same time the theories were created. The first time Shelby had sex with Patrick—the first time she did it with anyone—he went back to hovering around Leila within days. When she created the theories, Shelby used this as an example of typical high school boy behavior. And it wasn't the only example she had involving Patrick. He kissed other girls when Leila got too clingy for his taste too. And he always did this after having a fight with Leila about why he wouldn't be her boyfriend. Shelby shook her head like it was funny and laughed, claiming all she really cared about was having lost her virginity to Patrick Smith—the hottest boy in our class, the boy she'd had a crush on since third grade. Right after, she told us the girl code that stated we weren't supposed to hook up with boys our friends had previously hooked up with was outdated and unrealistic.

"When you live in a town this size, with a cute-guy list this small and an average dating cycle that's shorter than a menstrual cycle, outdated girl code just doesn't make any sense," she said. And we agreed. *It's all about the numbers.*

"Aubrey, please." Nathan grabs my hand, encasing it in both of his. "It might be nothing." He still thinks there's a possibility that this moment can fly by us like all the other awful moments before, and we can pretend it never happened, that we never caused each other pain.

But it's too late.

His eyes are pleading with me, his hand is tight around mine, and I know he doesn't get it. He doesn't know the core of the problem—the tipping point—the detonator that was activated the night Chiffon gave Ronnie Adams her phone number. He doesn't know because I never told him.

Instead we all did whatever we wanted, and didn't talk about what we were doing or not doing, because none of it was supposed to matter. We all kept secrets. If we didn't acknowledge our feelings, we couldn't be hurt by them. But they were there all along, buried and rooted and growing every minute. We never guessed what kind of feat it would be to keep them concealed, what an effort it would take to keep up the smoke and mirrors of our tricks.

We can't ignore this. We can't erase it or what it might mean. The theories are bullshit. They don't keep us from getting hurt. They deprive us of the right to our own feelings.

So I say something to Nathan that I should have said the second he started to move in on my best friend.

"Fuck you."

He drops my hand, but as soon as I take a step back he grabs my wrist.

"You realize I don't have any control here?" His grip tightens but I can still feel him trembling. "If the test is positive . . . it's not going to be up to me—I won't have a choice—"

I pull back at the word *choice*. I'm backing up and walking down the driveway, away from him.

"Aubrey—" He takes two steps toward me, and I bolt before he can tell me again that it might be nothing.

Choice. I know it's not the *choice* he's referring to, but all I can think about is Nathan's choice to have sex with Shelby, and Shelby's choice to have sex with Nathan, and my choice to think it wouldn't matter. I get in my car and slam the door, and drive as far away from him as I can.

CHAPTER
FORTY-FOUR

I drive and drive and drive and keep driving until I reach State. I haven't been here since I was thirteen and came on a field trip to see the greenhouse.

I park my car in the first available spot I find and call Trip. He doesn't answer, so I call him again.

"Yeah?" He answers on my third attempt.

"I'm at State. Where are you?"

"You're *here*?"

"Where's your dorm? What's your room number?"

He gives it to me and I hang up before he can ask any more questions.

The trees at State are tall and old, and the walking

paths are worn and cracked from where the roots have broken the surface. Redbrick buildings, coffee carts. Students carrying books, lounging on the grass, throwing Frisbees. It looks just like a college campus. I don't know why I'm surprised.

Finding Trip's dorm is easy. The girl sitting at the front desk in the lobby doesn't blink twice when I walk past. I ride the elevator up to the third floor. It creaks, but no one else panics so I decide this is probably status quo. Everything in Herbert Hall is worn. The tiles are faded, the walls are dull, the wood on the doors is no longer shiny. It even smells shabby. In a way this is comforting. It says people have been here before.

The door to room 358 is ajar. There's low music coming from inside, and low laughter. Trip is sitting in his desk chair, tipping it back so it's only on two of its legs. There's a girl in a red tank top with strawberry-blond hair sitting on the plaid comforter on Trip's bed.

"Hey, you found it." Trip greets me, both his hands in the air. The girl smiles at him, then at me. "Aubrey, this is Jill." Jill reaches out so I reach back. I let her shake my hand.

"So you're the reason Trip leaves us every weekend." She stops smiling for just a second to pout as she says the words *every weekend*.

"She's the reason Trip's no longer on academic probation," Trip says.

"But not the reason Trip is speaking in third person," I blurt out.

Jill and Trip laugh. I want to laugh with them, but I can still feel the tightening in my chest, the dip in my stomach.

Trip motions for me to take his seat so I don't have to stand awkwardly in the middle of the room, and he moves next to Jill onto the bed.

"To what do I owe this pleasure?" Trip says. Jill giggles at this and Trip smiles. It makes me want to scream.

"I was just bored."

"Then I'm afraid you've come to the wrong place," Jill says. "This one thinks sipping warm beer in the alley behind the student union qualifies as entertainment." She points to Trip when she says this to me. In case I didn't understand who she meant by "this one." In case I didn't already know what Trip finds, or doesn't find, entertaining.

Jill is sitting closest to me so I lean forward to look at Trip. "I need to talk to you," I say.

I hate Jill. I'm glad when she gets up to leave. She springs off the bed gracefully, and I hate her for that, too.

"I better get studying for chem. *Au revoir.*" She waves at Trip, smiles at me, and leaves.

Jill speaks French and is taking chemistry. She finds Trip *funny*. All signs indicate that Jill is a nice girl. A nice girl who can fill out a tank top. A nice girl with hair the color most people have to steal from a bottle. I hate her even more.

"So . . ." Trip leans back on his palms, stretches his legs out. "*You* want to talk? You never want to talk, Housing."

"I don't want to talk."

He raises his eyebrows in surprise. "Then what—" but that's all he can get out. One swift motion off the chair, my hands clinging to his shoulders for balance, and kissing him is easy. Kissing Trip has always been easy.

And Trip kisses me back because kissing me isn't easy, and he knows he should be glad for it. He loses his balance holding himself up, or he lets go all on his own, and we topple back onto his bed. It's irresistible, lying on top of each other like this, kissing. His hands are in my hair, then around my back, pulling me closer, holding me closer. I pull at his T-shirt until I get it over his head. Then he takes off my shirt too. When I finally feel his skin against mine, it's such a relief. This is Trip, this is what he is good at. Everything that happens next is going to make me feel better. I'm creating Nathan's worst nightmare, and that makes me happy too.

Then he's gone. He kissing my neck and then he's not. He's sitting back, his hand on my stomach, holding me away. I put my hand over his to move it and lean in to kiss him.

"Damn it, Aubrey." Trip turns his head. He puts his hand back on my stomach, firmer this time. "Stop for a second. Tell me what this is about."

"I don't have to tell *you*, of all people, what *this* is about."

"Tell me what's really going on." He sits up. My shirt is hanging off the edge of the bed. Trip grabs it but doesn't toss it to me. Not right away. "Why are you here?"

"I didn't think I needed a reason to see you."

"You don't, but if there is one, it'd be really shitty of you not to tell me."

I sigh. "Forget it."

Trip shakes his head. "You came all the way up here on a school night for *this*?" He gestures to us, the messy tangle of half-naked people on his bed.

"No." I put my shirt back on.

"Then why? What are you doing here, Aubrey?"

There's this feeling that I should go, that I'm supposed to leave. As angry as I feel right now at Trip for stopping us—something I didn't even think he was capable of doing—I can't make myself move. I don't want to. Did I want to be with him because I needed proof there was someone in the world who didn't want Shelby after they'd been with me? Did I want to be with him because I knew it would hurt Nathan? Did I want to remind him of all the reasons I was better than Jill? Yes. I wanted all those things, but before those thoughts entered my head, I came up here for one simple reason.

"I just needed a friend."

He breathes out a quick, defeated sigh, and pulls me

in, wrapping his arms all the way around me in a hug. I'd always thought Trip was safe because of the theories. But I was wrong. What if some people don't want to be erased or detached just as much as they don't want to feel pressure or confinement? What if the theories were never what brought people to us? What if there's something else inexplicable that puts people in our lives and keeps them there?

I wonder if Shelby has ever considered this possibility.

"Tell me what's going on," Trip whispers.

I stare at him. He holds the back of my head carefully, like he knows about the strain that comes from tilting my head to look at him when we're this close.

I tell him everything: about Nathan and Shelby, about all the ways I've lied to him and to myself. I even admit that I wanted to hook up with him to chase away the pain of what Nathan and Shelby did, and to make myself feel like less of a reject.

And I'm crying. Just a few tears at first, but with every admission, I lose more and more control. Trip rubs my back as I let it all out. Embarrassing sobs that can't be blamed on alcohol heave out of me. It's breaking all the rules to cry like this in front of a guy, about a guy, but somehow that fact makes it feel right.

CHAPTER FORTY-FIVE

A few hours later, when Trip is walking with me to my car, I get a phone call from Nathan. I ignore it.

"You sure you don't want to answer that?" Trip says, nodding toward my phone. Trip insisted on driving me home. He made some joke about how it was too late and I was too emotional, though I'm not sure he was really kidding. He opens the passenger door for me. My phone rings again as we get in. Trip's eyebrows go up. "Don't you think you should find out what you're actually dealing with?"

I already know what I'm dealing with.

The phone stops ringing and beeps to signal a voice mail. I listen to it because Trip has a point, and at least this way I won't have to talk back. Trip puts his hand on my shoulder and rubs. He looks out the window.

It's strange, but I don't feel much relief as I listen to Nathan tell me that Shelby's not pregnant and stumble over an apology about our fight this afternoon. Nathan doesn't sound very relieved either, though I'm sure he is. His voice is lifeless. Maybe he knows there's no going back. This pain was coming for us anyway.

"She's not pregnant," I tell Trip.

He turns to look at me, takes a moment to examine my face. He opens his mouth and I wait for him to tell me exactly what I need to hear, but he's quiet. Maybe for once he doesn't know what to say. Or maybe he knows there isn't anything he can say. I finally feel a rush of relief.

We drive off into the dusk, and the night catches us before we make it back.

Ten minutes from my house Trip says, "I don't know why you thought you could control anything."

And I get what he's saying to me, I really do, but still, there must be some things in life that we want and actually get to have. It's hard for me to accept that there aren't. Especially when I've got an acceptance letter to Barron hanging on my wall, and Trip sitting right beside me.

WHEN WE ARRIVE at my house a little after ten, my mother insists that Trip stay and eat something. When he's done eating the tuna casserole she reheated for him, she insists that it's too late for him to make his brother or his father come get him, and much too late to take the bus back to school tonight—which was his original plan.

"Aubrey, help me make up the bed in the guest room," she says. "You'll stay here tonight, Trip, and tomorrow I'll buy you a bus ticket. I won't take no for an answer."

But Trip argues with her about the bus ticket anyway. Just enough to show he's uncomfortable taking her money. In the end, she wins. As usual.

"Gregory, Jason, show Trip how to play your game."

Being handed over to my brothers is the highest form of praise or approval a boy can get from my mother. Trip smiles as he joins them, like he knows this. *Trip is a good guy; he drove your sister home because it was late; this is the kind of guy you should grow up to be*—this is what she's saying. Finally, he's acting like the kind of guy she'd like me to date.

It makes me wonder if I'm the type of girl anyone should grow up to be. I used to be so sure that I was.

My mother tosses me the edge of the white fitted sheet in our beige guest room, and I fit it over the corner of the mattress. It's so obviously neutral in here that I think it's kind of insulting—the way the room is trying so hard not to offend anyone.

"So do you want to tell me what's going on?" she asks.

I'm an open book. Everyone can read me. Trip knew there was a messed-up reason I kissed him. And now my mother knows that something is going on.

"Not really."

"I don't think you have a choice, Aubrey." She tugs the sheet and it falls out of my loose grip—as if to remind me who really holds the power in this situation. "Why did you drive all the way to State?"

"It's only an hour away."

"Aubrey."

"I just needed to see him." A half-truth.

"And why is that?"

"Trip is my best friend."

But this doesn't calm her. "No," she says, shaking her head. "That boy is not your best friend."

"Okay." I roll my eyes because *what does she know?*

"Oh, don't *okay* me. I'm not completely ignorant, Aubrey, come on," she whispers, which makes her sound only more urgent. "Tell me what's going on! I thought you were seeing Nathan."

"I'm not seeing Nathan." I tuck in the sheet. I concentrate on smoothing the edges. I had no idea I would feel so awful just saying his name. This sheet, its creases, the way it lies against the mattress, is all I want to think about.

"Well, that's probably best, given that your ex-boyfriend just drove you home from his dorm room." She says *dorm room* like it's a dirty word.

"Mom . . ." I'm about to explain to her that Trip was never my boyfriend. That technically, neither was Nathan. But I can't think of a way to do it that will make sense to her.

This won't look good on paper. I stumbled upon my boyfriend and my best friend about to meet up to find out if the night they had unsafe sex resulted in a pregnancy. Even if I tried to explain that I'd been wrong anyway to think Nathan would last beyond high school, and that I hadn't expected him to stay away from other girls, even Shelby, my mom would still only hear the betrayal. She wouldn't be able to see past my hurt, and then I would have to face it again too. And I can't bear to do that anymore tonight.

She walks into the linen closet. This conversation is not going to slow down her bed-making momentum.

"Well?" she says. "What happened? What happened with Nathan?"

It's easier to give her the unfiltered truth with her back turned like this. I take a deep breath.

"Nathan thought he got someone pregnant."

I think of Shelby standing outside my front door, spraying herself frantically with aerosol so my mother wouldn't smell cigarette smoke on her, and decide to leave her name out. "But it was a false alarm. I went to see Trip because I needed someone to talk to. Someone who might understand."

Her face is uneven, drained, worried, when she comes out of the closet. She's holding mismatching pillowcases.

"Aubrey—"

I hold up my hand and she stops talking, but it looks like it takes great restraint. I feel a twinge of guilt, having so much I haven't told her. And I feel worse for telling her about this at all, sad she has to hear it. "I'm sorry. I just can't talk about it anymore."

She nods. "And Trip understands because of what Zane went through?"

"Trip understands because he understands me." It's true, and I don't know when it became the truth—or if it's always been the truth. There's still a part of me that remembers when I thought there were never two people more alike than Nathan and me, and that we understood each other because we understood ourselves. But I don't know if we really did or we just understood the people we thought we were, the people we wanted to be.

She nods again and something passes over her face. Relief, maybe. "I'm glad you have someone to talk to," she says, but I know she's not totally comforted, because that night Trip falls asleep on two different pillowcases: one beige, one white.

CHAPTER
FORTY-SIX

I come downstairs around seven fifteen the next morning to my mother force-feeding Trip eggs, bacon, and orange juice. I notice the orange juice is untouched and feel the urge to laugh. Orange juice is a dinner beverage to Trip. What he really wants is black coffee, but my mother knows this. "I don't serve coffee to growing teenagers," she said once last year when she offered us sweet tea and Trip asked for coffee instead.

"That's nice," Trip says, nodding at me, his voice tired and low. The entire just-woke-up look is working for him in ways that make me embarrassed to be in the same room with him and my parents and my little brothers. "It's nice to see you smile like that."

I return this compliment with a cheese-tastic, over-the-top grin with my mouth full of toast, which makes my brothers laugh. Trip says, "Very classy, Housing."

My mother and Trip leave for the bus station at the same time that I leave for school. She called Trip by his actual name and to his face, instead of her usual way of talking to him: through me, addressing him as "your friend"—so I suspect she might drive him back to State herself.

I'M LATE GETTING to school on purpose. I haven't spoken to Nathan. I haven't spoken to Shelby, either, and though it doesn't seem like very long—not even twenty-four hours—it's the longest we've ever gone without a phone call or a text message or an email or some kind of correspondence, even talking face-to-face.

I arrive just a few minutes before the first bell. I don't look for Nathan. I walk right up to Melissa and Danica. They're laughing by our lockers. They stop when I walk up to them, and that's when I know they're both privy to Shelby's situation. Or, really, her nonsituation.

"Hi, Aubrey," Melissa says, her voice a mixture of enthusiasm and sympathy.

Danica doesn't say anything. She focuses on a renegade curl that's loose and hanging over her eye, pulling on its end and watching it spring back.

"How're you doing?" Melissa says. "Are you—" But

she stops. Danica is glaring at her. It's a warning look. I'm not supposed to be upset. It's not allowed. So acknowledging my bad behavior isn't allowed either. Danica's face suddenly loosens and she smiles. I don't even have to guess why.

"Hi, losers." Shelby bumps Danica with her hips, and the laughter of my best friends, loud and relieved, bellows around me. This is a sound that I love, these are the people who I love, but right now they feel like enemies. And the worst is that they're looking at me like I'm the traitor for not laughing with them about nothing, the way we always, always do when we're together. It was easy happiness, and now I have to take a stand against it.

"You heard the good news, right?" Shelby says to me. She's got a perma-smile on her face and all I can think is How is she going to look bored or displeased or indifferent when her entire glowing face screams: *I just dodged a bullet and I'm so happy.*

"I heard," I tell her.

"He said you were mad," Shelby says, her lips still curved up despite her flat tone. She shakes her head, rolls her eyes. I was being silly. I was having a moment. This is what she's saying with just one look.

It would be so easy to lie to them. Smile. Stick out my tongue to show I'm mad like a six-year-old. Give her a lecture about *wrapping the pickle* in a tight, urgent voice reminiscent of my mother's.

"I am mad."

Shelby is no longer smiling.

"She's not *really* mad," Danica says. It sounds like a command.

"She's recovering from the stress of it," Melissa says. She even reaches around to rub my back. "Nathan shouldn't have told you."

Danica nods in agreement. Shelby's face doesn't move; her gaze stays on me.

I don't know if this ever would have stayed a secret. I picture Shelby waving around the negative test in one hand, a bottle of champagne in the other, while Danica lights her a cigarette and Melissa ducks under the table because she's always afraid the cork will poke her eye out and Shelby is never careful about where she points the bottle.

It's easy to think nothing has changed. But don't they see how greatly and suddenly things *can* change?

"If only everything could be blamed on stress," I say. I arch my back so Melissa will stop rubbing it. "You guys don't understand."

"Understand *what?*" Shelby's voice sounds like venom, and I wish she'd play dumb with me because that would sting too, but in a different way.

The bell rings and I think we're going to separate, disappear into the crowded hallway, and go to class, and that we've been saved from this moment, but Shelby is still giving me the coldest stare I've ever seen. Danica is shaking her head like she's disappointed in me. Melissa is hugging herself since I won't let her touch me.

I don't know how to make them see. They're waiting for me to rise above this, get over it as if there was nothing to get over in the first place. The way they think I got over it when Nathan and Shelby hooked up.

"It's funny," I say before Shelby can say anything. And before I can think better of it. "It's miraculous, actually, that none of us except you has ever hooked up with Patrick Smith. Even though he's the hottest guy in our grade. Even though you told us he was really good in the sack, and that he was so easy and typical, someone who'd never accuse us of having the Girlfriend Stigma. No matter what—even if we called him twenty-seven times after we hooked up with him, or came to his house in the middle of the night, or showed up at Robert's every time he was there."

Shelby swallows, shrugs, and then shuts her eyes for just a second. "Are you upset that Patrick never wanted you or something?" I can see how afraid she is. Nervous that I'll reveal the truth about Patrick—the truth about her and the theories. It could have been so different. The same experience could have taught her how sometimes it's impossible to be indifferent, but instead she focused on all the reasons it was best to pretend that's what she was. Because even though Patrick was back with Leila, it didn't change the truth: Shelby wanted something from him—she needed to be treated a certain way. It makes me sick that she kept this from us.

I look at Shelby directly. "You should never have hooked up with Nathan in the first place."

Shelby's mouth falls open slightly, her eyes shift toward the crowded halls, like maybe for once she doesn't like that everyone watches her. I know what the answer's going to be before she tells me. "Why not?"

Melissa hugs herself tighter. Danica continues looking at the floor.

"We should get to class," Melissa says. The halls are nearly empty. Danica nods, and though they hesitate, they're eventually walking down the hall away from us, looking back every few steps when they notice Shelby and I aren't moving.

"You know I'm right." I don't know if this will make her run away or roll her eyes or if she'll finally be honest with me. She chooses the first option.

"You're pathetic," she says as she brushes past me, letting her history book clip me in the arm.

"I could say the same thing about you." I raise my voice so she'll hear me.

She turns around quickly and walks toward me, head tilted forward, eyes narrowing. "What did you just say?"

I don't repeat myself because I know she heard me. Now I know that she understands what it's like to want so badly to believe someone when they say they want you and that they don't want anyone else, even if she tries to never let herself feel that way.

"I shouldn't have to explain anything to you. Ever." She's so close to me now I can smell the hazelnut from her coffee clinging to her breath.

We hear a door creak open, a sharp squeak coming from the other end of the hall, where the office is. We could end it here; Shelby could go right and I could go left, and we'll avoid getting written up by whoever might be coming out of the office. But instead she nods toward the exit sign just a few paces away.

CHAPTER
FORTY-SEVEN

The morning is still in recovery from the rain of last night and the sun is having a hard time infiltrating the gray of the sky. I get a random thrill as we walk quickly through the parking lot, sliding around side mirrors and bumpers, not knowing if someone will notice us and make us go back in. Shelby and I have never cut class together. She does it sometimes with Danica and Melissa, and they spend the afternoon at the diner ordering coffee and pie, or they'll go to the movies and brag about matinee pricing and how they had popcorn and Junior Mints for lunch. It makes me sad that this is how we're doing it now.

"Where should we go?" I ask her when we're buckled in.

She shrugs and stares out the window, and I think that maybe she won't actually ever talk to me again.

The place I end up taking us is the park. There's a small lot on the north end, right along the river. The north end is the unpopular end. It's overgrown with shrubs, and unless you're fishing there's not really any reason to come up here. Shelby rolls down her window and I follow suit. I can faintly hear the sound of the river hitting the shore, sliding over the rocks.

"Why is the weather so shitty?" Shelby says. "It's ugly as hell up here, especially without the sun." She digs around in her purse and pulls out a cigarette, then raises the pack to me, offering. I shake my head. She doesn't look at me as she puts the cigarette in her mouth but doesn't light it. I'm not surprised. I can't remember the last time I actually saw Shelby smoke one of her own cigarettes. Usually she gives them away.

"Will you tell me what happened?" I say.

"I thought I was knocked up. I'm not. Fascinating, isn't it?" I have the urge to bash the cigarette out of her mouth. It makes her sound mean, the way it dangles against her lips while she speaks.

"I mean what happened with you and Nathan."

I need to know when I lost him, officially. When he chose to believe everything we'd said about nothing lasting. I want to know when my best friend and the boy I liked decided they wanted each other. It's the details that weren't important before that seem the most important now.

She breathes heavily out of her nose in a way that's supposed to be insulting and make me feel like a pain in the ass, and it does. She takes the cigarette out of her mouth and rolls it between her fingers.

"Did you really think hooking up with him wouldn't hurt me?" My voice sounds aimless, pathetic, even, but I can't stop asking the things I shouldn't ask. The things I shouldn't *have* to ask.

"It takes two to tango, Aubrey."

And it's true, but right now all I want is to know how she could have possibly overlooked that her best friend had found someone important. Even if he didn't get to be important forever. Why would she want to be the one who helped take him away? It's different than if after he detached he'd gone to Mary Ann or even Celine. Shelby and I are best friends.

"This is the worst thing you've ever done to me." As the words strangle out of my mouth, I don't know if I'm talking about now—how things with Nathan are so broken. Or if I'm really talking about the first time they kissed, the first time they hooked up, or that day on the football field when she finally convinced me that the theories were right and wounding each other was impossible.

"You don't think I'm sorry?" she says. "You don't think I would take it all back? Get over it, Aubrey, it's in the past. I can't take it back, so you can't be pissed about it anymore. And Nathan wants you. You're getting what you want."

"But why did it have to happen in the first place?" I talk over her. I'm almost yelling. Can't she see that she's known all along? The experience that made her the biggest advocate of the theories also proves the theories don't always work. She knew how easily it could all matter. How the high fives, and the never depriving ourselves, and the fun without the caring, couldn't really protect us.

"Is that why you came up with the theories?" I ask her. "If Patrick could hurt you, then everyone could."

Shelby rolls her eyes and holds her cigarette up like she's going to stick it back in her mouth, but she never does. She's too mad to do anything. "Patrick or Ronnie or Nathan. They could all hurt us, don't you understand?" *And they all have* is what she doesn't say.

"But now you've hurt me, too—"

Shelby interrupts me. "Do you want to know about the first time I kissed Nathan?" Her voice is cold. Her eyes are strained like I've never seen them before.

The thought of it makes me sick. But I want answers. "Tell me."

"The first time we kissed, we were at Patrick's."

"During spin the bottle." I nod. It seems cruel and

twisted that I had been there to watch it. That I'd thought it was just a game.

"Not during spin the bottle. That doesn't count." Shelby gives me a look that tells me I'm so wrong she can't even fathom it. "The next morning. Before he left."

"Why did he kiss you before he left?"

"Why do you think?"

But I have no idea what to think.

"Because we felt like it. He was awake before anyone and I couldn't sleep, so we sat in the living room talking for a little while before he left. He told me he was going back to San Diego for the week, but he wasn't excited. He said it felt like an obligation. He said you didn't ask him to stay. I told him that you wouldn't ever ask him to stay if he said he wanted to leave, and he told me he knew that. Then he asked me if I remembered our kiss during spin the bottle or if I was too drunk, and I said I remembered and asked if he did. He said, 'Not very well,' so I asked him if wanted to relive it." Shelby shrugs and looks away. "He did."

I touch my face to see if I'm crying. It feels like I am even though my cheeks are dry.

"But you're *with* him again, Aubrey. You wouldn't even care about what Nathan and I used to do if you didn't know about what happened yesterday," she says.

I take a minute to consider this. The truth is I'll never know if those weeks Shelby and Nathan were together would have made themselves known in other ways. If our denial about all the things that had happened before we left for Barron would have eventually been harder to ignore than a screaming baby.

"I always knew he'd go back to you," she says, her eyes flicking up to meet mine directly. "It was so obvious he wanted you. But he was still like everyone else. He was starving for other things."

I think she might be right, but I don't allow myself to think about that for very long. "I can't believe you kissed him at Patrick's" tumbles out of my mouth. I remember waking up alone in the cold, empty bed and having no idea. And Shelby never said anything.

"It was nothing." But her voice is too quiet to be convincing.

"Is that the evolved answer or the real one?"

"Both," she says with a straight face. She's holding my eye contact. Her mouth is a tight line. She looks strong, but now I know she's not.

"It wasn't supposed to be like this," she says. "Nathan and me, it was supposed to be random, and exciting. A quick fling, just for fun. Because he's different and funny, and . . ."

She doesn't have to finish because I know all the things that Nathan is.

"It was never supposed to be anything more than that." Shelby's face turns sad suddenly, twisting to reveal a kind of despair. It's shocking, coming that soon after resentment. I wonder if this is how her face looked on Tuesday.

I imagine her whittling her thumbnail down to nothing while she waited with Nathan, chewing furiously with her eyes shut so tightly her eyelids wrinkled. She probably hugged Nathan when she found out it wasn't true. Because then she could really say that it was nothing. It's a comfort to say something is less than it is. And even better if you can trick yourself into believing it. Then Shelby came to school and saw my face, and learned that I wasn't going to let her forget what she'd been through. I was going to make her explain it to me.

She's been failed too. The theories meant the most to Shelby. They were supposed to protect her—they were supposed to protect all of us. They were tricks and treats for boys, but they were shields for us. And they made Shelby feel invincible for a long time. It's so obvious now that it wasn't real, that we confused our power with acceptance. And Shelby had been the most desperate for it. We let people throw us away, all the while pretending that we were throwing them away too, because we thought that was the only way they would want us at all. I know Shelby was used to being thrown away. But this isn't supposed to be something we accept, and definitely not something we invite. I don't want to do it anymore. I don't want Shelby to, either.

"You could have told us you were upset about Patrick," I tell her. "You could have told us about your dad, and about the money." The theories made us keep secrets, even from each other.

"*You* could have told me that you and Nathan were . . ." She hesitates. "You should have told me how you felt about him."

She doesn't look convinced, though, about my statement or hers. It's not allowed, the things we're saying. To want the things that don't seem attainable—to be Nathan's girlfriend; for Patrick to be kind. Shelby, Danica, Melissa, and I didn't indulge each other in unattainable desires. But we should have realized that it's still worth it to try to get what we want, and we could have been there for one another if it fell apart.

"Why did you tell Nathan about your dad and about the money?" I want to know how she knew she could trust him. Despite the theories.

"Nathan was helping me figure out how to make it last, because it's not that much."

"I could have helped you with that."

She shakes her head, and I honestly think she's about to tell me she doesn't know why she chose Nathan. But then she licks her lips and looks as certain as she always does. "He asked," she says. "He asked what I was going to do next year."

"You always give a bullshit answer to that question."

"He asked until I ran out of bullshit answers and there was nothing left but the truth."

I take a deep breath and what comes out next is a groan. Nathan can be persistent. It hurts to think about him—about how we were right about him; about the worst things, and the best. It also hurts that I wasn't the one so persistent with Shelby that she ran out of bullshit answers.

"I already admitted that I'm sorry," Shelby says. "Do you want me to say that I was wrong, too?"

"But you *were* wrong," I tell her. "We were all wrong."

Shelby rubs her temples like I'm giving her a headache, and I probably am. But I want her to tell me that she gets it. The things we do matter. Even if we set ourselves up for the pain, even if we promise it will come and wait patiently for it, that doesn't numb it or dull it or stop it. It doesn't change what's done to us; what we do to each other.

That was probably the worst thing Chiffon did. Surprise us with pain.

"Have you talked to him?" she asks quietly. "I mean, besides when you told him to fuck off."

"Not really."

"You should."

I want to tell Shelby that I'm through doing what I *should* do, according to her. But part of me feels like she's still looking out for me, that even though we're fighting the way we never thought we would, and I've abandoned the theories, she still doesn't want me to feel like this.

"Maybe," I tell her. I start the car because there isn't anything else to say.

We're back at school a few minutes before second period is about to start.

"Aubrey," Shelby says, turning back to look at me with one foot out of the car. She doesn't look strong. She doesn't look certain. She doesn't look indifferent. "I'm sorry." Her voice gives out and I have the urge to cry.

She pivots again after she's taken a few steps toward the school, her mouth slightly open and her eyes wide, but I don't wait to hear what she has to say. I don't go inside with her. I just drive, and keep going.

CHAPTER FORTY-EIGHT

I head back to school later for Drama because my grade is based on participation, even if Mrs. Seymour sometimes doesn't stay for the last half of class. I don't sit with Nathan. I sit in the front row. During improv Nathan doesn't tag himself in when I'm in the middle of the circle. I'm trying not to look at Nathan, so I can't be sure if he's trying not to look at me, too.

At lunch, I wait until everyone is in the cafeteria before I go inside. The second I walk in, I wish I had left school. I can be chased away, and from people I was never supposed to be running from. I hate that.

Shelby is texting furiously to someone who's not

me. Maybe to no one, just to keep her thumbs busy so she doesn't chew her nails and give herself away. Danica stares vacantly at Robert as he tells her something he and Patrick find really amusing. Melissa is looking around the cafeteria, probably for me, her hair flipping over her shoulders as she turns her head. Nathan sits at the end of the table with his physics book open. Finals are coming up and Nathan is studying prior to the review sessions so that he can treat them like practice tests. I know he's doing this because it's what I do. What I don't know is why he's doing it here instead of in the library.

Across the cafeteria, closer to where the food is served, Marnie and Ella are sitting. I know the regulars who sit at their table—Ella's boyfriend, other people in AP classes—but right now it's just them.

"Can I sit here?" I ask, but I'm already lifting my legs over the bench, sliding in next to Marnie.

"Sure," Marnie says. They both glance in the direction of my friends at my usual table closest to the exit.

"So, what's up?" Ella asks. She gives one more glance toward the other table.

"I'm upset." It feels horrible to be so honest, but I go on, thinking maybe it will start to feel okay if I just embrace it. "I'm pissed off. I don't want to see Nathan right now. Or Shelby. Or any of them." Admitting the truth about why we're hurt is hard—embarrassing, even. It feels like the worst kind of exposure.

Marnie is nodding vigorously, her entire face like an apology. Ella looks back at them again.

"Did something happen?" Ella asks.

The answer to this will not be so simple to them. They probably noticed the Detach. They probably noticed those few weeks when Nathan and Shelby were inseparable. They definitely noticed Nathan's and my recent public displays of affection. But this is normal behavior for a high school boy. And for me. They don't know what makes this time different.

"I don't want to talk about it," I tell them.

"Of course," Marnie says. She reaches over and puts her hand on top of mine.

Ella doesn't seem so convinced, though. Or she's not pleased with my answer. There's a lot I've never told them. Ella's looking at me like she knows it. And maybe she doesn't like it.

"I thought it was pretty bitchy that she—" Ella stops abruptly because Melissa is standing there holding a tray with a half-eaten piece of pizza. She shrugs her left shoulder to keep her purse from sliding off.

"Can I sit down?" she asks in a small voice.

Ella nods. Melissa takes a seat across from me.

"Are you okay?" she asks me. I can tell by the way she's talking so quietly, and won't make eye contact with Ella or Marnie, that honesty makes her uncomfortable too.

"Not really," I admit.

"What did she say to you?" Melissa asks.

I just shake my head. Maybe it's important to tell Melissa that Shelby apologized, but I don't. Maybe it's important to tell her that the theories are wrong. I think she's probably been skeptical all along.

"She should have realized how much you liked him," Melissa says. "What she did . . . she's just as bad as Chiffon."

Ella and Marnie don't know anything about what this means, except that it's awful to be like Chiffon. To them, Chiffon is a trashy, slutty girl who has no respect for other girls or herself.

I can't take back the things Chiffon might've said to them in the past that weren't very nice, but I can take back what I've said about Chiffon. It doesn't really matter who started it, or if it's been a cycle of insults with no beginning and no end. I want to cut my part out.

I shake my head again. "Chiffon's not so bad." I'm staring at Melissa but I can still see Marnie and Ella turning to look at me, shocked. "I don't think she would have gone out with Ronnie," I tell Melissa. "If we had never stopped being her friend, I don't think she would've been his girlfriend before he left." It feels wrong to justify this, to admit there are stipulations that make us fragile to one another, conditions to friendship involving boys. That we sometimes have to choose between preserving what others want or taking what we want for ourselves—that boys can wedge their way in, and how we feel about them can make us hate the people we're supposed to cherish the most. "Or maybe she would have, but it would've happened differently. It would've been okay. Chiffon was a really good friend."

Marnie's forehead scrunches again. Ella looks away, glancing at the place Chiffon usually sits. It's empty today. I think they must get it: at least part of what they believe about Chiffon isn't true.

Melissa's eyes are watery as she nods.

Marnie fills the silence asking about our physics study sheet, and we spend the rest of lunch talking about school, acting like it's not strange that this is the first time I've ever sat with them in the cafeteria.

CHAPTER
FORTY-NINE

We meet at our spot in the housing development after school. It's not completely vacant anymore. Foundations have been laid, driveways and sidewalks poured. Some of the lots even have frames up, skeletons of homes. We don't stay in the car. We stand outside in the open.

"You have something to say." I can tell by the way Nathan keeps looking at the ground. The way he rubs his hands together as if he's chilly in this eighty-degree weather.

Nathan nods, squints against the brightness. There's something determined in his face, too, which gives him away.

"I'm sorry," he says. "I know I've already said it, but I wanted you to hear it again. Without all the noise." I think what he really must mean is without the expectation of him getting something out of it.

It's the first time I don't want an apology from him. I'm about to tell him so, but I decide against it. Maybe an evolved girl would accept the apology, and then trust the boy to never do anything to be sorry about again. Points for Team Girl, maybe, if boys knew that when they said they were sorry, they had to mean it.

"Will you be completely honest with me?" I ask him.

He nods quickly and I watch his throat hitch as he swallows. He's already been completely honest with me, about almost everything.

"Where do you actually want to go to school next year?"

His eyes dart away. He stands up straighter. A few seconds pass, and Nathan pushes his lips together. It makes me think he wants to laugh. He doesn't. He sighs. "Did I ever tell you what my safety school was?"

He didn't, but I still know. He's mentioned only one other school the entire time I've known him. The place his friend, who had the birthday party, would be going next year. "The university by your hometown with the *innovative* engineering program." That's what he said about it. It's in the opposite direction from Barron.

He nods, clears his throat. "It doesn't matter," he says.

"I'm going to Barron."

The thing I want to say, but don't, is: *Don't tell me you're going to Barron for me.* I think it might make him stop frowning if I say it—it might make him laugh, even—but self-deprecating humor has never worked for me, and even thinking about saying it makes me want to cry.

"Does anyone know where you really want to go?" I ask.

"Apparently, you do." He doesn't look at me when he says it. "But Barron's a great school."

"It doesn't matter how great it is if it's not what you want."

"It's fine," he says. "It'll be fine."

"Nathan." My voice sounds dry, like I need water. Our eyes meet—mine out of embarrassment, his out of concern. "You said you'd be honest with me."

He tugs on his hair, looking away, shaking his head slightly. "There is nothing about Barron that makes me want to spend the next four years there." The second he's done he runs his fingers over his lips.

There's a pause, a space of silence when the wind should pick up or a cell phone should buzz, but nothing happens. Just Nathan and me, taking turns looking at each other, and then the ground or the sky.

"It's really over between us, isn't it?" he finally says.

Even though Nathan and I are already cracked and broken and exposed, it still hurts. I hold my breath. I don't say anything. I don't even nod, though I want to. I keep thinking about what Shelby said. *I told him that you wouldn't ever ask him to stay if he said he wanted to leave, and he told me he knew that.*

"I've never done this before" is what he says next.

"Me neither." Admitting to good-bye, surrendering to it, is new and foreign and hard.

"Why'd you ask me about Barron?" he says. There's probably a part of him that thought my only questions for him would be about Shelby. But I know Shelby and I know Nathan, so I can make sense of it. And I'm tired of guessing their secrets.

"Because . . ." I'm not sure how to explain it to him. There's so much we can't dictate—and shouldn't—that the things we can control about our future, we should. We should at least make the attempt.

"Because it'd be stupid of you not to fight for what you want," I tell him. I feel the squeeze in my throat, a small tremble in my bottom lip. "Don't you know that by now?"

I hate that that's how I end our conversation, but I have to get out of here. I cry the entire drive home. I debate going around the block. Like maybe I can out-drive my tears. But in the end I just go home, fall into bed, and cry on my pillow. My mother comes in without knocking and climbs into bed with me. She rubs my head and doesn't ask me to explain.

CHAPTER
FIFTY

I eat lunch with Marnie and Ella the rest of the week, and I don't go out that weekend even though I don't have to work. I don't mind staying home. Melissa and Danica come over to my house on Sunday. I've been avoiding them at school. I think they understand. They don't ask me about Shelby. They don't mention Nathan or if he went out with them Saturday night. Danica's getting excited about next year. She turned in her dorm preferences this week. Melissa blushes and tells us about Tommy Rizzo.

"I'm not going to have sex with him before I leave," she blurts out. As if this question has been chasing her around and has finally cornered her. We laugh at this admission.

"You're so easy," Danica says. "We're *all* so easy. It's easiest for Melissa to just say no. It's easiest for me to just give them what they want."

I hope that when I see them again next year, we're all different. That we understand better what we want and what those things are worth.

Melissa raises one finger in the air. "Just to be clear," she says, "sometimes it's not *that* easy to say no to the Riz."

Their laughter explodes around me. I close my eyes. There's a part of me that wants to carry these moments with me, no matter the weight. There's a part of me that understands they're precious. I try to hold on to that.

I EAT LUNCH in the library the next week. It's the best place to prep for finals and I still don't want to sit in my old spot. I still don't want to be around Shelby.

I catch myself looking at her a lot, though. Watching her, just like everyone else. The way I've always watched her. But this time, what I see is different. I remember when Shelby was thirteen, her face beaming after Patrick kissed her at the pool. The way she used to frown when Patrick chose Leila. The way she laughed when she discovered she could have him whenever she wanted, she just had to throw him back.

I watch her exchange sly smiles with Patrick; poke

fun at Robert until he's laughing too hard to return her teasing; whisper in Sam's ear, making him blush; roll her eyes at the things Tommy Rizzo says to Melissa. She's biding her time. She's waiting for someone to surprise her.

Nathan saw through her, I think, the way I'm seeing through her now. Past that face no one can make sense of, past the mocking jokes, the razor-sharp tongue, and the cheeky commentary. The girl who says she doesn't believe in love but hopes she's wrong.

I think she must know the theories don't work, that they aren't real.

Sometimes I catch her watching me, too.

NATHAN EATS IN the library for the same reasons I do. We don't talk. On Friday, he's wearing a sweatshirt from his safety school. His dream school. His sleeves are rolled up. It's the middle of May, we're on the cusp of summer, and only the mornings and evenings are chilly. So I ask him. I think he probably wore it so that I would.

"We're no longer the only two students from Lincoln High in seven years to be attending Barron, are we?"

He smiles, closing his eyes a little. He shakes his head.

"Were they mad?" I ask.

"*Mad* is probably an understatement. *Disappointed* is the word they used the most."

I sit down across from him and he tells me about his

parents' reaction—his mother storming out of the room and refusing to make eye contact with him the next morning, his father shaking his head, saying "You're making the biggest mistake of your life" and "Education is the most important thing."

"That's not ideal," I say.

"No, no, it's not," he says, shrugging. "But they have no idea how disappointed they could have been." His lips turn up slightly, like he's smirking at himself. "I have a theory that everything is relative."

I stare at him for five beats too long.

"What?" he says. His lips are still curled up, but his right hand is tracing small circles on the table. He's not sure he wants to know.

"Never mind." I pull my physics book out of my backpack. I pretend not to notice that he takes a moment to watch me. We don't say anything else.

AFTER SCHOOL I go to my locker without waiting for Shelby to leave first. I'm standing right beside her before she notices me. I watch her eyes widen, just slightly.

"Hey, Brey," she says.

"Hi." After I shut my locker, I really look at her. She still looks like my best friend.

"We're on our way to my house. You should come," she says. She shrugs, but her expression is not indifferent. Her smile looks painted on; her eyes are searching me.

"Maybe," I tell her. And part of me thinks that I really will go over there. Have drinks. Eat pizza. Wait for someone to pick us up. Go to a party to experience all that I forgo when I stay home. Lie in Shelby's bed elbow to elbow with Danica and Melissa, laughing ourselves to sleep. There's a nagging sadness, though, because deep down, these are things I already miss. These are things I've already let go of. I can't see myself not being friends with Shelby, and I probably will go over to her house again one day. But I also know things will never be the same.

"All right," she says, waving before she jogs down the hall to catch up with Danica and Robert. They wave when they see me, too, and I feel dizzy with grief. *This is how it's going to be from now on,* I think. *People saying good-bye.*

CHAPTER
FIFTY-ONE

Trip is at my house when I get home from school. He's sitting on the front porch with three mitts and a baseball lying next to him. My brothers fight with light sabers on the grass. He's been defeated. I take a seat next to him.

"I should have told you about Nathan."

Trip gives me a small, crooked smile. "Not gonna argue with you."

I can't help but smile back. "So what are you doing here?"

"I haven't heard from you in a while."

"You're worried about me," I guess.

"Not really. That's the excuse I'm using."

"Why do you have to have an excuse at all?" I turn so I'm facing him.

His laughter is soft. "I don't know. I thought you wanted one."

He's probably right. "I was wrong about you," I tell him.

"Oh yeah?"

"Yeah."

"Well," he says, "that's because I've been trying to prove you wrong." He leans his back against the railing.

"I guess it worked."

Trip laughs again, louder this time. "You fell for some skinny kid who wears leather. It didn't work."

I don't know what to say, so I just shake my head.

"It's okay," he says.

"Trip?"

He raises his eyebrows in response.

"I really missed you after you left."

"I know," he says, closing his eyes for just a second.

It's the most infuriating thing he could say. It's also the most perfect. I laugh. It's the best I've felt all day.

"And Jill is just a friend." He says this slowly, with his usual confidence stemming from years and years of always saying the right thing. He taps my temple with his finger. *What's going on in there?* is what he's asking.

I tell him exactly what I'm thinking. "I'm glad there's

nothing between you and Jill." Because there will always be a part of me that's exhilarated by Trip wanting me. Maybe I'll never stop trying to be the girl I think boys see when they give me that look—*I'm all yours*. Maybe one day the visions will line up.

"But I think we should just be friends," I say. "Like we already are."

"Are you sure you'll be able to resist me?"

I must be blushing, because the corners of Trip's mouth turn up.

"Trip." Just like last year, he's leaving again, but this year so am I. The real difference is, now we don't have to lie about how it makes us feel. I know that when Trip thinks of next year, he's not thinking about what it would really be like to have a girlfriend ten hours away. Still, I ask him, "What do *you* want?"

He leans in close. "What I want is not something I'm going to say in front of your brothers."

I cover my mouth, hiding my smile and shaking my head because he said just the right thing. He smiles at me, though it's not as bright, like he knows I can't say the right thing back.

He shrugs. "But I like being your friend, too."

I take hold of his hand and squeeze, trying for a friendly gesture.

Trip looks down at my hand and smiles. "Although I still don't think you'll be able to resist me."

I drop his hand and swat at him; I'm laughing too hard to object.

Trip and I stay out on the front porch long after my brothers have defeated the Death Star and moved inside to fight their video game aliens. We even have dinner outside and my mother doesn't insist we come in. It's the first really hot day. It feels like the longest the weather's stayed nice too. But maybe I haven't been paying attention before. The flowers are in full bloom at our feet—yellow roses, my mother's favorite—and I wonder why I never noticed those, either. Endings, beginnings; before and after; coming and going; loving and leaving—it's all blurred together.

"Do you think it will always be like this?" I ask Trip. It's getting dark, but the sky still looks blue. Navy, like a veil is draped over it. "That everything will always feel like it's changing? We'll always be leaving, we'll always be moving on?"

"Not always," Trip says. "Not right now."

CHAPTER FIFTY-TWO

The hardest part and the easiest part about graduation night is that Nathan's not there. He went back to see his friends, to go to the graduation parties of his old school, his old life. To play Scrabble and wear Burger King crowns.

We throw our mortarboards into the air and duck as they fall right back down on us, faster and harder than the force we used to release them.

Graduation day is like a giant eraser. Nothing that's happened over the past four years matters, because now we're all in the same boat. And that boat is leaving.

We're all saying good-bye.

I hold hands with my best friends. Even Shelby. I let my mother cry on my shoulder and I cry a little on hers, too. I'm laughing in the picture I take with family because my dad whispered a corny joke in my ear right before the flash went off; something about *How many graduates does it take to change a lightbulb?* Jason is laughing too, and Gregory is rolling his eyes, finally acting like a proper middle-school boy.

I pose in a zillion photos and forget that Celine is passive-aggressive, or that Patrick uses girls, or that Leila is clueless. It doesn't matter that Marnie and Ella and I don't have anything in common except for which classes we took, or that Chiffon hasn't said anything to me since the day after she rescued me. I stand in a circle with Shelby, Melissa, and Danica, and we link hands and smile at one another. We don't mention the theories we used to follow to make ourselves invincible.

I COULD NEVER have predicted how fast summer would fly by.

I spend a lot of time at the French Roll, serving baked goods and coffee, and I leave every day smelling like cinnamon. Ella and Marnie come in when my shift's over to eat lunch with me, and we provide updates on things like how cool or weird our roommates seem. Danica joins us some days. All of us are still undecided majors, except for Danica, who knows she wants to be an English major. *There's no rush, there's no rush,* is what we tell each other.

I spend time at Shelby's, too, with Danica and Melissa, sitting on Shelby's front lawn playing cards while Melissa reads us our horoscopes and Danica braids the long strands of grass.

I hang out at the Chapmans', dining on fruit and red meat, and sitting for hours on the porch listening to Earl give out random advice about how to prepare for the weather at Barron—*it's a different altitude,* he claims. Zane and Trip decide to teach me self-defense—mostly things they've seen on TV—and we practice the moves in the driveway, kicking up gravel and clouds of dust until it starts to get dark and the bugs come out.

Sometimes Trip tells me, *They won't know what to do with you at Barron,* in a way that makes me smile and blush. I tell him, *It's fine, because I know exactly what to do at Barron.* And, sometimes, I even believe myself.

I DON'T GO to so many parties, but I do go to the going-away party Patrick throws for Nathan in July. Nathan's leaving early to start a summer internship with a civil engineering company by his new college. There are several internships he could've taken at the plant. That's why people move here, after all, to work for the plant—it's a pinnacle for people who study science or engineering, like Nathan's parents. But Nathan wants to leave. Robert and Patrick don't understand it. They only understand that it's a reason to throw a party.

Everyone comes. Even Chiffon. Shelby doesn't say anything to her. She doesn't give her dirty looks. I told Shelby about Chiffon coming to get me that night when I'd had too much to drink at Sam's. She was very still and quiet as she listened. She looked sad. I think she probably wishes she had been the one to take care of me, the way she's always the one to take care of Melissa when Melissa is drunk. The way she used to take care of me in so many other ways. She must've been thinking about Chiffon, too, about the friend we used to have.

Halfway through the party, Shelby leans forward, like she has a secret, so we form a huddle, my shoulders tight with Danica's and Melissa's.

"I heard she's no longer fucking Zane," Shelby tells us. The three of them look at me.

"It's true," I confirm. Chiffon broke up with Zane almost three weeks before graduation.

Shelby's eyebrows rise and she smirks. It's nothing like the face she makes when she's insulting someone. She's impressed, and looks at each of us, like this is a feeling we're all sharing. She doesn't mention girl points, none of us does, but I think we're all thinking about them.

At midnight, Leila, Shelby, and I walk in on Nathan making out with Mary Ann in the den.

"Oh myyyyyy!" Leila says, rushing to shut the door as Mary Ann scrambles to put on her shirt. Shelby and I laugh so hard we drop the vodka. Leila yells at us to be more careful with *her* vodka, and that makes us laugh even harder. We laugh so hard it's impossible to walk. So we roll around on the floor in the hall kicking our feet and holding our stomachs. Mary Ann storms out of the den, stepping over us as she walks down the hall.

"Mary Ann finally got what she wanted and now she's swimming away from him," Shelby says in between laughs. It's funny because Mary Ann moves her arms in long strides like she's always in water. What's really funny, though, is that Mary Ann is just going to be a senior and has no idea what it is to really leave. And she's walking away from Nathan like it's nothing.

Nathan comes out of the den and says, "Thanks a lot," but he slides down the wall so he's sitting on the floor with us. He starts laughing so hard that his entire body shakes and he has to cover his face because it's so red.

THE MORNING BEFORE Nathan leaves, I tell him it was the best party I'd ever been to. He thinks I'm kidding and tells me to knock it off.

He tells me to knock it off again when I start to cry. Nathan's room is like a fortress of boxes, half for storage, half to be mailed so they're waiting for him at his dorm, so all he has to take with him is a few suitcases. I'm transporting my things the exact same way. *Great minds*, Nathan said when I told him.

His room is so empty. There aren't even any sheets on

his bed. I tried to keep myself from crying, but nothing worked, so now I'm just letting the tears fall. Nathan's going to the place he really wants to be. He's fading from my life almost as quickly as he entered it, and I wonder if this place will ever be home to him because it's where his parents are, or if it will always be the place that built him up and wrecked him.

He hugs me until I'm not crying so much. We don't say anything. After he pulls away, I stare at him for a long time and he stares right back at me. It feels like a balancing act; we break the stare and Nathan really disappears.

My throat tightens like I'm going to start crying again, so I blurt out whatever pops into my head. "I have a theory," I start. My voice is shaking, but I keep going. "I have a theory that your new college will have a place where you can buy seven-pound burritos."

His face opens up, and he smiles, even though his eyes look like they're about to flood.

"I have a theory that improv is the most valuable thing I learned in high school," Nathan says.

"I have a theory that no one can ever drink too many strawberry milkshakes."

"I have a theory you're going to love Barron even more than you thought you would."

"I have a theory that nothing is going to turn out how we predict it will."

Nathan nods, then shakes his head. "But please, let

the strawberry-milkshake theory be fact." He shrugs and doesn't seem sad or scared, and I can't believe I always saw his bravery and his sincerity as things that were uncharacteristic to him, when really they were a part of him all along. According to Shelby, the longer you know someone, the longer they have to let you down. But sometimes, the longer you know someone, the more time they have to surprise you.

I say a final good-bye, and he walks me to my car. I feel a sort of shock as I drive away. Good-byes are sad, but they don't have to be. We always knew we'd be moving on, we just never understood what it took to do it, what it meant to do it, and what we got to take from the people and places we left. My first thought, after I've turned the corner and can no longer see Nathan in my review mirror waving at me from the sidewalk, is that I can't wait to call him in the fall, after classes have started and things about our colleges are still new and weird, but we're getting the hang of it too. To laugh at the things we predicted wrong, and to gloat about everything we saw coming. To make new predictions or just ramble about the present. I don't know if he'll answer when I call, but I hope he will.

CHAPTER
FIFTY-THREE

It's annoyingly hot outside when I leave for college. Trip helps us load up the cars with boxes to drop at the post office on our way out of town, and suitcases with my clothes and books that are too heavy and therefore too expensive to mail. I overhear Jason refer to Trip as "the muscle."

Shelby's here too, reading off my mom's checklist to her as she circles the boxes, examining their labels before Trip loads them. After the car is full, my mom brings us lemonade, and Shelby, Trip, and I sit on the front steps with our legs stretched out.

"Don't you have any advice or pearls of wisdom, or something to tell her, Trip?" Shelby says.

Trip shakes his head, but a small smile creeps over his face. "Try not to drink too much."

I shake my head at the reminder. I almost can't even laugh about it.

"Coming home is the best part about leaving," he says. "You'll see."

"I thought the unknown was the best part about leaving," Shelby argues. There's a real conviction in her voice.

"All right," Trip says. "The unknown. That's the best part about coming back too."

Last night Danica, Melissa, Shelby, and I exchanged gaudy silver friendship bracelets that look like chains, acknowledging that they are destined to be ugly and out of style next year and we'll have to buy new ones. But it still didn't feel quite like I was really leaving.

I feel it now, that I'm truly going away, as Shelby makes it official and says, "I'll miss you."

"I'll miss you, too."

Trip has his face turned away from us entirely. Shelby and I both notice at the same time. It makes us smile. "Are you going to be okay, Chapman?" she asks, patting his back as she stands up.

"I'll be fine, Shels," he says. He's smiling, but he won't look at either of us for longer than a glance.

"I'll see you tomorrow," Shelby calls to me. "I mean—you know what I mean." She shakes her head, and even though she's all the way at the curb, I can tell by the way she looks to the sky and bites her lower lip that she's fighting back tears. She waves one more time before climbing into the car she bought with the money from her dad and driving away.

Trip and I stand facing each other by his truck, just like we did last year when we said good-bye. And just like last year, I kiss him. He's Trip Chapman, and leaving without kissing him just doesn't seem right.

I wipe at my cheeks and sure enough, there are tears.

"Damn it, Aubrey," Trip says, looking away. His eyes are glassy.

"This is harder than I thought," I tell him. It's probably the last time we'll ever kiss and we both know it. We're not pretending that it doesn't mean anything, or that it means more than good-bye. We might make the same mistakes. We have scars, though it's easy to forget how they got there, how much they once hurt. This detach is different, but it still has to happen.

"We did all right," he says, opening the door to his truck. I think he's talking about how we managed to stay friends all summer, but then he adds, "That was a pretty great good-bye."

He gives me a look then, *the* look. The one that makes everyone blush and smile, and I am no different.

WE LEAVE FOR Barron that afternoon, stopping overnight just four hours away, and arriving the next morning. My brothers play Frisbee on the lawn outside my dorm while my parents help me unpack.

My roommate's name is Marie. She's from Florida, and her hair is curly like Danica's. She has more books than I do, and she smells like coconut. I wish I knew what she was noticing about me.

Our parents get along really well, and they stop helping us unpack halfway through to stand in the middle of the room talking like they're old friends who haven't seen each other in ages. Marie and I exchange a look— eyes wide, shaking our heads at them—and I feel the first pangs of homesickness. I wonder what Danica's roommate is like; if Melissa has started packing for State or is still putting it off. I wonder what Shelby's doing. If she's given up on theories or if she's made up new ones.

My parents leave to go to their hotel room and get cleaned up before we go to dinner with Marie and her parents. I walk out with them to collect the last few things I've left in the car.

"I'll see you in two hours," I say, waving to them. It's probably the tenth time I've said it since we walked outside.

My mother comes up to me and puts her hands on my shoulders. "Do you want me to stay?" she asks.

I do want her to stay, but I know she can't. "No, it's okay." I shake my head and say it again. "I'll see you in two hours."

I watch them drive away, seriously thinking about running after the car and taking back what I said about it being okay that my mother leave. I close my eyes and take a deep breath as I turn back toward my dorm room. The cement path leading up to it is new and smooth; the building is new, too, big and brick to match the others. But in the corner there are initials, probably drawn with a stick by students when the cement was still wet, reminding me: people have been here before you, and you're going to be okay.

ACKNOWLEDGMENTS

I must first thank my parents for always telling me that I could be anything I wanted to be.

An extremely large and very lavish thank-you to my incredible agent, Suzie Townsend, for understanding and loving this book and having the best plans for its future. And for that one particular editorial note that changed everything for the better. ☺ To Joanna Volpe, Kathleen Ortiz, Pouya Shahbazian, Danielle Barthel, Jaida Temperly, Jackie Lindert, Jess Dallow, and everyone at New Leaf Literary, Inc. I couldn't be in better hands.

Thank you to my editor, Rosemary Brosnan, for her amazing insight, for inspiring me to take this story the places it needed to go, and for being wonderful company. Thank you to everyone at HarperCollins: Renée Cafiero, Barb Fitzsimmons, Olivia de Leon, Jessica MacLeish, Andrea Pappenheimer and her sales team, and Kim VandeWater.

I am so grateful for the talented group of women I get to call my critique partners: Jean Marie Ayana, Shelley Batt, and Tanya Spencer. Thank you for "getting me," and for sharing your brilliance, for listening to me ramble, and, of course, for the laughter. A special thanks to Gloria Kempton, whose *Writer's Digest* class brought us together.

A huge thank-you also to Christa Desir, the first one to read this book; your notes made revising possible, even fun.

And another big thank-you for telling me to stop complaining about revising and just do it already (best advice), and for being so wonderful and teaching me more than you know.

Thank you!—to all the bloggers who helped reveal the cover, and to everyone who helped spread the word about this book.

This is in part a story about friendship, so I have to thank my friends who've impacted me so much: Lea, for being an awesome and supportive—and hilarious—cousin. Rowdy, for never leaving me "alone on the page." Karisa, for being just as infuriated about Joey choosing Dawson over Paris as I was, and for always wanting to talk for hours about life and books and "our stories." Lyndsey, for being my first writing partner—I swear we share the same imagination. Stefanie, for being my middle school writing partner who was just as obsessed with *Jurassic Park* as I was. Brittany and Kelsey, for all those nights spent overanalyzing and for "no rescue." Brienne, for book talk and real talk. Ashley, Alyssa, Amy, Andrew, Crystal, Emily, Jen, Leslie, Liz, Ryan, Val—we have too many stories to fit in one book. John and Luke, for support and for being great company eight hours a day five days a week. Sheri & Tom, Sarah & Lucas, for cheering me along, and for forgiving all those vacations I spent buried in my laptop.

And thank you, Justin, for calling me a writer out loud in front of everyone even when I insisted it was a secret. For taking me out of my comfort zone, for telling me "the stories behind the football game" so I could invest, and for always understanding when I disappear to write. And also, of course, for the first word in the title of this book.